THE RELEASE

ALSO BY TOM ISBELL

The Prey

The Capture

THE RELEASE

TOM ISBELL

HARPERTEEN
An Imprint of HarperCollinsPublishers

HarperTeen is an imprint of HarperCollins Publishers.

The Release
Copyright © 2017 by Tom Isbell

ISBN 978-0-06-221608-3 (trade bdg.)

Typography by Joel Tippie
17 18 19 20 21   PC/LSCH   10 9 8 7 6 5 4 3 2 1
❖
First Edition

To Paul and Mary Isbell,
who loved unconditionally.
And to Pat,
always.

PART ONE
ENEMIES

I know not with what weapons World War III will be fought, but World War IV will be fought with sticks and stones.

—ALBERT EINSTEIN

PROLOGUE

FROZEN SLOPES STRETCH THEIR icy fingers to leaden skies, and winter gales sweep clean the vast, white prairies. Though captured, he escapes. Though beaten down, he rises, even as the mountains rumble and the waters rush and roar.

But enemies persist. The dead and dying litter the long road to freedom, and many more must perish.

My beloved . . .

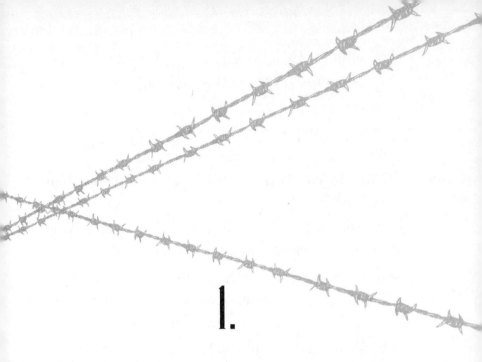

1.

THE NIGHT WAS COLD, and each time I breathed out, my mouth released a haze of frost. I squinted past the cloud of white, peering into the dark. They were out there. It was just a matter of time before they showed themselves.

A tap on the shoulder made me jump. Diana, come to relieve me.

"My turn," she said.

"Already?"

"Unless you want to stay longer."

"Nope, I'm good."

I pushed myself up from the snow and stretched. My toes and fingers were numb. My joints creaked. Argos uncurled from my side and also stretched, extending his back legs.

"Anything?" Diana asked.

"Some yellow earlier. Nothing recent."

"How many?"

"A dozen. Maybe more."

She nodded grimly. "They do anything?"

"Just circled." Then I added, "They came closer than last night."

We shared a look. Diana knew what I was talking about without having to say the words. *Yellow* meant *wolves*, the color referring to their eyes. The more yellow, the more wolves. Lately, the numbers were increasing, and the packs had started coming closer. The only thing that kept them at bay was an enormous ring of fire we'd built around our camp. We stoked it day and night like some primitive tribe from centuries past. So far, no wolves had dared go through it.

We intended to keep it that way.

The avalanche had wiped out all of Camp Liberty, flattening buildings, vehicles . . . and several dozen Brown Shirts. Their decomposing bodies released a sickening aroma of rotting, putrefying flesh. Just the thing to attract roaming wolf packs. Each night the wolves materialized from the mountains, alternately ripping at the corpses with their razor teeth and sending piercing cries to the starry sky.

As if the wolves weren't bad enough, just days after the avalanche, howling swirls of snow came racing down Skeleton Ridge and descended on the No Water, wreathing our shantytown in five-foot drifts. What was cleared away one morning was buried in snow the next. Between the snow and wolves, we were prisoners in our own camp.

Diana took my place on the ground, folding her willowy body behind the barricade. She pulled her auburn-colored hair back into a ponytail and readied a bow and arrow. I found some logs and tossed them onto the nearest bonfires. Five hundred embers danced to heaven. I was about to go but found myself lingering, wiping the bark from my hands.

"What?" Diana asked, noticing I hadn't left.

It was a long time before I answered.

"How's Hope?"

Diana gave a small sigh. "She's fine, Book."

"She's really okay?"

"No better or worse since the last time you asked— which was last night."

"Have you seen her?"

"Hardly anyone sees her. You know that. Now get out of here."

I started to leave.

"And Book?"

"Yeah?" I turned to her, hopeful.

"Stop thinking about her."

That was what Diana told me every night. *Stop*

7

thinking about her. There was little chance I could follow that advice.

I shuffled back through the snowy labyrinth of Libertyville. That was the name we gave our makeshift town of rickety huts. The buildings were an unsightly collection of recovered pieces from Camp Liberty. Bits of planking here, corrugated metal there, tree branches acting as joists and beams. A ramshackle village whose blue-tarped roofs dipped low from snow. Temporary housing.

Although we often talked about marching out of there, it would have been mass suicide. It was the dead of winter, and there were still Less Thans so emaciated they could barely walk. We'd rescued seventy-five of them from the Quonset hut that night two months ago, but malnutrition and sickness had taken the lives of four the first week alone. The long winter claimed three others. We couldn't be on our way until all sixty-eight of them regained their strength—whenever that was.

Argos and I stepped into the shack that we called home. It was nearly as cold inside as it was out.

On the floor were seated Twitch and Flush, bent over a sheet of paper. Flush read a series of numbers out loud.

"Any progress?" I asked.

"There's gotta be a pattern," Twitch answered,

tapping the paper with his fingers. "I just can't figure it out."

"And you're sure they're not random numbers?"

"Two people with the same series of thirteen numbers? Not likely."

Back when we had been digging through the snow looking for building materials, we'd come across Colonel Thorason's body. In his front shirt pocket was a slip of paper. On it was written a long string of numbers.

4539221103914

When we uncovered another Brown Shirt and found the exact same numbers in his shirt pocket, we figured it was a code of some kind. So far, we'd had no luck translating it.

"I keep hoping it's a letter-number cipher," Twitch went on. "Those aren't so tough to crack. But if it's a letter *shift* cipher, then things get tricky. You gotta create a whole grid to solve it."

Leave it to Twitch to know all this. He'd been blinded by a mortar when the Brown Shirts ambushed us last summer. Although it slowed him down physically, it didn't faze him a bit when it came to problem solving. The code was just another puzzle he was determined to break.

In addition to Flush and Twitch, Red was also in the room, carving a cedar branch. Like Flush and Twitch, he had been in that original group of Less Thans who escaped Camp Liberty. His shame for abandoning us in favor of Dozer was as easy to read as the radiation splotch on his face. There was never a moment when he wasn't making arrows or tending to the survivors.

"Anything?" he asked. The same question we asked one another every night.

"Some yellow a couple hours ago."

"More or less than last night?"

"Definitely more. And getting closer."

It was not the answer anyone wanted to hear.

I tossed some wood into the stove and poked the logs. As I stretched out before the flames, pinpricks of heat danced up my toes and fingers. Argos circled and lay down. He was practically fully grown now, the scars from various wolf attacks pockmarking his fur like badges of honor.

Cat entered and we went through the same series of questions. *Any yellow? How many? How close?* That kind of thing.

The fact was, we were fixated on wolves—could think of little else. They circled us each night, taunting us with their howls, their greenish-yellow eyes poking through the dark like devil fingers. There was never a time when they weren't on our minds.

"How much longer?" I asked, absently petting Argos.

"Till what?"

"Till they finish off the corpses?"

Cat shrugged. "Another day. Maybe two."

He bent down and picked up two rocks—one quartz, one flint—and began knapping them together, making arrowheads. He held the flint by wedging it between his armpit and artificial limb. His movements were so effortless, you almost got the feeling he'd been missing an arm his entire life. Typical Cat.

"And when they're done with the corpses?" I asked.

He shrugged. "I guess they'll look somewhere else." The fire crackled and Cat knapped the rocks. Then he turned to Flush and asked, "We're still waiting for spring?"

"As soon as the snow melts," Flush said.

"We can't leave any sooner?"

"Not as long as there are LTs who can't get out of bed."

"We could build a sled and drag them along."

Flush shook his head. "Better to wait until we can all walk on our own."

I knew what was going on in Cat's mind. It wasn't just wolves he was thinking about. We had seen for ourselves the realities of the Republic of the True America: Hunters tracking down Less Thans, experiments on Sisters, Brown Shirts locking up LTs and letting them die in their bunks.

Since Chancellor Maddox had somehow escaped the avalanche—Dr. Gallingham, too—we knew we couldn't remain in Libertyville a second longer than necessary. Our only salvation—and *curse*—was the snow, which kept the Brown Shirts away . . . but also kept us captive.

To lift people's spirits—and also celebrate a year's worth of birthdays—we'd decided to throw a party the next night. It wouldn't solve our problems, but maybe it would get our minds off wolves and a dwindling food supply—at least for one evening.

When I climbed into bed, Cat continued to strike rocks, and Flush and Twitch were still poring over numbers. As I settled into sleep, it wasn't wolves or Chancellor Maddox or Dr. Gallingham I thought about.

It was Hope. I hadn't seen her since we'd rescued her from the bunker. For the past eight weeks, she had spent her days hunting game in the foothills, returning only when the sun was setting and she could cloak herself in darkness, closeting herself in her tent on the far edge of Libertyville. I wondered when I'd see her again.

If I'd see her again.

My eyes drifted shut and I fell into a deep sleep, only partially aware of the wolves' haunting howls from the other side of the ring of fire.

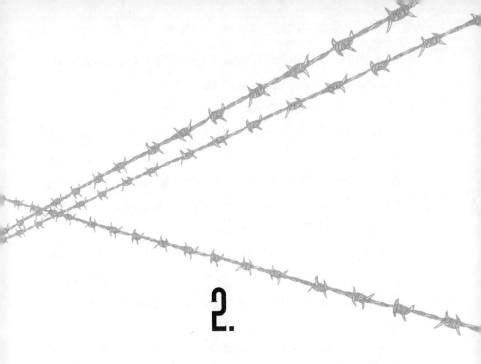

2.

AFTERNOON SUNLIGHT BOUNCES OFF the snow as Hope field dresses a squirrel. Her hands and knife move in an acrobatic flurry. She's done it so many times, it's become a kind of dance. Knife in the underside, tug at the skin, slice off the front legs, remove the skin, dig out the entrails, chop off the head, cut the back feet, pull out the organs—*done*. She can do it in her sleep.

Hope does all this in the privacy of an aspen grove. Anything to hide herself. While she's never considered herself a vain person, there is something about these scars—these twin Xs on her cheeks—she finds disgusting. Repulsive, even. They're like brands for marking livestock, as if she were someone else's property. The thought sickens her.

It's why she keeps to herself. Why she wears a hoodie

and pulls the drawstrings tight. Why she avoids the stares of well-meaning friends.

Why she avoids Book.

Hunting is her refuge. It not only lets her provide food for the others, it gives her an excuse to get away from camp. And the fact is, she's good at it. Setting traps and tracking prey have always been her specialty. She can thank her father for that.

It's the only thing she can thank him for. Now that she knows he collaborated with the enemy, working alongside Dr. Gallingham and injecting patients with experimental drugs, she finds it best not to think of him. Yes, she'll use the skills he taught her, but that's it. No more honoring his memory.

She plops the skinned squirrel in her pack, resets the trap, and notices the late-afternoon sun sneaking past the tree trunks, announcing the coming dusk. Time to return to Libertyville. Skeleton Ridge is no place to be after dark.

Her lips purse and she gives a sharp whistle. A moment later, a whistle answers. It's Diana, hunting on the other side of the aspens. That's their signal to start back down the mountain.

Hope reaches back and removes the pair of skis strapped to her back—skis she made from birch planks. She slips her boots into the bindings, pulls them taut, and takes off down the mountain.

Her hair is longer now, black and flowing, and the crisp winter wind sails through it. It's not as long as her mother's was, but it's getting there. Closer to how it was before Chancellor Maddox ordered it chopped off way back when.

Partway down the mountain, something catches Hope's eye: two dark objects, not much bigger than her hand, lying still and silent atop the snow. She angles the skis in that direction, *shoosh*ing to a stop. It's obvious what she's looking at: two field mice, their bodies stiff from death. Hope looks around. The mice aren't from any trap, and it's unlikely they died from natural causes one right next to the other. So what are they doing here? More importantly, why haven't they been eaten?

She grabs one by the tail and lifts it in the air.

"What've you got there?" Diana asks, appearing at her side.

"Nothing," Hope says, startled. She throws the stiff rodents into her pack. "Just a couple of mice."

"Better than nothing. And it wouldn't hurt for you to eat some of that."

"We'll see."

"I mean it."

"I know."

It's an ongoing debate. Diana is convinced Hope isn't eating enough, and Hope tells her there's hardly enough food for the sick and wounded, let alone the healthy ones.

She's still thinking about the mice when Diana says, "Book was asking about you last night."

"So?"

"So what I do I tell him?"

Hope pulls up her hoodie and tightens it. "Tell him whatever you want."

"But he keeps asking and I don't know—"

"Tell him I'm busy," she snaps. "Tell him I'm trying to feed two Sisters and seventy-three Less Thans. Tell him someone needs to do the hunting around here."

Diana looks down at her hands before asking, "And tonight? I can't change your mind?"

Hope gives her head a shake and turns away. She has no interest in going to parties. Has even less interest in being seen.

"You know, you're going to have to go out sometime. You can't stay shut up the next couple months."

"I get out," Hope says. "I'm out now."

"You know what I mean."

Hope says nothing. The sun angles lower.

"Suit yourself," Diana says, "but I hate being the lone girl." Ever since Scylla was killed by the avalanche, Diana and Hope are the only two Sisters, surrounded by all these Less Thans.

"I'm not worried about you."

16

"I'm not worried about me either. It's those poor LTs I'm thinking about." She shoots Hope a wink and pushes off.

As they ski single file down the mountain, headed for the ring of fire encircling Libertyville, Hope thinks about Book. The truth is, he can ask about her all he wants, but Hope won't let him see her this way. She won't accept his pity. As much as she likes Book, as much as she remembers every last detail of their time together, she knows there's no going back. Not now. Not ever.

She zips down the mountain, ignoring the tears that press against her eyes. She blames them on the cold, on the setting sun, on anything but the truth.

Live today, tears tomorrow.

Later, after Diana has gone to the party and Hope can hear the muted, faraway sounds of laughter and music, she reaches beneath the tarp wall and sticks her hand into the snow, fishing around until she finds the two dead mice. She hasn't had a chance to examine them since they returned, and the thought of them bothers her. At a time when every single person and animal is foraging for food, how is it that two mice died so oddly, and are left uneaten? It doesn't make sense.

She pinches one by the tail and dangles it. It exudes a whiff of rot, and her eyes pore over the brownish-gray rodent. Although there's no blood, she spies something she didn't notice before: the belly puckers unnaturally, as though the two seams of skin don't quite match up. She lowers the mouse to the table and pokes at it, revealing a razor-thin gash that runs from head to tail. An eviscerating slice like from a sharpened knife.

Or a wolf's claw.

She examines the other mouse and finds the same. Another slit that runs the length of the tiny animal's belly.

Okay. So a wolf killed these mice. But why go to that trouble and then not eat them?

Hope has heard the wolves at night, gobbling up the avalanche victims. If they're as famished as the LTs and Sisters, why leave two mice to fester and rot?

Unless. . . .

The hair rises at the back of Hope's neck as she comes to a sudden realization. A moment later, she rushes out of the tent.

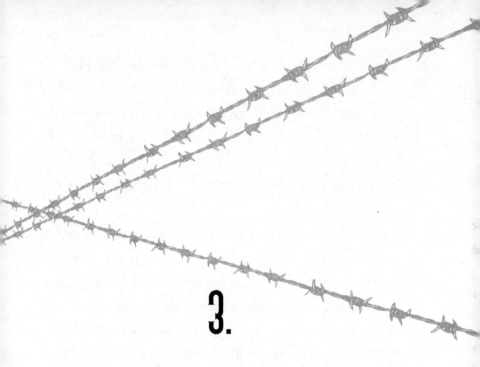

3.

GROWING UP IN CAMP Liberty, we never celebrated birthdays. The only exception was when we turned seventeen, because that was the day we went through the Rite. There was a big ceremony on the parade ground, and following that, the birthday boys—the graduates—were shipped off to become the new lieutenants of the Western Federation Territory.

Or so we were told.

The truth was that the Less Thans were sold off to Hunters to be tracked down and slaughtered like prey. A very different future than what was promised us.

But now that we were free of Camp Liberty and there were a number of us who had turned or were about to turn seventeen, we decided to throw a proper birthday party. This was going to be a genuine celebration.

A couple of the guys even made decorations out of paper they'd found blowing around in camp. Personally, I enjoyed the irony of it. I doubt that anyone ever dreamed that the official Republic of the True America stationery would be turned into party hats and paper chains.

Some of the LTs had created a stage at one end of the mess hall and were performing skits. At the moment, two guys were prancing around in an improvised horse costume, and that was getting huge laughs, especially when the rear of the horse got separated from the front.

I found Flush and Twitch sitting at a table in the very back of the mess hall, poring over sheets of paper.

"You're missing the fun," I said.

"Some of us are preoccupied," Flush said, cocking his head toward Twitch.

"I can still hear, you know," said Twitch. "I know you're talking about me. And I bet you're cocking your head in my direction."

Flush's face turned bright red, and Twitch pointed at the paper.

"Look at this," he said. "We've started working out some combinations."

I bent down and inspected the paper. An elaborate chart showed numbers along the side and letters across the top.

"If we choose the column where 'four' is 'n,'" Twitch went on, "then that means that 'five' is 'o,' 'six' is 'p' and so on. So then we get something like—well, read it, Flush."

Flush picked up the paper and tried to pronounce what they'd come up with. "Nomsllkk-mskn," he said.

Nomsllkk-mskn. If it was a word, it wasn't an obvious one.

"I admit," Twitch said, "it's nothing definite yet, but if we added some more vowels in there, who knows?"

"You might be onto something," I said, patting him on the shoulder. "Keep at it."

Flush rolled his eyes. "Now we'll never enjoy the party," he moaned good-naturedly.

"When we get to the Heartland," I said "the first thing we'll do is throw a real party. And we'll have those foods we've always read about."

"You mean like cake and ice cream?"

"And cookies and brownies and everything else we can think of."

Flush turned back to Twitch. "What're you waiting for? Let's crack this code so we can get out of here and celebrate."

I turned back to the stage. The rear of the horse was chasing the front, trying to catch up. It had been a long time since I'd heard my friends laugh so much.

The one actor had just about caught up with the

other when a voice interrupted them.

"We need to leave."

I knew that voice. Had *dreamed* about that voice.

The actors hesitated, unsure if they should go on or not.

"We need to leave," the voice said again, and the audience laughter came to an abrupt halt.

Heads turned. Standing by the back door, concealed in shadows with a hoodie drawn tight around her face, was Hope. It had been forever since I'd seen her, and I could feel the butterflies in my stomach.

"We know that, Hope," Flush said, stepping toward her. "That's what we've been talking about in our meetings."

"I mean *soon*."

"Exactly. Once the snow melts—"

"Tomorrow. The next day at the latest."

Jaws hung open. Eyes widened. We'd just lived through the most dangerous year of our lives . . . and she was proposing something to top even that.

"You're kidding, right?" asked Flush.

"I'm not."

"But we've got three Less Thans who can barely get out of bed. It's the middle of winter, the snow's practically to our knees, and we don't have nearly enough food to take with us on a trip."

Others began chiming in; everyone had an opinion and wanted to voice it.

Hope listened to it all, calmly nodded, then walked down the aisle toward the front of the mess hall. She tossed two objects onto the stage, where they landed with a muffled thud. The two actors backed up and everyone grew quiet.

"What are those?" Flush asked.

"Mice," she said.

"So?"

"The wolves killed them."

He shrugged. "Wolves kill mice all the time."

"They didn't eat them."

It slowly sank in what she was getting at.

"They've developed a taste for humans," she went on, her voice eerily calm. "They're no longer interested in other animals. It's people or nothing."

Her words were followed by a silence louder than the avalanche.

"That may be true," Flush said, "but that doesn't mean—"

"We leave tomorrow," she insisted. "We rejoin the Sisters we left behind at the lake and go from there."

An LT named Sunshine let loose a high-pitched laugh. "Now you're dreaming. Like we're gonna be able to make it all that way—especially with *them*." He pointed in the direction of the infirmary, housing those Less Thans still too weak to walk.

"We'll get there," Hope said.

"Right. And the world's flat."

I understood where Sunshine was coming from, but Hope was right. If we didn't leave soon, there was a chance we wouldn't leave at all.

Again, a chorus of voices chimed in, most claiming that Hope was being alarmist. Chicken Little, and all that.

I listened to the debate, then looked at Hope to gauge her reaction. But she'd already gone, slipped out without anyone noticing.

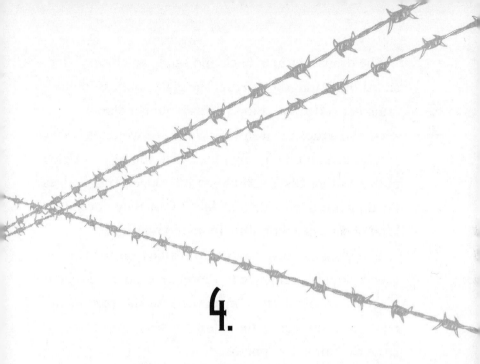

4.

IT WAS FOOLISH, LEAVING the tent like that, exposing herself to the stares of others. But after examining those mice, Hope knew things that others didn't. If she didn't say something, they'd wait until springtime to leave and then it'd be too late. That's why she spoke up.

Well, that's the main reason. There's also the matter of unfinished business.

She's preparing to go to bed when she catches a glimpse of herself in the shard of mirror that hangs on a side wall. She stands there a moment, studying her face. Each time she happens to see her reflection, she is startled. The Xs are as unsightly as ever. As though it's someone else she's looking at, some stranger. Definitely not Hope.

She draws her arm back and sends an elbow flying, smashing it into the mirror. The glass shatters, obliterating her reflection. Blood drips from her elbow.

As she wraps the wound in cloth, she wonders if they can do it. Can they really make it all the way to Helen and the other Sisters, huddled in Dodge's Log Lodges on the shores of a distant lake? Can they cover that kind of distance with little food and no shelter?

She snuggles beneath a thin blanket on the floor—a bed would be entirely too foreign—and as she does most every night, she fingers the locket around her neck. She can sense the stares of her mom and dad from the miniature photos.

Not for the first time, her fingers edge away from the locket and move toward her face, tracing the raised scars on her cheeks, down one diagonal and up the other. The two Xs remind her of what she wants.

Revenge.

For her mother. For her father. For her sister, Faith. It's not that she doesn't want to escape from the territory and save the country and all that other *rah-rah* stuff. But mainly she wants revenge. And she will get it . . . or die trying.

She settles in for sleep, comforted by the soothing *tap tap* of raindrops on the tarp. As she's drifting off, she remembers Book's expression when she threw the mice on the stage. He was as surprised as everyone else, but she got the feeling, from a single glance, that he agreed with her. Which is why she was hurt he didn't say anything in support of her. Still, even if he had—

She jolts up in bed.

Something's not right. She replays her thoughts, stopping when she remembers the soothing sound of raindrops. Straining to listen, she hears it again: *tap tap*. It sounds like raindrops, but there's no way it can be raining—not in the dead of winter. She whips into her clothes, grabs her bow and a quiver of arrows, and hurries out of the tent.

The night is cold and clear. No moon, which makes the stars glimmer extra bright.

Now that she's outside, she can hear the sound more clearly, and she realizes the *tap tap* is more a pitter-pat, a muffled padding. As much as she doesn't want to believe it, she knows the sound. A wolf. When they run, they do so on their toes, but when they stalk, their whole pad hits the ground.

This one's stalking.

Hope follows the sound, her moccasins slipping through freshly fallen snow. The tendons of her knuckles glow white as she grips the bow. She still can't believe it. How did a wolf get past the ring of fire?

She comes upon a single set of tracks. Even in scant starlight, she's able to make out the distinctive wolf print: the triangular pad, the four oval toes in perfect symmetry. The good news is that it's just one wolf. The bad news is that it's big. The paw prints are larger than the palm of her hand.

She picks up her pace, her breath ballooning in front of her. Rounding the corner of a hut, she comes to a small intersection. Before her is the infirmary. The wolf prints lead right to the flap that serves as the lone entrance.

Hope tiptoes forward, parting the flap with an outstretched elbow.

Her eyes adjust to the dark, and it takes her a moment to locate the wolf. It's as big as she feared, and prowling the aisles. Its fur is singed from where it went through the fire. She assumes that at any moment it's going to stop and attack one of the three Less Thans there, but instead it keeps moving—as though it's checking out the situation. *Counting its prey.*

The wolf rears back its head and sends a piercing howl toward the ceiling. The sound sends a shudder down Hope's back.

The emaciated Less Thans start to wake. One sits up in bed.

"Don't move," Hope whispers fiercely.

They obey. The wolf turns and stares at her, just as she stares at it. For the longest time, neither of them moves. Then Hope slowly nocks an arrow and draws the bowstring back. But just as she's about to shoot, the wolf leaps forward, landing on the Less Than who's sitting up. Hope wants to release the arrow, but the wolf is smart enough to get behind the LT, shielding itself.

Trying to get a better angle, Hope runs to another aisle. But every time she moves, so does the wolf, repositioning itself behind the sick LT. Hope could run back in the other direction, but the wolf will just move again. Meanwhile, it continues to howl, its piercing wail blasting her ears.

"Have it your way," she mutters, and draws the bowstring back until her thumb tickles her cheek. She waits until the wolf is midhowl, and then she sends the arrow flying. It zips through the infirmary in a horizontal blur, missing the LT by an inch and impaling the wolf in the neck. It shrieks, then crumples to the ground.

The infirmary comes alive. The Less Than is sobbing hysterically, and there are startled cries as other LTs race in from the party. But even as they come running to find out what's going on, Hope is headed the other way. She's taken care of the situation, and now she's getting out of there.

Picking her way through the snowy back alleys of Libertyville, Hope's heart races. The thing she can't let go of is that howl. That wasn't some mournful wail, some aimless baying at the invisible moon. That was a call to arms.

A signal to attack.

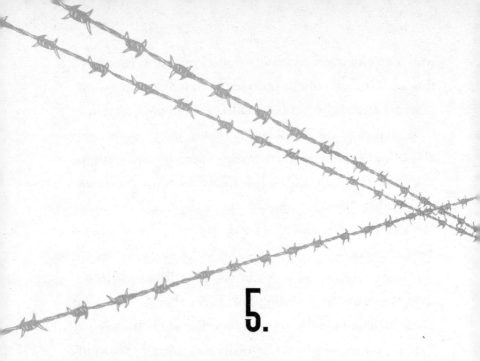

5.

WE LEFT THE NEXT morning.

There were those who disagreed with our decision, but Hope was right. We had to get out of there.

"That wasn't a wolf attack last night," Hope said as we were tying up the last of the packs. "It was a scouting mission. That thing was here to let the rest of the pack know what it'd seen."

It was crazy what she was saying. Ridiculous, even. But I knew that she was right. Like her, I had seen the attack on Skeleton Ridge.

That didn't mean we were ready to leave. For all the reasons Flush had voiced earlier, we weren't even remotely prepared for this. But the alternative was worse.

The LT who'd been pounced on by the wolf died

30

during the night, as much from shock as from the attack itself. With no shovels and little time, we topped the grave with rocks to prevent the wolves from unearthing the corpse.

"What's the point?" Sunshine mocked. "If those wolves want him, they'll get him. Nothing we can do to stop 'em."

"The rocks'll stop them," I replied.

"The rocks'll *slow 'em down*." Then he added, "Probably better for us if the wolves *did* get him. That way they won't come chasing after us."

No one bothered to respond, and Sunshine ran a hand through his greasy hair. It was so blond it was practically white, and when he laughed, his cheeks turned bright red. He looked like a demented elf. Although he was one of the emaciated ones we'd rescued from Liberty, you wouldn't know it now. He was brash to the point of cocky. People put up with him because he was a fellow Less Than . . . and because he was good with a slingshot. We had a feeling we'd need every fighter we could get.

When we finished creating the burial mound, a number of us stood awkwardly around the grave while I recited a poem.

No man is an island,
Entire of itself,

31

Every man is a piece of the continent,
A part of the main.

A little John Donne to feed our souls—not that any-one had the faintest idea what the poem was or who wrote it.

Our number was down to seventy-four.

After placing our few belongings in the middle of tarps and bundling them into Yukon packs, we squinted into the morning sun.

"Let's get out of here," Cat said, impatient to get going.

"Which direction?" Flush asked.

"Where else? East to the river." It's how we'd gotten here, and it was how we'd get out.

Cat took the lead, finding an opening in the ring of fire's dying flames, and everyone else followed. We carried supplies and dragged the two wounded on tri-angular stretchers through the calf-high snow.

I was the last to leave. I turned and took a final look at Libertyville, at what had once been Camp Liberty. I hoped to never lay eyes on this part of the Western Federation Territory again.

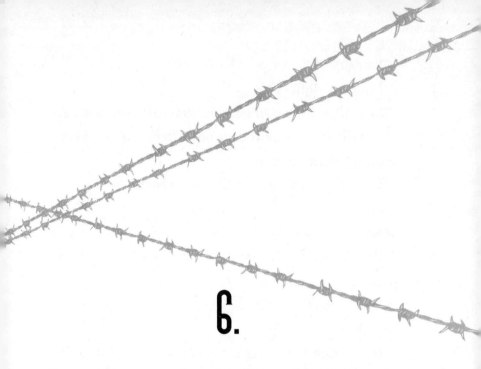

6.

THE SNOW IS DEEP, the going slow, and by the time they reach the river—a winding sheet of ice—they're huffing for air. They head south along its banks.

The sun is a blinding splotch of yellow that bounces off the snow and spears their eyes. Hope is glad for the hood. It shields her eyes from the glaring sun . . . and conceals her scars from others.

"Hey."

Book is suddenly walking alongside her. She angles her head in the other direction.

"You doing okay?" he asks.

"Doing fine." There is defiance in her voice. Even a touch of contempt. Only the weak and helpless accept pity. Hope is neither of those.

"You sure?"

"I said so, didn't I?"

Book allows the silence to stretch between them. All around them is the muffled thud of footsteps as seventy-four stragglers wade through snow.

"What do you want, Book?" Hope finally asks.

"Isn't it obvious?"

"Not to me, it's not."

"I'm looking for someone—someone I used to know who's gone missing."

"Who's that?"

"A girl named Hope."

Hope gives her head a violent shake. "Not gonna happen."

"Why? Because of those?" He gestures vaguely to the Xs on her face. "You think you're the only one around here with scars?"

"No. . . ."

Book tugs up a sleeve and displays the crisscrossing lines on his wrist. "What do you call these?"

"Sure, they're scars. . . ."

"But?"

"They're hidden. You're not disfigured like me."

"Right, because yours are on your face, that makes them somehow worse," he says sarcastically.

"That's right."

"Because everyone can see them, that somehow

34

makes them more noticeable than everyone else's."

"Exactly."

"And my limp?"

"That's different and you know it."

"Is it? What about my internal scars? How about those?"

"What're you talking about?"

"Feeling responsible for the deaths of my friends. Those scars don't heal."

"You think I don't have those, too?"

"I *know* you have them. That's my point. All of us do." She stops abruptly. "So these are just nothing?"

"I don't care about those. No one does."

"I do!"

Her voice carries farther than she intends, and Diana makes a move to come to Hope's side. Hope shakes her off.

"I care about these scars," Hope says in a fierce whisper. "I care because I know that's all that people see. They can say they don't, that they can look past them, *that all they really see is my soul*, but that's bullshit and you know it." She whips the hoodie back so that the Xs catch the full brunt of sunlight. The scars pucker the skin; shadows crisscross her cheeks. "Tell me you don't see these."

Book shrugs. "I don't see them."

"And you see into my soul."

"I see into your soul."

Hope grabs Book's hand and slaps it against her cheek, resting his fingers on the cold, raised edges of her scars. "And now?"

"They don't exist."

She throws his hand away. "You're crazier than I thought."

Then she pulls the hood around her face and stomps off, joining the seventy-some others who trudge past Book in the vast expanse of snow.

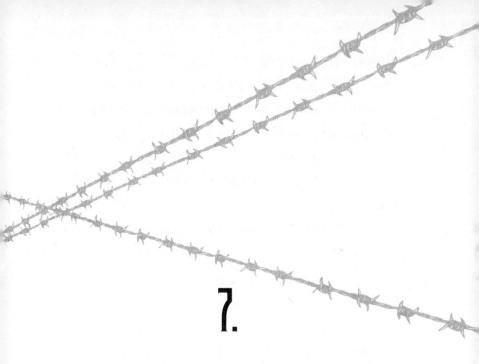

7.

HOPE WOULD HAVE NOTHING more to do with me the rest of that day. Or the day after that. When we set up camp each evening, I put my bedroll on one arc of the circle, and she put hers directly opposite. Then she'd go off in search of food, not returning for hours.

Each evening, we huddled around our fires, pockets of muffled conversation drifting from one group to the other.

"What do you think it was like?" Flush asked out of the blue one night.

"What *what* was like?"

"The day the bombs fell. Omega."

"Frightening," an LT said.

"Confusing," another added.

"Terrifying," a third chimed in.

"For the living, yeah," Twitch said.

We turned to him. His blind eyes probed the night.

"Ninety-nine percent of the earth's population was probably eliminated in a matter of seconds. They didn't feel a thing. They might have been the lucky ones."

His words settled on us. The fire popped and crackled. The world had never seemed so still.

"I wonder which country started it," Flush said.

"Why's it matter?" Cat said, whittling a branch. "What matters is it's left to us to pick up the pieces."

"Yeah, but aren't you curious?"

"Why? There's no way we'll ever know."

Cat was right—we'd never find out the answer to that—but it did make me wonder about something else.

"Why do they hate us?" I asked. The question had burned within me ever since I found out we were considered Less Thans. As I spoke, I petted Argos. I could feel the ribs protruding beneath his fur.

"Who?" Flush asked.

"Everyone. Brown Shirts, Hunters, Crazies. Why do they all want us dead?"

"You know what they say," Twitch said. "There are three reasons to hate someone. Either we have something they want."

"Yeah, right," Flush said sarcastically.

"Or we're a threat."

"Not likely."

"Or we're just different."

Flush didn't respond to that one. No one did.

"But why the Hunters?" I asked. "I mean, I can maybe understand the Crazies not liking us—they're just crazy. And the Brown Shirts have somehow been indoctrinated to think we're evil. But what do the Hunters have against us? What's their deal?"

"Maybe they just like shooting defenseless people," Cat said.

"Yeah, maybe." But we all knew there was more to it than that.

By the fifth day after leaving Libertyville, our pace had become glacial—a combination of fatigue and lack of food. Although Hope often returned with a rabbit or a squirrel, sometimes even a porcupine, it wasn't enough. Not to fill over seventy bellies. We were slowly starving to death.

Our rest breaks dragged out. We covered fewer miles. Each day started later and ended sooner. Although the sun brought warmth, its sharp rays bit our skin, chapped our lips, burned our cheeks red. Our eyes formed a permanent squint from staring into sunlight.

It was obvious we couldn't go on like this.

"We need to go to the Compound," I said on the sixth afternoon, as we were gathering wood.

"What're you talking about?" Flush asked.

"The Compound—where we were held captive by the Skull People."

"I know what it is."

"We need to return there."

Everyone around me stopped what they were doing.

"But that's, like, miles and miles out of the way," Flush said.

"I know."

"The fastest way to Dodge's is if we cut across the river and head east, not go south to the Compound. And for the sake of the sick, for the sake of *all of us*, we need to get to Dodge's as soon as possible."

"I don't disagree."

"Not to mention the fact that the last time we were at the Compound, the Hunters and Crazies were having a field day massacring the Skullies."

"I remember."

"So why do you think—"

"There might be food there." That was the magic word: food. "You're right, the Compound was attacked. But that place was so well stocked, there have gotta be some hidden rooms where there's still food. Just imagine what that could do for us."

The thought of eating smoked meats and canned vegetables made my mouth water.

"But Book, we don't know who controls the Compound," Twitch said.

"True, but what if the Hunters and Crazies just attacked and left? What if they're not there anymore? Not only that"—here I hesitated—"what if there are survivors? Skull People, still alive. If so, we could bring 'em with us."

Flush cleared his throat before speaking. "I don't mean to sound heartless or anything, but why would you want to do that?"

"First of all, because they helped us escape."

"After they locked us up."

"And secondly, because they have skills. They're smart—they can help us."

"If you're thinking of your little friend Miranda," Diana said, "don't forget she was a traitor."

It was the first time anyone had uttered her name in months. Miranda. The girl who'd kissed my cheek as we watched the sun set. The same girl who'd been spying for her father.

"At first she was, yeah. But if it wasn't for her, we wouldn't have gotten out of those caves. She created the diversion." No one responded—not Diana, certainly not Hope—and I went on. "Listen, we're not going to make it out of this territory unless we get some food. Like, soon. And the Compound is the only possibility I can think of."

"But if the Crazies are still around—" Flush began.

"We take that chance. We don't have a choice."

The silence stretched, and it was a long time before anyone else spoke. I squinted into the distance. The setting sun erupted in an explosion of orange.

"I love it," Sunshine said. "We're screwed if we go, we're screwed if we don't. Welcome to the life of a Less Than." He brayed like a donkey.

"What're you thinking, Book?" Cat asked.

"It wouldn't be everyone," I said. "Just a small group. Whoever wants to join me. The rest of you go on to Dodge's and we'll meet up there. Hopefully with a whole mess of food."

Now I needed volunteers. I shot a look to Hope, hoping she would say yes. She met my stare with narrowed eyes.

"Go," she said. "We'll continue on without you."

"That's what I'm suggesting," I said.

"Then do it. You don't need my permission."

"Fine."

"*Fine.*"

I didn't disagree with her, but it hurt, the way she said it. Like she wanted no part of me.

"I'll go," Red said.

"Me too," Flush added, although not with as much conviction.

So that was the group: Red, Flush, and me. And of course Argos. Everyone else would cross the river and head straight for Dodge's.

"If you want, I can join you," Cat said later on, when it was just him and me.

"No, better that you're with the others. They need you."

"You sure about this? You don't have to go back there if you don't want."

"It's best this way," I said, and left it at that.

That night I had watch, peering into the dark for any sign of yellow. I wondered if the wolves were content now, if they had just wanted us to leave Libertyville so they could reclaim that part of Skeleton Ridge for themselves. Or were they trailing us across the frozen tundra, waiting for the right moment to attack?

Soon, it wasn't wolves I was thinking about, or Skull People, or even Hope. It was my grandmother. The woman with the long black hair whose final words to me had been *I haven't been guiding you, Book. You must be listening to your heart.*

But at that particular moment, I had no idea what my heart was telling me. It felt like I knew less than ever.

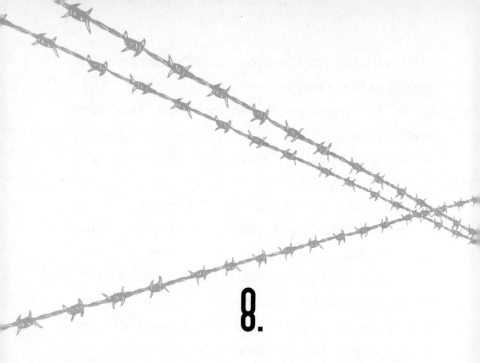

8.

THEY SEPARATE THE NEXT morning. After an awkward round of good-byes, most of them cross the frozen river to the other side. The only ones who don't are Book, Red, Flush, and Argos. Hope and Book don't exchange any final words, but when Hope reaches the opposing riverbank, she catches him watching her. At the same moment they both look away.

Hope agrees that they need food, and she can't fault Book's plan to return to the Compound. Still, she can't help but wonder if his ulterior motive is to find Miranda. It angers her that she feels a stab of jealousy.

For the first part of the morning, the two groups are a mirror—three on one side, seventy-one on the other—trudging through snow on opposite banks of the river. The trio moves at a far quicker pace, of course, and soon they forge ahead. When they eventually disappear into the horizon of white—Argos's muffled bark a final good-bye—Hope is surprised to feel a sudden emptiness.

Later that day, Hope hears a distant sound. It takes a moment to identify it, and when she realizes it's the growl of a Humvee, the Less Thans and Sisters scurry for cover, throwing themselves to the ground. Cat is atop a ridge, and Hope crawls forward until she's next to him. They peek their heads above the snow.

A lone Humvee appears in the far distance, and they watch as it snakes its way across the snow-blasted prairie. What Hope can't figure out is why it's out here, where it's going. The one-lane road appears to dead-end at a small, snow-covered mound. There are no buildings here—no structures of any kind. Just a rusted chain-link fence encircling a tiny hill.

"Launch facility," Cat explains.

"Huh?"

"It's where they fired the missiles that day. My dad took me to one once."

"There's a missile there?"

"Used to be, in an underground silo. Nearly five thousand of them, scattered across the country. That's how the world blew itself up."

Hope has often wondered about Omega. She was young when her father first explained it, but somehow she envisioned airplanes dropping bombs from the air, not missiles erupting from the prairie.

She studies the hill. It's a good quarter mile away, but she's able to make out an upside-down dome on top of the mound. Burn marks scorch its edges.

"What's in there now?"

"Not a missile, that's for sure."

So why is the Humvee headed there?

They watch as the military vehicle nears, then passes through the fence, skidding to a stop when it reaches the small hill. Three Brown Shirts emerge, cracking jokes, their laughter bouncing off the cloudless sky. One lights a cigarette before they disappear behind the far side of the mound.

"Where are they going?" Hope asks, more to herself than Cat.

Five minutes pass before the soldiers return. They each carry a large wooden crate. Stenciled on the sides is the distinctive symbol of the Republic: three inverted triangles. Beneath that are a series of letters and numbers. *M4. M16. AK-47.*

Military weapons.

The three soldiers slide the wooden crates into the back of the Humvee and then return to the mound. Hope rises to her feet.

"Where're you going?" Cat asks.

"I want to see what they're doing."

Cat looks at her like she's crazy. "You want to go inside a missile silo?"

"That's right."

"Where there are three Brown Shirts with weapons?"

"Yup."

"Why?"

She's not sure she knows the answer, but it has something to do with unfinished business. *Everything* has to do with unfinished business.

Cat turns to the Less Thans behind him. Their hunger and exhaustion are obvious; many have fallen asleep in the snow. Cat points to the LT named Sunshine.

"Sunny, get up here," he says.

Sunshine crawls forward. "What's up, el bosso?"

"You're good with a slingshot, right?"

"I'm good with any weapon." He says it loudly, as if for Hope's benefit. She rolls her eyes.

"Great. Then you're coming with us."

"What? I—"

"We'll move in on their next trip."

They wait for the soldiers to return.

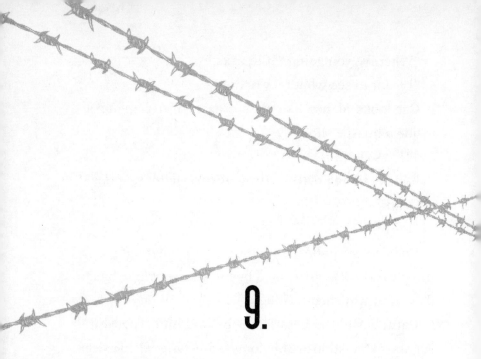

9.

IT WAS STRANGE TO be following the same path we'd used to escape from the Compound. Once more, we were racing *to* something we'd already escaped *from*. I longed for the day when we could just live in one place.

Red raised his hand and motioned Flush and me to stop. He pointed to Argos, who was sniffing the ground with a sudden intensity. When he lifted his head, snow encrusted his muzzle.

Directly next to his front paws were human footprints.

I lowered myself to the ground and analyzed the treads; they weren't from the moccasins of the Skull People nor the rags of the Crazies. These were pre-Omega shoes: Brown Shirt boots.

Soldiers.

My body gave an involuntary shudder.

"How many, do you think?" Flush asked.

"Looks like two."

"Recent?"

"Recent enough."

The footprints veered inland, away from the river but in the direction of the Compound.

"Do we follow them?" Flush asked.

"Do we have a choice?"

We shared a look, and Argos took off at a trot.

The footsteps were easy enough to track, and by midafternoon Flush pointed to the far horizon. Squinting across the flat tundra of snow, all I could make out was a speck of a distant object, sparkling sunlight.

"Solar panels," Flush explained. "I used to clean those things."

That was his job at the Compound. While I was working in the Wheel, he was helping harness energy.

"So we're close?" Red asked.

"Not just close," Flush said. "We're probably above the Compound right now." We all looked at our feet, envisioning what was on the underside of the ground.

We marched on, eager to reach the Compound entrance . . . and dreading it just the same.

It was the smell that suddenly led us forward. The footsteps were still there, of course, but we could have reached the Compound from the scent alone.

No, not scent—more like *stench*.

"What the heck?" Flush said.

Neither Red nor I answered, because we each had a suspicion we didn't want to voice. The Brown Shirts' rotting, putrefying bodies outside Libertyville had taught us what death smelled like. But why was that smell so strong out here, especially the closer we got to the Compound?

When the footsteps forked in the direction of the Compound's main entrance, we abandoned them and went the other way, following the smell instead. We needed to see where it led us.

We were now in a field of corn stubble, dead stalks jutting from the snow. With each passing step, the bile rose in my throat, and my imagination was working overtime. Did we really want to discover the source of this awful stench?

Argos stopped and began to whimper. At first, I thought he was picking up the scent of more footsteps. Then I saw the black oval—a small hole in the middle of the field. It was nearly invisible to the naked eye . . . and just wide enough in diameter to allow a human body.

"Good boy," I said, and nudged him out of the way.

I got down on hands and knees and inched forward, then stuck my head into the opening. There was a long wooden ladder that descended into darkness. Where it led was impossible to see. All I knew was that a wave of rancid smells gushed through the narrow opening, like lava spewing from a volcano.

I recoiled, breathing through my mouth to avoid gagging. It was rotten eggs and dead skunk and over-flowing outhouses all mixed together. My eyes watered after a single whiff.

"Where's it lead?" Flush asked.

"Hell," I answered . . . and then started making my way down.

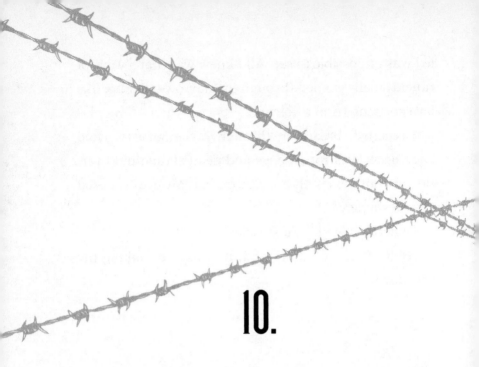

10.

THE THREE BROWN SHIRTS reappear, once more lugging wooden crates that they slide into the Humvee. When they return to the silo, Hope, Cat, and Sunshine rise to their feet and scamper across the snow.

They enter through the open gate and ease around the mound, stopping when they reach a thick metal door. Cat nods and the three of them step inside. When Hope's eyes adjust to the gloom, she sees that they're in a small antechamber. An elevator door stands straight ahead; to the side is a tube with a metal ladder descending straight down. She bends her head and listens. Voices spiral up.

With a series of hand gestures, Hope motions that she'll go first, climbing down the ladder into the heart of the silo. She has no idea who's down there . . . or what she's getting into.

When she reaches the bottom, the first thing she sees is an open reinforced steel door. It's easily two feet thick. Beyond it is a series of tunnels branching off in varying directions. Soldiers' voices echo from a nearby chamber.

When Cat and Sunshine join her, they head toward the voices. On the way, Hope spies a side room, stacked with dozens and dozens of crates. More weapons.

Hope looks at Cat. *Are you seeing all this?*

He gives a nod.

As they tiptoe through one of the tunnels, still trying to follow the soldiers' voices, Hope knows they're buried beneath countless tons of earth and steel and reinforced concrete. Even if this place took a direct hit during Omega, it would have come out just fine.

They reach a cramped soldiers' quarters: a couple of bunk beds, a primitive lavatory, a small kitchenette. In former times, soldiers lived here. Now, it's just storage space, filled floor to ceiling with more crates.

The Brown Shirts' voices grow suddenly louder, and Hope, Cat, and Sunshine duck into the nearest doorways. When the soldiers approach, Hope lets them walk by . . . and then she tiptoes forward, following. Just as her hand reaches for her knife, her shoes make a squeaking sound from the melting snow. The trailing

Brown Shirt turns around.

His eyes open wide when he sees her. "Hey, you can't—"

Hope sends her foot into the soldier's groin. "I just did."

His face turns strawberry as he collapses to the ground. Cat and Sunshine leap forward. The other Brown Shirts throw their crates and make a run for it, drawing weapons as they do.

"Damn it!" Cat curses, dodging the tossed crates and taking off after the soldiers. Sunshine follows.

At the first intersection of tunnels, one Brown goes right and the other goes left. With a quick nod of his head, Cat motions for Sunshine to follow the one to his right while he goes the other way.

No sooner does Cat step into the tunnel than it goes black; the soldier switched off the lights. Cat freezes, willing his eyes to adjust to the black. He tilts his head to the side, straining to hear. All he can make out is the steady, muffled, faraway sound of the soldier's breathing. And then the click of a pistol being readied.

Cat freezes. One series of blind gunshots down this narrow tunnel and Cat's a dead man. He presses himself against the wall.

He stands there, trying to come up with a plan. More than anything, he needs to see. From far behind him, he hears the sound of a scuffle. He can only hope

Sunshine subdued the other soldier, leaving just this one.

His body folds in on itself as he lowers himself to the ground. Lying flat on the concrete floor, he removes an arrow from his quiver and nocks it. He reaches out to the side walls and gets his bearings, determining the tunnel's direction. The fingers of his artificial arm hold the bow in place as he slowly draws back the string, aiming down the center of the tunnel. At the last moment, he alters where he points, so that when he releases the bowstring, the arrow travels no more than fifty yards before it hits a side wall.

"Shit!" the soldier cries, and takes off running.

Cat nocks a second arrow and sends it flying, then hears the satisfying sound of arrowhead entering flesh. The soldier stumbles to the ground, his gun clattering. Even in the dark, Cat is able to race forward and find the wounded soldier lying sprawled in the middle of the tunnel. Cat drags him back to the others.

When all three Brown Shirts are trussed up, Hope interrogates them.

"What's going on here?" she asks.

The soldiers sit on the floor, wrists and ankles tethered together. They don't answer her.

"Where's your camp? Where're you taking those crates?"

The Brown Shirt with the arrow jutting from his

shoulder blade actually laughs. "Why should we tell you?" he says. "The only reason you're still alive is because my gun jammed."

He begins to turn away, but Cat grabs the soldier's nose with his wooden pincers. "She asked you a question. Now, are you gonna answer her or not?"

His face goes pale. He tries to squirm free, but Cat's grip won't allow it. "The Eagle's Nest," the Brown Shirt sputters.

"What's that?"

"Headquarters."

"For who?" Again, the Brown Shirt tries to pull his nose free. Cat just pinches harder. *"For who?"*

"Chancellor Maddox. Who do you think?"

The hair rises on Hope's arms, and although she knows it's her imagination, it feels like both her scars itch at the mention of the chancellor's name.

"You can say good-bye to those plans," Sunshine says. "You're not going there ever again."

"Actually, they are," Hope corrects him. "And they're taking us with them."

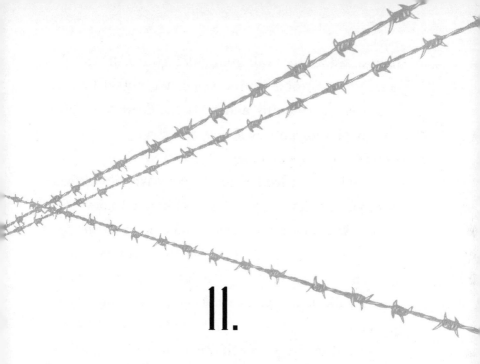

11.

THE LADDER GROANED BENEATH my weight. My guess was that this was one of the escape tunnels Goodwoman Marciniak had told us about. Except instead of escaping, we were using this tunnel to enter. A nasty habit we kept falling into.

When my feet landed on solid ground, I whistled for Flush and Red to climb down. Argos stayed up above.

The three of us began feeling our way around in the dark, trying to get a sense of where we were and how we could reach the heart of the Compound. Along the wall, a torch sat perched in its holder, as cold and lifeless as the winter itself. We could have lit it, but a fire would only announce ourselves.

Waving our outstretched hands like branches in a

breeze, we let the wall guide us forward. It was slow going, made worse by the smell. We pulled bandannas over our mouths and noses, and every so often we stopped to spit—as if that could rid us of the foul stench.

Finally, we noticed a far-off glow. We moved faster now, aided by the distant light. Although I knew there were soldiers up ahead, I also thought about the food we would find. I could imagine the countless jars of green beans and blueberry jam, the strips of dried meat hanging like icicles in the smokehouse. The more I envisioned them, the more I could practically taste them.

I was thinking so much about my next meal that I stopped paying attention to where I was going. I tripped on something and went flying. When I reached down to push myself up, my hand went *squish*. I tried with my other hand, but it went *squish* as well. Then I realized why.

I'd landed on a person.

A dead person.

Many dead persons.

I was elbow deep in decaying corpses, and only the possibility of being discovered by Brown Shirts prevented me from letting out a horrified scream. I clamped my mouth shut and tried to steady my breathing.

"Oh . . . my . . . God," Flush said. "Are those what I think they are?"

I nodded dumbly.

Easing to a standing position, my eyes peered into the dark, head swiveling first one direction and then the other. We were smack-dab in the middle of a burial ground, surrounded by hundreds and hundreds of lifeless, bloated bodies.

Although we wanted to turn around—wanted desperately to get the hell out of there—we knew we couldn't. We had come this far; we had to see it through. So we inched forward, tiptoeing around and over the piles of bodies.

What I couldn't figure out was what it was supposed to be. Was this a cemetery—some sacred place of honor—or just a dumping ground? There was no way to tell.

We headed for the faint glow at the end of the tunnel, hoping to get as far away from the bloated corpses as possible. But of course, just when we thought we'd cleared the last of them, there were still more—piles of bodies stacked like firewood stretching as far as we could see.

"Who are they?" Red asked. I understood what he was getting at. He hadn't been with us when we'd been imprisoned in the Compound. He didn't know what Skull People looked like.

But when I bent down and tried to examine the dead

bodies in the dark, I suddenly wasn't so sure myself. On the one hand, it seemed their clothes were leather sandals and wool robes and toga-like garments, which made me think Skull People. But right next to them were men wearing rags, their beards long and matted, which made me think they were Crazies. I couldn't figure it out.

A noise from farther down the tunnel grabbed my attention. Perhaps the very Brown Shirts whose footsteps we'd been following.

The more we tiptoed forward, the brighter it got . . . and the more we tried to avert our eyes. It was bad enough we were traipsing through this grisly graveyard—no point making things worse by staring at the corpses themselves. And yet, I caught myself glancing down from time to time, looking for people I might recognize. Like my grandmother. Or Goodwoman Marciniak.

Or Miranda.

It didn't help that every corpse's expression was the same—one of horror and fear.

In the near distance, torch flames caressed the cave walls with strokes of flickering light. Flush pulled to a stop, and I followed his gaze . . . to the bloated face of the chief justice.

My heart gave a lurch. I had no reason to feel any sympathy for him. After all, he was the one who'd sentenced us to thirty years' imprisonment. But he was also the man who'd changed my sentence from the

Wheel to the library—and was Miranda's father.

So maybe she was here as well. My eyes roamed from one face to the next, and while the bodies were discolored and disfigured, there wasn't one that looked remotely like the girl who'd kissed me as we watched the setting sun.

I breathed a silent sigh of relief.

We moved on. The only sounds were the quiet shuffle of our feet, a persistent dripping from the ceiling, the steady huff of breathing through our mouths.

When we reached a high-ceilinged chamber at the end of the tunnel, we expected to see the soldiers, but they weren't there. No living person was. Just hundreds of scattered corpses.

"Where'd they go?" Flush whispered, but I didn't know. I wondered the same thing.

Red pointed to the side. "Was it always like that?"

He was referring to an enormous rock pile that blocked a far entrance, boulders strewn in every direction. I gave my head a shake. "The Crazies were blowing up the place as we were leaving. Guess that's what happened."

We eased forward and began exploring. Some of the tunnels were completely closed off, barricaded by heaping mounds of rock. Others looked remarkably the same. The Crazies had managed to destroy only a por-tion of the Compound.

Flush began winding his way between a series of scattered objects, bending down to inspect a stack of items in the very center of the chamber. "What's this?" he asked.

I turned and looked . . . and my heart stopped. I needed no refresher course to know what I was looking at. It wasn't just dozens of cans of gasoline, but also explosives—C-4 and sticks of dynamite, heaped atop one another like a jumbled pyramid.

Someone intended to reduce the Compound to a pile of rubble.

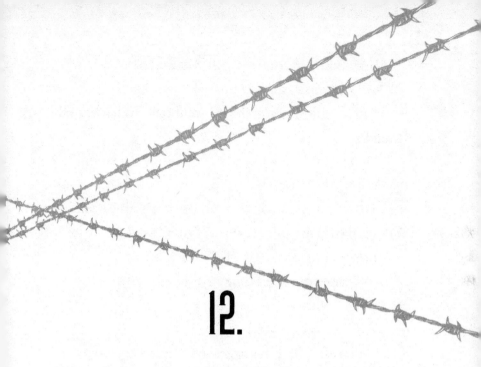

12.

HOPE SITS IN THE passenger seat while a Brown Shirt drives. The other four are crammed in back. Whenever the driver peeks to the side, Hope raises her crossbow so it's aimed at his chest. The message is clear: *Don't try anything.*

Before leaving, she instructed Diana to lead the sixty-some Less Thans to Dodge's Log Lodges. Hope, Cat, and Sunshine will catch up when they can.

"How often do you make these deliveries?" Hope asks the driver. When he doesn't answer, Hope nuzzles the crossbow against his side. "I asked you a question."

"Get that thing outta my ribs, and maybe I'll tell you."

"Why don't you tell me and then I'll get it out of your ribs." She presses it into his body.

"Just started," he says, writhing. "Last week."

"How many more trips will you make?"

"Till the silo's empty, I guess."

"You're taking *all* those weapons to Chancellor Maddox?"

"That's right."

"Why?"

"Got me," he says, and Hope jams the crossbow between his ribs. "I'm serious! I don't know."

For some reason, Hope believes him.

"Tell me about the Eagle's Nest," she says.

"What about it?"

"What kind of place is it?"

"A fortress you'll never get into," he says smugly.

Questions swim through Hope's mind. Why are all those guns in an abandoned missile silo? Why are they being transferred to the chancellor's headquarters? And why now?

The miles slip by—endless fields of white—as they veer farther and farther north, up toward the rolling foothills of Skeleton Ridge.

It's late afternoon when the vehicle slows to a stop, and Hope realizes she's been daydreaming. Something to do with Book. A part of her tries to shake the memory away.

Another part doesn't.

"There," the driver says, and Hope looks at where he's pointing.

Perched atop a nearby mountain peak, swathed in swirls of clouds, is a fortress. Its walls are made of stone, and crenellated parapets give it the appearance of a medieval castle. Hope can't believe it. What's something like that doing in the Republic of the True America?

"What is this place?" she asks.

"I told you, the—"

"Eagle's Nest, I know. But *what is it*?"

"A ski resort back in the day. Now it's the chancellor's HQ. That's all I know."

Hope studies it a moment. The turrets seem to snag the clouds, tugging at wisps of white. The Brown Shirt wasn't kidding; the place is impenetrable.

"How do we drive up there?"

"We don't."

Hope turns to him and presses the crossbow into his chest.

"I'm not kidding," he sputters. "There're no roads up there in winter."

"So how—" Hope doesn't finish the sentence. At just that moment her eyes land on a tiny red square dangling in the sky. It's an aerial tram slinking up the mountainside on a thick black cable. The soldier was right; there is no way in the world they'll get up there—not if they have to ride in that.

"Told ya," he says.

Hope sends an elbow into his side, and the Brown Shirt doubles over.

"Oops," she says.

As her eyes follow the tram to the top, she tries to figure out how the three of them will make it up there. Because if that's where Chancellor Maddox is, that's where Hope needs to go.

"Well, I guess that's that," Sunshine offers from the backseat.

"Not necessarily," Hope says. Even as she says it, she knows what she's thinking is wildly dangerous and ridiculous even to consider. Still, what does she have to lose?

Three Brown Shirts shuffle through the snowy streets of town. Vehicles pass, weary salutes are exchanged. No one gives them a second glance.

A good thing, too, because wearing the uniforms are Hope, Cat, and Sunshine. The original soldiers are currently hog-tied in the back of the Humvee, down to their boxers, T-shirts, and socks. As a courtesy, Hope threw a blanket over them so they wouldn't freeze to death.

Sunshine tugs at his uniform. "This thing is scratchy. And two sizes too big. And frankly, I don't think the color becomes me."

"I don't think *talking* becomes you," Cat growls. The younger LT shuts up.

Hope barely hears them; she's thinking about Chancellor Maddox. Hope's parents always taught their daughters to avoid the whole "eye for an eye" thing. They never said anything about "cheek for a cheek."

A military transport passes, and Hope and Sunshine bow their heads. The fact that she's a girl and has tea-colored skin makes her more than slightly conspicuous. Cat, the former Young Officer, fits right in.

"Uh-oh," Sunshine says.

"What?"

"See for yourself."

They're within sight of a small brown building not much bigger than a shed—the tram station—and Hope's heart sinks. Two armed Brown Shirts stand guard, checking the papers of everyone who intends to board.

"What do you think?" Cat asks, once the trio duck into an alley.

"I'm working on it," Hope says.

Hope knows the smart thing would be to abandon their plan, to join back up with the others and head for Dodge's and not worry about Chancellor Maddox and Dr. Gallingham and a silo full of semiautomatic weapons. The important thing is to get out of the territory.

But Hope Samadi is the first to admit she's never been about the smart thing. Especially when it comes to avenging her family's deaths.

They crouch in shadows, eyes trained on the two soldiers guarding the tram station.

"You sure about this?" Cat asks.

Hope gives a fierce nod.

"Okay then," he says. "Let's do it."

He gets up and exits the alley, walking purposefully toward the station. When he's halfway there, Sunshine exits the alley out the other way. Hope takes a deep breath, then rises and shuffles down the street, head lowered. Her short black hair is tucked under her soldier's cap.

"How's it going?" Cat asks one of the soldiers at the tram station, an older man with a pockmarked face.

"Papers," the soldier commands humorlessly. He steps from the shed and extends a hand.

"Right." Cat pats his pockets. "Now where did I—"

"No papers, no tram. You know the rules."

"I know. Oh, here. . . ." He removes a folded bundle and passes it to Pockmark.

The Brown Shirt examines the papers carefully, especially the picture. His eyes dart back and forth between the photograph and Cat's actual face.

"I know, I know," Cat says, "it doesn't look like me. That's what a lot of people say."

Pockmark grunts. His gaze lands on Cat's artificial hand. "What happened there?"

"Hunting accident. No biggie."

Pockmark shuffles through the papers. "How come it's not listed?"

"It's not?" Cat asks innocently. Out of the corner of his eye he notices the other soldier inching closer, his index finger gripping the trigger of his M4.

"You sure this is you?" the first soldier asks.

"Of course it's me. Who else would it be?"

Just as the second Brown Shirt exits the shed and begins to bring the barrel of his gun toward Cat's chest, a thin wire wraps around his neck and is snapped back. The soldier's mouth opens and the assault rifle clatters to the ground. Hope pulls at the wire until the soldier's eyes bulge.

Pockmark drops the papers and reaches for his pistol. Sunshine appears with a wire of his own, and Pockmark has no choice but to drop his weapon.

Cat begins binding the soldiers' hands.

"Fine, you tied us up, you win," Pockmark says with a smirk. "But there are a lot more soldiers up top than just the two of us."

Hope's doubts start to overwhelm her. What was she thinking, trying to get past the Brown Shirts and enter a secure fortress? Is she really willing to say good-bye to everything—her friends, Book, *life itself*—just for revenge?

"So I guess that's that," Sunshine says.

Hope gives her head a shake. "Nothing changes. I'm still going up there."

She doesn't know how, she doesn't know what she'll find. She's not even sure she'll succeed. But unfinished business is unfinished business, and there's no turning back from that.

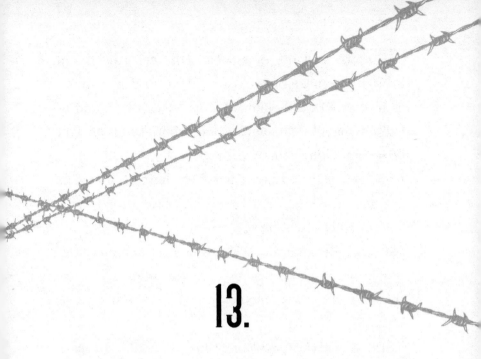

13.

"Freeze, Flush!" I commanded, and he could tell from my tone I wasn't kidding around. "Now, slowly step away. No big movements."

"Is it . . . ?"

I gave a nod.

"What'll happen if it goes off?"

"Let's not find out, okay?"

I knew what TNT could do. And with that many pounds of explosives—and all those cans of gasoline— the Brown Shirts weren't just looking to blow up a single chamber; they meant to destroy the entire Compound. *Leave no trace.* If we didn't get out of there, we'd be buried beneath tons of rock and earth. Not an image I wanted to dwell on.

Flush backed up, eyes wide. His feet guided him through the maze of explosives. At a turn in the path, his foot accidentally nudged a can of gasoline, and we inhaled sharply. The can teetered but stayed upright. We let out a long, slow breath.

"What now?" Red asked, when Flush finally joined us.

"Forget the food," Flush said, still breathing heavily. "We gotta get out of here."

It was hard to argue. We'd come here hoping to find something to eat, maybe even recruit an army. It was obvious neither wish would come true. We had to get out while we could.

Still, there was maybe one thing we could salvage.

"You go on ahead," I said. "I'll join up later."

Flush looked at me like I was crazy. "What're you talking about? They're going to blow this place to smithereens. We've gotta get out of here."

"I know, but there's something I need to do." He was about to protest, but I didn't let him. "I'll be quick. Promise."

Shaking their heads, they eased back down the tunnel and were swallowed by black. I took a deep breath, then scurried across the chamber.

There had been a time when I'd worked in the Compound. Not just the Wheel, but also the library. It was where I was headed now.

Like a rat in a maze, I raced down one tunnel after

another, backtracking whenever I ran into a dead end. I'd never approached the library from this direction, and it took me a while to get my bearings. Every so often I heard the two soldiers' voices, and I flattened myself against the damp limestone walls, praying for invisibility.

When I finally found the library, I yanked a torch from the wall and lit it with my flint, and the flame cast a flickering light on the countless shelves of books. A thick layer of dust coated everything in sight: books, tables, chairs. My eyes darted across the titles. In the background, the soldiers' voices grew louder. I had to work fast.

Twenty years ago—following Omega—the country that was formerly the United States of America established a new government. They created new borders, wrote a new set of rules, and confiscated all the maps. It was a new country, they told the citizens. The Republic of the True America. There was no point living in the past. No place for old geography.

For nearly a year, we had been blindly traipsing across the Western Federation Territory, trying to get from one point to the next. But if we actually *knew* where we were going, wouldn't we stand a better chance? If the Compound couldn't give us food or armies, it could at least give us knowledge.

My eyes landed on an oversize book. Its jacket was

torn and faded, but the title was clear enough. *Atlas of the World*. Even though it was decades old, it was exactly what I was looking for.

I slipped the torch into a holder and then pulled the atlas from the shelf. As I laid it on the table, an explosion of dust mushroomed up. My fingers raced through the pages, not stopping until I reached the desired page.

The United States of America.

Poring over it, I took in the green of the South and East, the rugged browns and purples of the West, the five enormous lakes at the top of the page, the vast expanses of blue to the east and west. There was something about it that seemed so different from the world I knew. Organized. Unified. Serene.

I knew it couldn't have been as idyllic as it looked on the page, but a part of me ached for a return to that life, when everyone was a part of the whole and there weren't men on ATVs hunting down the weak and different. A return to a world without Less Thans.

Soldiers' voices broke me from my reverie. I had to hurry.

The book was way too big to take with me, so I ripped out the map's two adjoining pages, then folded and stuffed them into a back pocket. For good measure, I found a map of the entire world and tore that out as well. Maybe there would come a day when we could safely explore other parts of the planet.

Yeah, right.

Retracing my steps, I made my way back through the Compound, easing around corners to avoid being seen. Despite the cold of this subterranean world, perspiration dotted my forehead, slid down my jaw.

I had just reached the far side of the central chamber when I saw them—the two Brown Shirts whose footsteps we'd trailed here. I ducked behind a boulder and watched as they strode toward the center of the room, joking and laughing. As long as they were there, I was stuck. The tunnel I needed to exit from was on the very opposite side of the chamber.

The soldiers inspected the gas cans and dynamite, taking their time.

Come on, I silently pleaded. *Get out of there. Go away.*

While I waited, my eyes took in my surroundings. As in the rest of the Compound, there were bodies scattered everywhere, resting atop pools of dried blood. Their stiff limbs were splayed in multiple directions, as if they were reaching for one last gasp of life.

And that's when I saw her.

Miranda.

She was curled on her side as though she'd just lain down to take a nap—like I could nudge her shoulder and she would wake. But of course she was dead, and had been for some time.

I bent down beside her, easing her body over until

she rested on her back. Her hair was pulled back in its customary ponytail, and her face was pale and gaunt. Smudge marks dotted her cheeks, just as they had when I'd seen her last in the Wheel, running off down the tunnel to distract the Crazies.

Even though death had bloated her body, and dried blood smeared her chin and neck, she was still recognizable, her metallic pendant around her neck.

It was Miranda and at the same time it wasn't. Without her jokes and smile, she was just the empty shell of a body. Not the same Miranda at all. And then it hit me—I would never fully know whether she had actually liked me or if that was just an act. She took those answers with her to the grave.

I have no idea how long I knelt there, taking in Miranda's face, waiting for her eyes to flutter open. They never did.

It was the sound of the soldiers' footsteps that brought me back to the present. I peeked around the corner and watched as they made their way to a wall sconce. One of them grabbed the torch and then they left. Silence followed.

I waited for the echo of their footsteps to fade away before I emerged. They were gone. If I hurried, I could carry Miranda through the chamber and back down the tunnel, laying her to rest at her father's side. It seemed the right thing to do.

I took her cold, stiff hand in mine, and was just pre-paring to lift her lifeless body into my arms when I heard a new sound. It was distant and faint and oddly urgent, and its muffled quality made it hard for me to identify. I froze in place, trying to figure it out.

When the sound emerged from the tunnel—the very one the two Brown Shirts had departed through—I could suddenly hear its high-pitched crackle. Its racing sputter. Its snakelike spit and sizzle.

It was a fuse . . . making its way to the cans of gas and TNT.

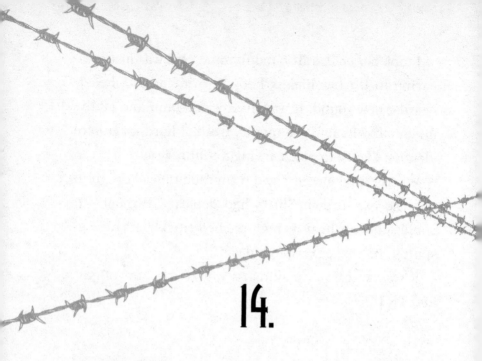

14.

Hope realizes there's no way she can make it up to the Eagle's Nest riding in the tram. Once the door opens at the top, she'll be captured and probably killed. So if she can't ride up in the tram, maybe she can ride up *on* it.

That's why she grips the metal plates that connect the tram car to the cable.

"See you in exactly one hour," Cat says, synchronizing his watch. They know the tram runs exactly every fifteen minutes.

Just as Hope wonders if she's making a huge mistake, the tram gives a jerk and she is on her way. No turning back now. As the tram rises above the snow-covered boulders and trees, soaring up the mountainside, Cat and Sunshine get smaller and smaller until they're no bigger than ants.

What she hadn't counted on was the wind. It was breezy down at the base of the mountain, but up here it's howling. Gusts tear at Hope's fingers and screech between the cables. Blankets of snow swirl in mini tornadoes.

The tram sways and lurches, rocking violently side to side. It's everything Hope can do to hold on. Her fingers are numb from clinging to the biting-cold metal.

She lifts her head and sees a tiny red spot coming her way: the other tram. When one tram goes up, the other automatically comes down. Which means that in a couple of minutes, the two cars will pass side by side, and if there are Brown Shirts in the descending tram, what's to prevent them from seeing her?

Her mind races, even as the other tram grows larger. Digging her numb fingers into the metal plate, she inches her legs around until the lower half of her body hangs over the far side of the tram. There's virtually no feeling in her fingers at all, and it's a minor miracle she's able to hold on. She doesn't let herself look down.

The two trams grow close, then near . . . then pass. Two red squares passing high above the mountainside. No shouts of alarm. No gunshots. Hope lets out a long breath.

A quick glance shows the descending tram is

crowded with Brown Shirts, too occupied with their own conversations to spy her. When they're far away, Hope manages to climb back on top of the tram. The top of the mountain can't come soon enough.

Although the Eagle's Nest looked impressive from the bottom of the mountain, it's even more menacing from up close. Stone walls jut from the cliff face. Spires rise to the skies. It's an impregnable fortress perched atop a steep mountain.

The tram slows, and Hope can make out the station now. There are two Brown Shirts there, each with an M4 slung over his shoulder. There's no way she can stay on top of the tram without being seen. She'll have to think of something else.

Live today, tears tomorrow.

Before the tram shudders to a stop, she leaps from the top, flying through air and landing in a deep snowbank. Of course, just beneath the snow is a granite boulder, and her impact is harder than she expects. It takes everything in her power not to cry out.

She lies there a moment, waiting for the pain in her ankles to subside, listening to hear if the Brown Shirts spotted her. Their laughter and jokes continue as before.

A glance at her watch tells her ten minutes have passed. That leaves only fifty. She needs to get going.

She scrambles up the mountainside, pulling herself up to a ledge. To reach the interior of the fortress, it appears as though soldiers have to walk through a long, damp tunnel burrowed within the mountain. She's thankful that the few lightbulbs that do work are dim and spaced far apart.

She tugs her cap low and enters the tunnel. The walk seems to take forever, the sound of her footsteps echoing against the stone. The arched stone ceiling drips water.

At the end of the tunnel is a large elevator, and when the door opens she steps inside, admiring the polished brass walls, the immaculate interior. Not what she expected. She presses the button for the top floor, and her stomach drops as the elevator shoots upward. Her hand rests on the handle of her knife, jutting from her waistband.

When she steps out of the elevator, breath leaves her. The exterior wall of the Eagle's Nest may be a medieval fortress, with its thick stone and crenellated parapets, but the inside is all twenty-first century. Buildings made of chrome and glass reach for the sky. Tinted windows glint in the late-afternoon sun. Everything sparkles and shines.

A glance inside the buildings shows atria with water-spewing fountains, escalators moving people effortlessly up and down, coffee shops and bakeries, banks and grocery stores. It's like she's landed on another planet.

And the people—not just soldiers but men and women in suits and lab coats, all in a hurry, moving briskly atop paved, spotless streets. No one pays Hope the least bit of attention. Keeping her head lowered, she edges her way through the fortress, trying not to gawk.

Rounding a corner, she spies the most prominent structure of all: a towering, white, cylinder-shaped building, located in the very center of the Eagle's Nest. It's over a dozen stories tall, and its top floors are circled by walls of darkened glass. Judging by the guards standing at the entrance, Hope guesses that's where Chancellor Maddox keeps her headquarters. Maybe she's staring down at Hope this very instant.

Hope glances at her watch. Thirty minutes have passed. Time is running out.

She makes a large loop within the Eagle's Nest, walking by a sophisticated power grid, a soldiers' barracks, and a bare area at the very edge of the fortress walls where Brown Shirts patrol with binoculars pressed against their eyes.

Eventually, she's drawn to a back alley by a series of loud sounds: clanking of metal, drone of generators, electric fizz of welders. The buildings are more industrial in this part of the fortress, and the workers wear coveralls and hard hats.

Hope stops when she spies a large garage filled with military trucks. Several dozen mechanics scramble under engine hoods and chassis, stripping the trucks' flatbeds, leaving solid sheets of dark steel in their place. She wants to watch longer—to figure out what they're doing—but there's not time.

She walks toward a central courtyard, her attention grabbed by throng of bystanders. She can't tell what they're up to, only that they've formed a tight circle and seem to be enjoying themselves. She drifts in their direction, ducking her face beneath her hat to hide her tea-colored skin.

As she nears the edge of the circle, she can hear taunts, jeers, mean-spirited laughter.

"You missed a spot!"

"Still dirty!"

"No stopping until you get it clean, you filthy Less Than!"

Her heart thumps against her chest, and she's suddenly not sure she wants to go any farther. But just at that moment the crowd parts and she's afforded a glimpse.

Crouched in the middle of the circle, on hands and knees and surrounded by the taunting mob, is a girl about her age, scrubbing the pavement while men and women spit on her. The closer Hope looks, the more she realizes she's seen this girl before. *Knows* this girl.

It's Scylla!

Because the Sisters and Less Thans never found her

body, they assumed she had been killed by the avalanche. But here she is, with a pail of water in one hand and a filthy rag in the other, while the crowd peppers her with kicks and insults.

"Better get it spotless, you subhuman mongrel!"

"If you can't clean it with that rag, we'll make you lick it off!"

Although she is still all muscle, she has clearly lost a good deal of weight since Hope saw her last. In addition, bruises color her face. Scylla survived the avalanche, only to be captured by Brown Shirts and forced to endure *this*.

Anger boils inside Hope, and she reaches for her knife. But even as her fingers wrap around the handle, she realizes there's nothing to be done. Not now. Not one against a mob. As she comes to this decision, her heart goes out to her friend, wondering what she did to deserve this.

Then again, Hope knows the answer to that. Scylla was born a twin—a prized commodity for the likes of Chancellor Maddox and Dr. Gallingham. And because she's been experimented on, she's no longer pure. She has no value. She's a Less Than—the greatest crime of all.

Hope has to get back down the mountain. There's nothing she can do for Scylla. Not now. She's sorry to leave, but she has no choice. Maybe she can come back later and try to rescue her friend. She hopes so.

She turns back around . . . and there he is.

Dr. Gallingham. He is standing on the very edge of the circle, watching this drama play out with a pleased expression, his hands folded tidily across his bulging paunch. He is just as she remembered him: obese, smug, his thin lips pressed together in what passes for a smile. He dabs a soiled hanky at an eye.

One look and it all comes flooding back. The experiments. The drug-induced fevers. The freezing tank of water.

Faith.

This time, Hope's hand clasps the knife handle and doesn't let go. She could kill him here and now, but then she'd be taken prisoner. Probably executed. That doesn't bother her so much, except it would leave Chancellor Maddox alive and well. She doesn't mind sacrificing her life to accomplish her task, but only if she knows both monsters will be destroyed. No good if one is killed and the other survives.

She removes her hand from the knife and hurries out of the fortress.

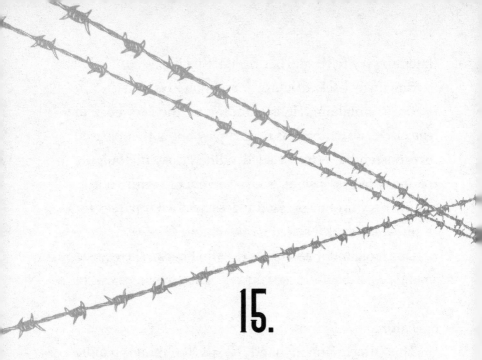

15.

I RELEASED MIRANDA'S HAND and placed it on her stomach, tidying her final posture.

"I'm sorry," I said. There was more I wanted to say, of course, but there wasn't time—not with a fuse racing for explosives.

I ran back the way we came, scrambling through the pitch-black tunnel, hurtling over piles of corpses as best I could. At one point I slipped and fell, doing a face-plant into a disintegrating corpse. I threw up, disgusted, and started running again.

However long it had taken Red and Flush and me to get through the tunnel from the other direction, it seemed to take me twice as long from this end. The stench, the blackness, the echo of my chugging, heavy breaths made it seem like a race through hell itself.

"Come on," I heard Flush yell, and when I looked up toward the ceiling, I saw his face poking through the hole.

A moment later I was at the ladder, the wood creaking beneath my weight. I climbed as fast as I could, smelling my own sweat and vomit.

The ladder sagged, the nails screeched, and I prayed it would hold out long enough for me to climb to the top. My heart slammed against my chest, just waiting for the awful explosion I knew would come at any second. Every so often my eyes traveled above me, to that small hole in the earth and the oval of shining sky.

Argos was up there, barking his head off. *Hurry up,* he seemed to be saying. As if he knew the dangers even better than the rest of us.

I was nearly three-quarters of the way up when my foot slipped out from under me. Before I knew it, I'd lost my balance and was sailing backward through air, plummeting to earth, legs and arms splayed.

When I landed with a *thud* against the hard-packed ground, the air rushed out of me, and I thought I'd never breathe again. I lay there, stunned, like a swatted fly. Panic gripped me as I struggled to inhale.

I rolled to the side, my body damp from perspiration. Nausea rushed through me like a wave. Somehow I had to get up the ladder. With stiff legs and tingly hands, I once more began to climb.

The going was slow, molasses-like. When I glanced up to the distant opening, I saw the heads of Red and Flush, looking down and urging me on.

"Come on, Book!" one of them yelled. "You can do it!"

Argos barked his head off.

I could do it . . . as long as there was time.

But there wasn't time.

Not five feet from the top, I felt it—an enormous *whoompf.* The fuse had reached the explosives.

Other muffled explosions followed, each louder than the first. *Whoompf! Whoompf! WHOOMPF!*

I thought maybe that was it. Just the central chamber had felt the blast. Maybe I'd been spared.

But then a wave of furnace heat slammed into me, pushed forward by a cannonball of flame, racing down the tunnel, its orange and red flames molded by the cave itself. It was consuming everything in its path, searching for oxygen and a way out—and it was on me before I had a chance to blink. I grabbed the ladder, tucked myself into it, and said a single word.

"Hope."

And then it hit.

The heat from the inferno in the Brown Forest had been unbearable; this was worse. It was a scalding blast of furnace air—like being dropped onto a sizzling griddle. Heat and fire consumed me.

But it was more than just heat—it was wind, too. A fiery tornado ripped me from the ladder's rungs and carried me along like some insignificant speck. Breath was impossible—the air way too hot to inhale—and my arms flailed as the flaming whirlwind spun me around and vomited me through the escape hole like lava from a volcano. Like Jonah from the whale. I shot up straight in the air, hovering for what felt like forever, kept aloft by the rushing wind and scorching heat, reaching for the sky itself.

And then I landed. Hard.

The world was suddenly muffled, encased in a thick blanket, and I saw the racing footsteps of Red and Flush as they hurried toward me.

Their mouths were open, but I couldn't hear, couldn't understand.

They helped me sit up. Argos was there, too, licking the side of my face, cooling me with his slobbery tongue.

My eyes landed on my two friends. Their faces were scorched—but they were laughing and patting me on the back. We were alive. Somehow, against the odds, we survived.

But when the earth began to rumble, I realized it was too soon to celebrate.

Far behind us across the frozen field, puffs of white lifted to the sky. And then the fields themselves seemed to disappear from view. It took us a moment to understand what we were seeing. The ground was falling into the Compound, the earth collapsing like a row of falling dominoes.

And coming right for us.

Red and Flush helped me to my feet, and we took off in a dead sprint, racing atop the frozen corn stubble. Three charred figures in a field of white.

Our feet kicked up the snow. My right side radiated pain, and my body screamed with every footfall. Red and Flush were far ahead. A glance over my shoulder told me the ground was gaining, racing after us like an incoming wave. The sound was unlike anything I'd ever heard; the heavy *thwump* of earth slamming earth. It tossed me like an exploding kernel of popcorn.

This time I landed on my stomach and chest. Argos stayed with me, pressing his snout against my face and neck, making sure I was alive.

"Good boy," I said, although I couldn't hear my own words.

I sat up and looked around. We were submerged in an enormous crater. Before us, the earth continued to roll and buckle, collapsing in on itself, erupting snow and dirt. My arms encircled Argos, waiting for the shaking to stop.

When the ground stopped roiling and finally settled to an uneasy rest, Red and Flush came running back and knelt by my side.

"I'm okay," I said.

We took off in a hurry, heading for the closest ridge.

Reaching the bluff, we allowed ourselves a moment of celebration, marked with deep breaths, drinks of water, and the occasional hug. We walked down to the frozen river and crossed its icy pavement. And I knew, in that moment of escaping certain death, in my final seconds of life, I had uttered one word: Hope's name.

16.

HOPE REUNITES WITH CAT and Sunshine at the bottom of the mountain. They dodge patrolling Brown Shirts and find their Humvee, dumping the three hog-tied soldiers out of it before taking off.

Cat drives—a skill he learned at Young Officers Camp—and they return the way they came. Once they're far from town and the shadow of the Eagle's Nest, Hope describes everything she saw.

Their mood is dark, the silence broken only when Cat explains that while Hope was up the mountain, he found something in one of the soldiers' pockets—a slip of paper with a line of numbers. The same code found on Colonel Thorason.

4539221103914

When they run out of gas, they dump the Humvee and rush to catch up with the other Less Thans, joining them the next day. Diana is happy to report that there's been no sign of Hunters, Crazies, or wolves.

"How about Book?" Hope hears herself ask.

"No sign of him either."

"Just wondering," Hope says, a little too hastily.

It's evening when they reach a small ridge, and Hope motions for them to stop. Below them, covered in a blanket of snow and ice, lies a large lake. Next to it, shrouded in a tangle of overgrown trees, is Dodge's Log Lodges—hardly noticeable to the naked eye. It's where they left Helen and the emaciated Sisters last fall, and Hope's heart stirs at the sight of it. But the longer she observes the group of run-down cabins, the more she realizes there's no movement there. No signs of life at all.

She shares a glance with Diana. They've been through this before—returning to Camp Freedom only to find it empty, its prisoners evacuated on a death march.

Not again, she wants to say, feeling a sudden, painful ache. Poor Helen and all those dying Sisters. Hope regrets leaving them.

Hope, Diana, and Cat decide to check it out. They ease down the hill, hiding in the shadows of thick underbrush. Hope's crossbow is slung over one of her shoulders; in her hand she grips a spear.

They reach a small clearing and hesitate. Moonlight silhouettes them, and they'll be sitting ducks in the open. Still, it's the only way to get across. Hope takes a deep breath and hurries forward. She doesn't exhale until all three reach a grove of trees on the far side.

"Come on," she whispers, and the words have barely left her mouth when she hears a tiny, metallic *ping*— the sound of something snapping. Out of instinct, she runs . . . just as a large net plummets from the trees and lands on her two friends. The rope is thick, the knots small and hard. Cat and Diana struggle to free themselves, but their desperate attempts only make things worse.

"Go," Cat commands.

"Not without you," she says.

She draws her knife. It won't be easy cutting through the tangled web, but she can do it if she hurries. She takes a step in their direction . . . and falls through space, arms and legs flailing. She lands with a hard thud. Snow and leaves rain down on top of her, and she lies there a moment, shaking away the pain.

A deep pit surrounds her. Her hands and fingers claw at the earth, but the surface walls have been smoothed like marble. There's no chance for handholds or climbing up. To make matters worse, her crossbow is shattered and she's separated from her spear. It lies directly above her, the spear tip dangling above the hole, the rest of it out of sight.

She hears the muffled sound of her two friends scraping against the net, trying to free themselves.

Now other sounds, too. Hushed voices. Muted footsteps in the snow. When the footsteps stop, the spear is suddenly yanked away, disappearing from sight. Hope's heart sinks.

Like a cornered beast, she backs up, tucking herself into shadows, making herself as small as possible in the deep, dark trench. She'll not go down without a fight. She still has her knife, and she grips it tightly in her palm. Wondering if these are her last moments on earth, she whispers aloud one word.

"Book."

A head appears, its outline barely visible against the night sky. Another head as well. Then still more after that. Hope can't tell if they're Crazies or Brown Shirts— although neither possibility is good. Tears sting her eyes as she readies for a fight.

"You lose this?" a voice taunts, and a hand holds out her spear high above her.

Hope doesn't answer.

"I said, did you lose this?" the questioner repeats, and Hope realizes the voice is familiar.

"Is that who I think it is?" Hope asks.

"Who else lives here?"

Hope breaks into a deep smile and lets herself

breathe again. It's Helen. After all this time, the Sisters are reunited.

While Hope is lifted from the trap, Cat and Diana are extracted from the net. The Sisters retrieve the other sixty-some Less Thans and bring them back to camp. As Helen leads the way—skirting sharpened logs and booby-trapped pits—Hope can only marvel. When they were last here, Helen was the only healthy Sister alive, and Dodge's Log Lodges was a crumbling resort, near collapse.

All that's different now.

The buildings have been repaired and camouflaged, new structures erected, and fortifications placed all around: pickets and moats and trap holes, all designed to hold the enemy at bay. Helen has transformed a series of dilapidated buildings into an actual fort.

"But it looked deserted from the ridge," Hope says, pulling the hoodie tight around her face.

"Good," Helen answers. "That's the way we want it."

Sure enough, the front windows are painted black and no repairs have been made on that particular exterior. All the expansion has taken place *behind* the existing structures—hidden from view.

Hope realizes there is something serene and peaceful about the place. Moonlight splashes the frozen lake, and the cabins themselves are like an oasis in a scarred landscape. For the moment, at least, there are no rabid wolves, no half-mad Crazies, no assaulting Brown Shirts.

Even more remarkable is how Helen has brought the Sisters back to life. There were sixty when Hope, Scylla, and Diana left here last fall. Although five didn't make it, fifty-five of them did. And they're getting healthier with each passing day.

But perhaps the greatest transformation is Helen herself. No longer the shy twin who could barely look another Sister in the eye, she is now the camp's undisputed leader. As she shows Hope around, she moves and speaks with a quiet confidence.

Later, as she helps Helen in the kitchen before preparing for bed, Hope still can't get over this new Helen. It's like a different person altogether.

"You shouldn't be ashamed, you know," Helen says out of nowhere. Her eyes are on the birch roots she's dropping into a giant cauldron.

"Of what?" Hope asks.

"Those." She gestures to Hope's two Xs.

At first, Hope doesn't respond. Her scars—and Chancellor Maddox—are the last things she wants to talk about.

"We all have scars," Helen says.

Hope bristles; it's what Book said too. "As visible as this?"

"The size of the scar isn't what matters."

"Easy for you to say."

"Maybe." Helen gives the cauldron a stir. An earthy mist rises from the boiling mixture. "But if you're interested, I do know how to make them disappear."

"How?" Hope asks, turning expectantly. She'd give anything to have her face look the way it used to look.

"By not trying to hide them."

Realizing what Helen is getting at—that she doesn't have some miracle cure—Hope gives her head a disappointed shake.

Helen goes on. "I know, I haven't experienced the kinds of things you have, but I do know that when we try to cover something up, it only draws attention to itself. But if you uncover it and show it to the world, well, it becomes invisible. Like Book's limp. When's the last time you noticed that?"

It drives Hope crazy that Book said some of the same things.

"So why do the Sisters stare at me?" Hope asks.

"What do you mean?"

"I saw how they looked at me when you brought us into camp. How their gazes lingered longer than they should've."

Helen laughs.

"What's so funny?" Hope asks, defensive.

"That's not why they're staring."

"Then why?"

"Don't you know?" Helen says. "You're their savior. You're the reason they were rescued. If it weren't for you, they'd all have been killed by Brown Shirts. And every single one of them knows it."

Hope waves away the compliment, but when she opens her mouth to speak, she can't. The lump that has lodged in her throat won't let her.

17.

IT WASN'T DIFFICULT TO track the other Less Thans' footprints in the snow, and when we finally made it to Dodge's a few days later and the two groups reunited, there was much hugging and congratulations all around. Argos got the best of it, with every single Sister wanting to pat his head and scratch behind his ears.

I spied Hope and went to thank her for escorting the Less Thans back to safety. Just as I approached her and opened my mouth to speak, she turned away. We didn't even say hello.

That evening, we all crowded into the main lodge, and following a feast of venison and rabbit stew, each group told of the gruesome things they'd seen. When

I finished describing the Compound with its piles of corpses, a thick silence hung in the air.

"No sign of your grandmother?" Cat asked.

"No sign of *any* living people," I said. "And the only body we recognized was the chief justice." I didn't tell them about Miranda. It still hurt to think of her lifeless body, lying crumpled and still like a fallen bird.

"So what do we do now?" Flush asked.

I knew what he was getting at. Brown Shirts had blown up the Compound, tons of weapons were being moved to the chancellor's fortress, and the same unbreakable code had been found on three separate people. So where did that leave us?

"Maybe we stay here for a while," I suggested. "Lie low and get our strength back before heading out in the spring."

The nods from the others told me they agreed.

"There's something you should know," Helen said, and all eyes turned to her. "Yesterday, one of the girls on patrol came across some tire tracks."

It was amazing how quickly 120-some bodies could get so quiet.

"Who saw them?" Hope asked.

A small girl named Sarah raised her hand.

"Did you see the vehicles?" Hope wanted to know.

Sarah shook her head. "Just the tracks. About a mile from here."

"What type of land? Was it on a hill? In a valley? What?"

"Maybe on a hill. I can't remember."

"You don't know?"

"I'm not sure."

Hope let out an exasperated sigh.

"Go easy on her," I said to Hope. "Why does it matter?"

"It matters because someone might be spying on us," Hope answered. "And if they were on a hill, they obviously wanted the best vantage point." Her words challenged me to contradict her. I didn't.

Despite the blazing fire in the fireplace, it felt as though the heat had been suddenly sucked out of the room. The warmth of our reunion was a thing of the past.

"So what do we do?" Helen asked.

"We figure out who they are and what they want," Hope said.

"And then?"

"And then we go from there."

That night, sitting beside the fire's dying embers, a group of us tried to crack the code, substituting letters for numbers until we were dizzy from trying. Even though we came up empty, it seemed obvious that the Brown Shirts were up to something. But what that was, we still couldn't tell.

When I finally fell asleep, I dreamed of Chancellor Maddox. She was far away from me, but even from the distance I could tell what she was doing. She was carving Xs into Hope's face. I took off running, trying to get there in time to stop her, but I wasn't fast enough. When I finally reached Hope, Maddox was gone and blood was streaming down Hope's cheeks. She refused to look me in the eye.

I'd never felt so powerless in all my life.

A group of us set out the next morning: Cat, Hope, Red, Sarah, and me. Once again, Hope found a reason to be as far away from me as possible.

Overnight, a frost had painted all the trees and bushes white, and it was like walking in a world without color. Dense thickets hid us from view as we made our way up a snow-covered hill. When the thicket cleared, Sarah pointed to a series of lines arcing through the snow, and it was easy to identify the tracks.

ATVs. Hunters.

As we studied them, we saw where the tracks converged . . . and where the riders had dismounted. It was clear they'd been looking down the hill in the direction of the lodges. Just as Hope had guessed, they were spying on us.

My stomach dropped as we eased back through the thicket, and no one said a word. We strode into camp, and Sisters and Less Thans emerged from the buildings, gazing at us expectantly.

Helen was the last to appear, wiping her hands on her apron. "Well?" she asked.

"We need to get busy," Hope said. She walked right by her, not even stopping to talk. Instead, she headed for the supply closet and began handing out axes, shovels, and saws.

18.

THEY WASTE NO TIME building their defense. Some arm crossbows, others sharpen logs, still others dig pits, covering them with false blankets of leaves. Twitch and Flush head up a crew tasked to build a series of small catapults. There were hidden pits and booby traps before, but if the Hunters are daring enough to attack Dodge's Log Lodges, they'll have to work their way through twice as many of them.

The woods are filled with the sounds of hammering and sawing.

At one point, Hope finds herself next to Book, setting traps at the camp's outskirts. For the longest time they work in silence, spreading out nets on the snow.

"So you're not talking to me anymore?" Book finally asks.

She shrugs and keeps working, bending branches to attach to the corners of the nets.

"Or do you think I'm invisible?" he goes on. "'Cause I'm right here, you know."

"I can see that."

"So?"

"Maybe I don't have anything to say."

She slips a knot around a corner of netting and pulls it taut.

"So what happened between us, what was that?" Book asks.

"The past. That was then, this is now."

"That kiss on the plateau—"

"The past."

"The one in Camp Liberty after Cat killed Dekker—"

"The past."

"Lying together in the tunnel, holding you—"

"Let it go, Book! All of it!"

A couple of Sisters glance in their direction.

"Why?" he asks.

She sighs noisily and lowers her voice. "We're too different. We don't have anything in common."

"Sure we do. I don't believe in myself, and you don't believe in me either. I'd say we're perfect for each other."

If he's hoping that she'll smile, it doesn't work. Her mouth is a straight, unwavering line.

"My feelings for you haven't changed," he whispers. "Have yours?"

She looks up at him. Her mouth opens, but no words come. Instead, she flings her net to the ground and stomps off, leaving Book alone, his breath pulsing slow and steady in the winter air.

That night, it takes Hope forever to get to sleep. It's not soreness from work, it's not even the gnawing hunger. It's the conversation; she can't get it out of her head. Although she regrets her words, she can't seem to make it clear to Book that things are different now. Two scars have changed everything.

When she finally falls into a sleep, it's a deep and soundless one. Diana has to nudge her to wake her up.

"Morning already?" Hope asks, her words slurred.

Diana presses her finger to her lips and whispers, "Shh."

An oblong of moonlight splashes the floor—enough illumination for Hope to see Diana's worried face. Hope quickly throws on clothes and grabs her weapons. They slip into the dark, snow crunching beneath their feet. Others are up as well, moving soundlessly between cabins. Hope wonders what's going on. Why does everyone seem to be creeping to the lake, to the back edge of the resort? If they're about to be attacked, shouldn't they be getting into position?

When they crouch on the snowy beach, Hope is surprised that everyone else is already there, their breaths ballooning in front of them. What Hope can't understand is why their backs are turned away from Dodge's.

"What's going on?" she asks.

Cat points across the frozen lake, but Hope doesn't know why. Finally she sees them: a series of dim yellow lights, small as fireflies, wavering like mirages just above the surface of the ice.

ATVs.

But they aren't coming from the surrounding countryside where the Sisters and Less Thans expected them to come from; they're riding across the frozen lake for a sneak attack.

"What do we do?" one of the younger Sisters asks. It isn't just panic that laces her voice, it's more like terror. She's heard the stories of how the Hunters have massacred Less Thans.

"Just turn around," Sunshine says. "Hide ourselves behind trees and boulders and fire at 'em from this direction."

"It won't stop 'em," Cat says.

"But if we take cover and our shots are good—"

"You haven't seen these people."

Sunshine has the sense to realize no one else supports him—especially those who fought the Hunters in the Brown Forest. They know this enemy.

"We could run," someone suggests, but that won't work. The Hunters have vehicles. They have guns. It wouldn't be a fair fight at all.

"So if we don't face 'em and we don't run," Sunshine says, "what do we do?"

"The only thing we can," Hope says. "We surrender."

They take pillowcases and tie them onto sticks. A dozen of them venture onto the beach, waving flags of surrender. The white cloth snaps in the midnight air.

The four-wheelers draw closer. There are several dozen in all. The rumble of their engines is muffled and far off. Hope tries to see the riders' faces, but only their silhouettes are visible, wreathed by headlights and exhaust. If the Man in Orange is among them, she can't yet tell. In the past, he's been their leader—the one who seems to take the most pleasure in killing Less Thans.

"You sure this is the right thing to do?" Sunshine asks.

No one answers him, in part because no one knows. Besides, it's too late to change plans now. They've made their decision.

"Will they honor our surrender?" Diana asks.

"They'd better," Hope says.

"And if they don't?"

Before Hope has a chance to answer, the first bullets go whizzing by, embedding themselves in trees and the backs of buildings. Shards and splinters rain down. A window shatters. The Sisters and LTs scramble for cover. They had never intended to surrender, but they'd hoped to trick the Hunters longer than this.

When the firing comes to a lull, Cat yells out, "Rocks!"

A long line of Less Thans springs up, each holding a miniature boulder. The line stretches far and wide, and when they step onto the frozen lake, it's a struggle to maintain their balance while lugging the heavy stones.

"Arrows!" Hope shouts.

Another line pops up behind the first. These are the archers—Sisters mostly—who nock their arrows quickly, efficiently.

"Draw!" Hope yells, and the archers do.

The four-wheelers near. Their rumble vibrates across the ice.

"Fire!"

A rush of arrows sails through the sky, their *whoosh* like a flock of screaming birds. When the arrows strike, their flint points clatter against the frozen lake, a hailstorm of stone on ice. Not a single Hunter goes down. The ATVs slow but keep coming.

"At will!" Hope cries, and the night rains arrows. *Whoosh whoosh whoosh.*

Led by Cat, the Less Thans have ventured out to a good twenty feet from shore. He motions them to stop. A couple crumple to the ice when hit by bullets. The others hold their ground. Then Cat hefts the rock above his head and counts out loud. "One . . . two . . ."

On three he brings the boulder down with all his might, chucking it into the ice in front of him. The rock breaks through the frozen lake and sends up a fountain of slushy water. The other Less Thans do the same. The ice is suddenly dotted with a series of boulder-sized holes. It's one thing to walk or ride atop a frozen lake; it's something else altogether to hurtle small boulders into it.

The LTs race back to shore, passing a second line of LTs who also carry boulders. They venture to the same place as the first group and heave their heavy rocks into the ice. Geysers arc skyward as more holes mar the surface. Bullets strike two more Less Thans, and their friends drag them to shore.

The Hunters keep coming, their headlights growing sharper.

Cat's group returns with another set of rocks.

"Throw!" he shouts, heaving his rock through air. The other Less Thans do the same.

Hope has that coppery taste of fear in her mouth. They had hoped the holes would connect, creating a chasm of frozen water between the Hunters and them. But it hasn't worked that way. The ice is too thick, and all they've done is make a series of gaps. It's enough to slow the Hunters down . . . but not enough to stop them.

Out of instinct, Hope looks at Book, just as he looks at her. For the briefest of seconds, their eyes lock, and then he rises from behind an overturned picnic table and yells at the top of his voice, "On the ice!"

19.

EVERYONE LOOKED AT ME, confused.

I ran forward on the lake, sliding to a stop just shy of the holes. A couple of the LTs reached for rocks, but I stopped them.

"Just you!" I said. "Nothing else!"

They still had no idea what I was thinking . . . until I began jumping up and down on the frozen lake.

"Come on!" I screamed, desperation growing. Hope was the first to understand what I was getting at. She ran from the cover of a log until she was by my side. Once the others saw her, they came out as well, until we'd created a massive line of Sisters and Less Thans that stretched as far as we could see.

"As one!" I said, and began jumping up and down. Others gradually joined me, and in no time the ice dipped and swayed, water sloshing from the holes and soaking our shoes and numbing our feet. The four-wheelers grew closer. For the first time I realized how many of them there were. Not just a couple dozen like our previous encounters with them, but fifty or sixty— an *army* of Hunters, each one atop an ATV.

"Higher!" I said, and all of us began leaping into the air in unison as though on trampolines, the ice undulating beneath us.

And then we heard it. The sound of a crack, louder than any rifle shot, like an enormous tree being ripped in half. We watched a gap run from one end of the lake to the other, connecting the holes we'd created earlier. It shook the ice beneath our feet, and many of us tumbled and fell. No matter. A watery abyss revealed itself, and the gap widened, slowly at first and then faster, until several feet separated our shelf of ice from the ice the ATVs were on.

Some of the Less Thans started to cheer.

"Get back!" I yelled, and we scrambled for cover on the rocky beach just as the four-wheelers reached the edge.

When the first Hunters arrived, they tried to brake, but their vehicles skimmed across the ice, unable to stop. As they tumbled into the icy water, we responded with a flurry of arrows.

The other Hunters slid to a stop, and they stared at the watery gap that separated them from us. Even in the dark, I could make out the Man in Orange: the burn on his face from the propane explosion, the scar where the arrow had nicked him in the Brown Forest.

"We can do this the easy way or the hard way," he called out over the idling engines. "You choose."

We didn't answer.

"All right then," he said. "Don't say we didn't warn you." He turned and nodded, and bullets raked the ground, the trees, the lodges. Every lake-facing window exploded into shards.

We stayed hidden behind boulders, logs, overturned picnic tables—anything we could find.

When the barrage finished, the Man in Orange said, "We can wait you out, you know. I can send some of my men back around so you'll be surrounded. And then there's nothing you can do."

He was right. We had won this battle, but not the war. We were fortified but also trapped. That gap in the lake meant one less exit out of there.

"Starvation is such a gruesome way to die," he said, as the other Hunters chuckled. "Or we can talk about this. Give yourselves up, and we'll work out a deal."

We looked at one another but said nothing. The wind shook the surrounding trees and sent snow ghosts skittering across the frozen lake.

"Fine," he said. "Your funeral."

He made a motion to his fellow riders, and they

began turning their vehicles around.

But I had something else in mind.

I read in a book once about Molotov cocktails, how they got their name during a war in the 1930s when Finnish soldiers used improvised bombs against Russia. Dodge's Log Lodges just happened to have all the necessary ingredients.

As part of our plan to "surrender," we had emptied out the wine bottles in the cellar, replacing the alcohol with gasoline from lawn mowers in the shed. Once we stuck in bits of kerosene-soaked cloth, our bombs were ready. Meanwhile, others began turning the catapults around.

"Light cocktails!" I yelled, and small blue flames erupted up and down the line. I waited until all the four-wheelers were facing the other way, and then I cried out, *"Now!"*

Some of us raced forward, past the beach and onto the ice. It buckled and dipped beneath our feet, cracking and sloshing water. Still we ran, the burning cocktails gripped in our outstretched hands, not stopping until we reached that watery line where ice ended and lake began. Once there, we heaved the flaming bottles over the Hunters' heads. The catapults did the same, even more effectively landing cocktails well behind the enemy. There was a sound of shattering glass, followed seconds later by igniting flames.

Whoompf. Whoompf whoompf. Whoompf whoompf whoompf!

A line of fire spread in a distant arc.

The Man in Orange turned around. The flickering flames caught his scornful expression.

"You missed," he said drily. "Too bad."

But we hadn't missed.

When the fire began eating into ice—right down to the lake itself—the Hunters began to panic. Some revved their engines and tried to make it across. They weren't successful. The gap was far too wide, and those who attempted to fly from one scrap of ice to the other ended up in the water—an immediate and icy grave.

Four-wheelers suddenly buzzed around in a noisy panic, only gradually realizing they were imprisoned on a circle of ice. They throttled their ATVs, looking for a bridge where they could get across.

It didn't exist. With rocks and fire, we had managed to create an enormous island in the lake . . . and they were stuck on it.

The Man in Orange glared at us.

"Starvation is such a gruesome way to die," I yelled.

And then we turned and walked away, taking the four dead LTs with us so we could give them a proper burial.

20.

DAYS PASS. A THIN skin of ice forms on the open water, but nothing thick enough for a person to walk on or an ATV to drive on. The Hunters remain stranded, huddled behind their four-wheelers like a circled wagon train on the Oregon Trail.

Hope and the others go about their daily activities, gathering food, building defenses . . . and keeping one eye on the Hunters. If they even think about crossing the ice, the Sisters will open fire.

On the fifth day, the Man in Orange rises from the circle and walks to the edge of the ice floe. He raises his arms and waves a white handkerchief.

"We want to talk," he calls out. His voice is raspy, and he looks pale and weak.

Diana is on watch. Instead of responding, she makes a motion to Sarah, who goes loping off. A few minutes later, Hope, Cat, and Book return, followed by a couple of dozen Less Thans and Sisters.

The Sisters and LTs regard the huddled Hunters, and then Hope steps onto the beach. "We're listening," she calls out. "What do you want to say?"

"We're starving and freezing. We need food and blankets."

"Why should we trust you?"

The Man in Orange scowls. "Look at us. There's nothing we can do."

"You still have guns—there's plenty you can do."

"So what do you want?"

"What else? Put down your weapons."

The Man in Orange turns to the other Hunters. With his back to the shore, it's impossible to hear what he's saying, but a moment later the Hunters raise their hands high in the air.

"Not good enough," Hope says. "You need to actually drop your weapons. All of them."

The Man in Orange sighs, lowers his hands, and then his gun goes clattering to the ice. Others follow.

"Better?" he asks.

"Almost. Now kick them in the water."

Heads snap in Hope's direction.

"Are you kidding?" Sunshine whispers. "Those could

be our ticket outta here."

"No. Those could be our downfall," she says grimly.

She doesn't bother to explain, but both Book and Cat nod their heads in support.

"Throw them in the water," Hope calls out again, "and then we'll talk."

"Who do you think you are?" the Man in Orange growls. "Some girl telling us what to do?"

"We're the people you've been hunting the last two decades. And as long as you have weapons, you're not getting any food."

The Hunters don't bother to hide their anger. Still, what choice do they have? They're hungry, shivering, gaunt from cold and lack of sleep. One by one they stumble to the icy edge and slide their rifles into the lake. The water swallows the weapons with a thick *kerplunk*.

"All of them!" Hope calls out.

Several of the Hunters remove hidden pistols from shoulder straps and drop them in the water as well.

Satisfied, Hope turns to Sarah. "Get every single person. And someone find a ladder."

When she runs off, Hope makes her way out onto the ice. "So what do you wanna talk about?" she asks.

Even from where she stands, Hope can see the Man in Orange's jaw working back and forth in humiliation.

"You know what," he says. "Let us off of here and we'll return to our homes and won't bother you again."

"Why should we trust you? Aren't you the same guys who burned down a forest to get to us?"

"Do you want to negotiate or not?"

Hope cocks her head as if considering the offer. "Dump your vehicles and we'll consider it."

His eyes go wide. "Listen, we already threw away our weapons. We're unarmed. We don't have anything—"

"Roll the vehicles into the lake."

The Man in Orange gestures to the ATVs. "Do you know how rare these things are these days? How *valuable*?"

"Dump 'em, or this conversation's over."

The silence lengthens to something long and unbearable. Then the lead Hunter nods to his comrades.

One after another, the Hunters shift their four-wheelers to neutral and wheel them over the edge of the ice. They plunge beneath the surface of the lake. The icy water roils as it swallows them.

"Satisfied?" the Man in Orange asks bitterly, when all the vehicles are gone. Fifty-some stranded Hunters stand in the middle of an ice floe. They look naked without weapons and armor-plated ATVs.

Hope motions for the ladder. It's slid over the chasm of icy water, and the Man in Orange is the first to crawl across on hands and knees. When he reaches the other side, Less Thans tie his wrists with a stretch of rope.

"I thought you said we were free to return to our homes," the Hunter demands.

"No, that's what *you* said. I think you need to be our prisoners—at least until we're out of the territory."

"Then the deal's off."

"Fine." Hope turns to the Less Thans. "Remove the ladder. Leave the others out there."

The LTs start pulling it back.

"Wait!" the Man in Orange shouts. He hesitates. "We'll do it your way. But you can trust us."

Hope doesn't even bother to respond.

One by one, the Hunters crawl across the ladder. As each one reaches the Sisters and Less Thans, he's tied up and hobbled like a horse so he can't attack or run away. Then they're all searched a final time. There are still a couple of concealed knives, a small pistol . . . and a slip of paper, found in the Man in Orange's front pocket.

On it are the same numbers from before.

4539221103914

"What is this?" Hope asks the Man in Orange.

He sneers, the lopsided smile tugging at his burn. "Wouldn't you like to know?"

Hope motions for them to be taken away.

As the Man in Orange is about to walk by, Hope puts

a hand on his forearm, whips him around, then slaps him as hard as she can. Her icy fingers dig into his scar-pocked face.

"What was that for?" the Man in Orange growls.

"Wouldn't you like to know?" she says, and walks off.

21.

WE LOCKED THE HUNTERS in a cabin and set up guards. We put the Man in Orange in a separate cabin, far away from the others. The less contact he had with his friends, the better. The day after their surrender, Cat and I entered his cell.

"What's this mean?" Cat asked, sliding the piece of paper across the table. A couple of Less Thans stood guard outside the door.

"We know it's a code," I went on. "We just don't know what it says."

The Man in Orange's eyes bored into the table. His burn was pink and shiny and glistened with secretions. He hadn't shaved in days.

"If you tell us," I said, "we'll help you out."

"Yeah, right," he scoffed.

"In case you haven't noticed, you're our prisoners here."

"Maybe now," he said with a smirk. "Not for long."

His words sent a shudder down my back. I tried to hide it.

"So are you going to tell us or not?" Cat asked.

"You gonna release us?"

"No."

"Then I'm not gonna tell you."

He sat opposite us, his ankles and wrists tethered together with rope. Even though he was the prisoner, something about his tone made it feel like he was the one in charge.

"What do you aim to do with us?" he asked. He tilted back his chair on its rear legs like he owned the place.

"What do you mean?" Cat said.

"You captured us, but we all know you can't keep us here forever. I'm guessing you'll want to leave come spring. So it's a pretty simple question: what're you planning on doing with us?"

Cat and I didn't answer.

"You gonna turn us over to the government? 'Cause in case you hadn't noticed, Chancellor Maddox is a friend of ours."

I could feel my face burning hot. I had no good response, and he and I both knew it.

"Anything else you want to know?" he mocked. "Or is that about it?"

"You never answered my question—"

"And I don't intend to. Not until you release us."

My chair squealed as I pushed it back. Maybe someone else would have better luck talking to him. I certainly wasn't getting anywhere.

My hand was shaking as I placed it on the doorknob, but before I opened it, his voice called out behind me.

"You think 'cause you got us locked up you've won? You think Chancellor Maddox has *forgotten* about you? 'Cause in case you didn't know, it was the government that brokered the deal with us. They not only gave us permission to hunt you down, it was their idea. No different from deer season back in the day, they told us. Just thinning the herd."

His words turned me around.

"But w-we're people," I stammered.

"You're Less Thans. There's a difference."

My fists kneaded my face, as though trying to massage away his words.

He leaned forward. "And I'll tell you something else, *Less Thans*. Your little summer camp here ain't as secret as you think."

My heart thunked to a stop.

"What're you saying?" Cat asked.

"Once we found you all, you think we kept that

information to ourselves? By now, our riders have reached Chancellor Maddox and told her all about this tree house of yours. I'm sure she'll be thrilled to know exactly where you are, especially before the Conclave begins."

Dread settled in my stomach. Cat and I shared a look.

"Why should anyone care about us?" I asked. "We just want to get to the next territory and start a new life."

He laughed long and hard. "It doesn't matter what you *want*. You really think Chancellor Maddox will let you leave now that you know about the Final Solution?"

His words were a slap to the face.

"What's the matter?" the Man in Orange sneered. "Not so cocky all of a sudden?"

I found enough voice to ask, "What's the Conclave?" I'd heard the word twice before: once as Goodman Nellitch gripped my ankles on the cliff face, before he fell to his death. The second time was when Chancellor Maddox threatened me at Camp Liberty. In both cases, I'd had no idea what they were talking about.

The Man in Orange chuckled. "You really don't know shit from Shinola, do you, boy?"

He continued to laugh, and when it was obvious he wasn't going to answer me, I stumbled outside, sweat pouring from my body. Cat was right behind me. The Man in Orange's laughter seeped through the door, the walls, the ceiling—the haunting sound soaring to the heavens.

But of course it wasn't just his laughter that worried me, it was our new reality. We had hoped to stay here at Dodge's until the spring thaw—just like we'd hoped to stay at Libertyville before that. But if the chancellor was bringing her Brown Shirts after us, we had little choice but to pack up and leave. Once more it would be a race to the next territory, and this time with an entire army on our tail.

PART TWO
ALLIES

He who conquers others is strong; he who conquers himself is mighty.
—LAO TZU

22.

Two DAYS LATER WE left Dodge's Log Lodges. There were approximately 175 of us: 125 Less Thans and Sisters, and another 50 or so Hunters.

"If you're thinking of leaving the Western Federation Territory, you'll never get out alive," the Man in Orange said as we shackled him and the other prisoners together.

"We'll see," I said, trying to sound confident. But it was hard to disagree with him.

We retraced our steps from a lifetime ago, back when we'd rescued the Sisters from the death march. Around the lake, through the woods, down one gravel road after another. For obvious reasons, we avoided Camp Freedom. The town of Bedford, too. Crazies lived there. And we wanted nothing to do with them.

"Hey!" one of the Hunters shouted at dinner one night. He was a round man with a square head and triangle ears. Like the others, he reeked from not bathing. "You expect us to eat this swill?"

"It's the same swill we eat," Sunshine said. The rest of us had pretty much learned to tune the Hunters out.

"What is it?"

"Rabbit stew—what do you think it is?"

"It looks like shit to me. Tastes like it, too."

"It's better than what you had on the ice," Sunshine said. "Which was *nothing*."

"Sounds like something a Less Than would say. A Less Than who's used to eating *shit*." Triangle Ears slung his stew across the fire, and it landed with a *splat* on the LT's face.

Sunshine jumped to his feet, ready to fight, and Cat and Red had to restrain him.

"Don't," Cat said. "It's what he wants."

"He can't get away with that! It's not right!"

"Let it go."

Sunshine's eyes darted back and forth between Triangle Ears and Cat. When Cat finally got him to sit back down, the Man in Orange spoke up.

"Hey, Limp," he called out. "You really think you can make it all the way to the next territory?"

"We did it once," I said.

"Yeah, but I bet you didn't have wolves trailing you the whole time."

He picked up on my surprise.

"Don't tell me you didn't hear the howls this morning," he asked. "They're close. *Real* close. I'd say you all are sitting ducks—unless you release us and let us help you fight 'em."

"Not likely," I said.

"Suit yourself."

I tried to concentrate on eating, but all I could think about was wolves. Had I really missed hearing them, or was he just making it up?

"What's your deal, anyway?" he asked.

"What're you talking about?"

"You know *exactly* what I'm talking about, Limp. You and the chick with the Xs on her face. I'm guessing you want her, but she wants nothing to do with you. Am I right?"

He laughed, and the food got lodged in my throat. I felt heat prickling the back of my neck.

"I got news for you, sonny boy. You ain't gonna get her. She's got eyes for ol' One Arm over there. In fact, I think I might've seen 'em kissing behind the shed at your little hideout."

Cat reached out a hand, but there was no stopping me. I threw down my food and went racing across the circle, lunging on top of the Man in Orange and hitting him as hard as I could. He was tied up, so I had no problem getting the better of him—one punch after another, slamming my fists into his face until my knuckles bled.

But Cat was right; it was exactly what the Man in Orange wanted.

Once I started hitting him, the other Hunters made a break for it. Some of them had managed to loosen their knots, and there was suddenly chaos—Hunters running in fifty different directions, and LTs and Sisters fumbling for weapons and racing after them.

The snow allowed us to track them down, but even then, the Hunters were big and strong and didn't go down without a fight. There were bruises and bloody noses on both sides, and only the threat of knives and arrows convinced the Hunters to finally give up. It took us a full hour to corral them all.

The Man in Orange's face was a bleeding mess, but he didn't seem to care. Just the opposite, in fact. His smile, showing bloodstained teeth, mocked me as though the Hunters were the ones who'd just won this latest skirmish.

"Let it go," I heard Cat say, but whether he was talking about the Man in Orange or him and Hope I didn't know.

I shook off his grip and hurried away, wondering if the day would ever come when the Hunters would be punished for what they'd done to us. Wondering also if what he'd said was true: Was I really wasting my time with Hope? If so, why did I even bother?

23.

ONCE AGAIN, HOPE SLEEPS hardly at all. It's not just what the Hunter said but other things, too. Like the memory of the Heartland.

They'd made it there once before, and not a day goes by when Hope doesn't remember the life they glimpsed that night. Families having picnics. Children playing tag. Musicians in gazebos. More heaven-like than any heaven she could imagine.

They'd done the right thing. Crawling under the fence and coming back for the others. Trying to save the Less Thans and Sisters. Still, Hope longs for the day when she can have even a fraction of that happiness . . . with someone by her side.

She runs her hands through her hair and then lets

them linger on her face. Who is she kidding? There's no chance of that. Not with these two grotesque scars.

Morning comes and Cat returns from watch. "There's one out there," he says.

Heads turn. They know exactly what he's talking about.

"Close?" Flush asks.

"Close enough."

"Could just be a loner," Flush says hopefully. "Not from the Libertyville pack, just one on its own."

"Could be."

But then again, probably not, Hope thinks.

They break camp and set out. They're getting good at these hasty departures. The snow comes down hard, falling throughout the day. When they left Dodge's Log Lodges, it was up to their ankles. Now it's nearly to their knees.

Book takes point, the first to burrow through the thick drifts. Cat offers to take his place, but Book refuses. It's like he's driven to get out of here. Hope wonders if he's trying to get away from Dodge's . . . or her.

The blizzard still rages when they stop for the night, and their clothes are plastered in white. They look like mythological creatures.

There's no way they can go on a hunt, and all they have left is a dwindling supply of onions and potatoes. After tying the Hunters to a grove of trees, the Sisters and Less Thans huddle together against the side of a cut bank, trying to ignore their gnawing hunger. Book is as far away from Hope as possible. When Hope gives him a glance, he looks in the other direction.

"You're not going to make it," the Man in Orange calls out gleefully, just as everyone's about to fall asleep. "You should've let us kill you when we had a chance." He leans his head back and lets out a mocking laugh.

Hope grits her teeth but says nothing. She doesn't have the energy or desire.

An hour or so later, when most everyone's asleep, Hope pushes herself to her feet and walks the length of the cut bank. She wends her way between sleeping bodies, careful not to nudge anyone awake.

She can see his outline against the fire, the flames' flickering lights tousling his brownish-black hair. He's keeping watch, his eyes staring intently at the black beyond their camp. With no greeting whatsoever, she plops herself down beside him.

"Why'd you do it?" she asks.

Book is startled to see her. "Do what?"

"Come back from the other side?"

Book's eyebrows arch in surprise. "That was last summer. You're asking about that *now*?"

"We were there—we reached the Heartland—and then you decided we needed to come back to save the others."

"That's right. Do you regret it?"

"I'm not saying that."

"Then . . . ?"

"I just want to know what you were thinking."

He lets out a long breath. "I saw those families and how happy they were, and I figured that'd be us pretty soon. It just didn't seem fair that that's the life we were going to be leading while we had friends stuck back in camp. There wasn't really any choice in the matter."

"Sure there was a choice. You didn't hear the rest of us suggesting we cross back over."

"Maybe not then, but once reality set in, your conscience would've gotten the better of you. I know you."

"You do, do you?"

"A little bit, yeah," he says. "It was the right thing to do and you know it."

The light from the fire dances on Book's cheeks. Hope turns away.

"Why're you asking me this?" he wonders.

"Just curious."

"Maybe, but we haven't spoken in days, so I bet there's a reason."

Hope feels her cheeks burning and is grateful for the dark. She angles her face away from him.

"So what is it?" he presses.

Hope is suddenly unable to speak. She has the sense of what she wants to say, but somewhere between her brain and her mouth, the words are getting stuck. It's like there are too many and they're all jumbled together and she couldn't form a sentence if her life depended on it. If she attempted to talk, it'd just be gibberish.

"Are you gonna tell me?" Book prompts.

"It's like I told you," she says, then quickly rises. "I was curious. Good night."

Before Book can stop her, Hope slips into darkness, pulling the hood tight around her face.

As her fingertips trace her scars, she vows she will do whatever it takes to finish off Dr. Gallingham and Chancellor Maddox—even if it means sacrificing her life in the process. *After all,* she thinks, *it's the right thing to do.*

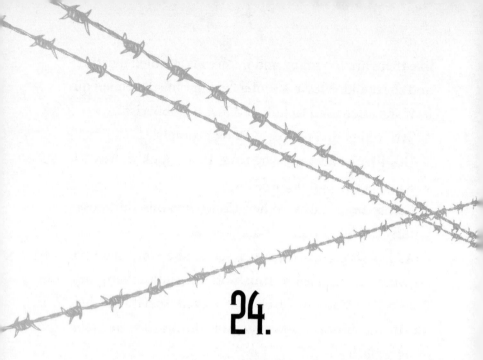

24.

THE NEXT DAY, AS we trudged through falling snow, I thought of Hope. I wondered why it was she'd come to talk to me. Wondered what it was she couldn't say.

"I have some thoughts about those numbers," Twitch said, suddenly appearing by my side. One hand rested on the shoulder of Flush, who guided him forward.

"I'm listening," I said.

"If it's a code, it can't be too complicated, because too many people seem to have it. And if they're all expected to solve it, then there's gotta be a simple solution."

"Makes sense."

"Which makes me think it's gotta be a cipher—each number represents a different letter of the alphabet. The problem is, there could be any number of choices."

140

He recited the numbers; at this point, of course, he knew them by heart. "But maybe we're thinking about them wrong. Like the four numbers in the middle. We're assuming they're 'one, one, zero, three,' but maybe they're actually 'eleven, zero, three,' or maybe 'one, ten, three,' or maybe even 'one, one hundred and three'? There's just no way of knowing, except by going through and doing a literal translation. Which is what we've been working on."

"Okay. So did you find anything?"

"Nothing definite, but I think we're getting closer." He looked to Flush, who removed a crumpled piece of paper from his pocket. It was the chart, now more elaborate than ever.

"If we start with one as 'o,' then two becomes 'p,' three is 'q,' and so on," Flush explained. "And if we think of the beginning numbers as four, fifty-three, ninety-two, twenty-one, one hundred and three, ninety-one and four, then we get something kinda interesting."

"What exactly?"

"Robimar," Flush read.

"Robimar?" I asked.

"Robimar," he repeated.

"Is that even a word?"

"Not that we know of," Twitch said. "But maybe it's the name of a town. Or a person." His excitement was palpable. "What do you think?"

"I haven't heard of it, but it sounds like you might be getting close."

"We think so, too." And with that, he and Flush headed off, talking excitedly. It sure seemed that cracking the code would reveal what the Brown Shirts were up to.

When we stopped late that afternoon, we tied the prisoners to a grove of birch trees, and I removed the map—the one of the former United States. It had been living in my pocket ever since I'd ripped it from the atlas back at the Compound. Its creases were sharp to the touch.

I ironed it out on a rock while my index finger traced one town after another, looking for anything resembling Robimar. The names of the cities were exotic and foreign-sounding.

Great Falls. Excelsior Springs. Butte. Paradise.

I suddenly wondered what the name was of the town we'd seen in the Heartland. Maybe that was Robimar.

I had just returned the map to my pocket when Cat made a sharp whistling noise. Everyone stopped what they were doing, and the howls began a moment later. Wolves. Not just one lone wolf as Flush had hoped, but a pack. And there was something urgent in the cries. Desperate.

Sisters and Less Thans exchanged panicked glances and Cat took charge.

"Form a circle," he said. "Then arm yourselves."

Everyone scrambled to the grove of trees and got into position. With the prisoners in the middle, we all sat down around them, our backs to one another, our weapons out. And then we waited, listening to the mournful wail of howling wolves.

When darkness came, the yellow appeared.

Wolf eyes. I'd never seen so many in my life.

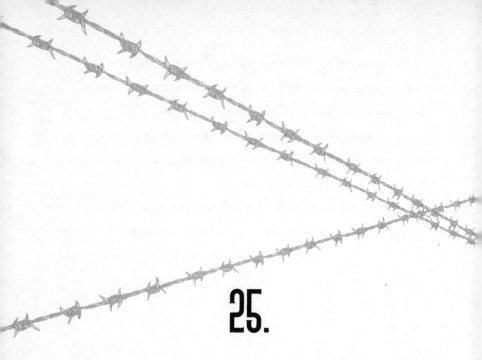

25.

HOPE COUNTS FOUR PAIRS of eyes—an easy enough number to bring down. Then a fifth pair appears. And a sixth. And soon it's not just six wolves, but twenty. And then not just twenty, but fifty, then a *hundred*, all circling the Sisters and Less Thans, snarling and growling and nipping at the wind.

"Why don't you untie us?" the Man in Orange suggests. "We're pretty handy with weapons."

"So we've seen," Flush says drily.

"Then the smart thing would be to let us help you. There's no way you can take those wolves down on your own."

No one says anything, but Hope knows he's right. On their own, the LTs and Sisters may be able to bring down several dozen wolves, but there are far too many to defeat them all. Eventually, the wolves will reach them.

Eventually, the wolves will win.

"Be smart," the Man in Orange pleads. "Untie us now and we'll never bother you again."

Other Hunters say the same, begging to be let free. Hope hears them tugging against the ropes, the hemp scraping the bark of the trees.

She looks to Cat. He gives his head a shake, and it's clear what he's thinking. Arming the Hunters is just as suicidal as facing wolves.

"Come on!" the Man in Orange screams. "You need us!"

Maybe, Hope thinks. *But if we're going to die, better that it's on our terms. Not at the hands of the Hunters.*

The wolves continue to circle, launching their frenzied howls into the night. The sound raises goose bumps on Hope's arms.

Without warning, three wolves make a dash for the circle. Arrows bring the first two down, but the third makes it through. He goes straight for a Less Than's throat, and it's a good twenty seconds before a Sister manages to kill it with her knife. The wolf collapses with a sigh.

The wolves continue to circle, and again a small group makes a break for it. Four wolves this time. Two make it to the circle and latch onto Sisters' arms. The surrounding Less Thans and Sisters have to scramble to beat them away.

Hope shares a look with Cat. They're being tested. The wolves are seeing how many they have to sacrifice to get through. Even as the pack continues to make revolutions in the snow, drools of saliva hanging from their teeth, they seem to be calculating their odds.

"Why don't they just do it?" Sunshine asks. "What're they waiting for?"

"The right moment," Cat says, and leaves it at that.

The Sisters and Less Thans try to stay alert, but it's difficult, mesmerized as they are by the circling pairs of eyes. Yellow dots in a black surround.

"Come on!" Sunshine shouts. "Just do it! Come and get us!"

The wolves' howls sound like laughter. Finally, Sunshine can't take it any longer. He throws himself to his feet and darts away from the circle before anyone can stop him.

"Sunny, don't!" someone yells.

But he's rushing straight for the pack of wolves, brandishing his knife, waving it rapidly back and forth.

Six wolves are on him before he can bring the blade forward. The beasts tear him limb from limb, ripping off arms and legs and hands and fingers, burying their snouts into the flesh of his skin and yanking out organs and entrails.

Hope can't turn away fast enough. It's an awful sight . . . and sound. A couple of the Sisters retch.

Sunshine might have been brash, he might have been a bit of a braggart, but he was a Less Than just the same. He was one of them. It's no longer just fear that hangs over the Sisters and Less Thans; it's an overwhelming sadness.

"No one else goes anywhere," Cat says.

But before anyone can stop him, Book rises and heads for the very center of the circle: the prisoners.

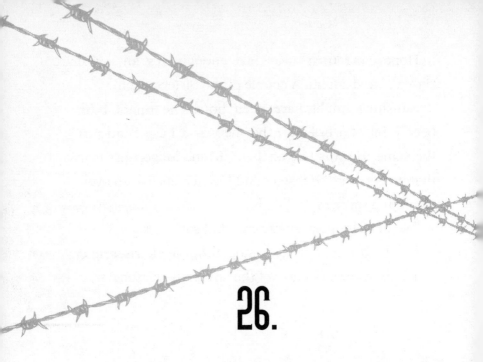

26.

IT WAS CRAZY WHAT I was thinking—downright stupid, in fact—but I knew we had to do something. Sunshine's death proved that.

My hands were shaking when I reached the Man in Orange.

"Thank you," he said, his voice brimming with relief. "You won't regret this."

He extended his body forward so I could slice through the ropes behind his back.

I withdrew my knife. But instead of cutting the ropes, I placed the knife tip at the top button of his coat and sawed downward.

"What're you doing?" he asked.

I didn't stop until his coat and shirt opened up like a

robe, sliced through from top to bottom. Snow pelted his chest.

"Hey!" he yelled, straining against his ropes. "What the hell do you think you're doing?"

I didn't answer. Instead, I went to the next prisoner and did the same, cutting his coat and shirt from top to bottom. And then the prisoner next to *him* and the one after that until I'd gone to all of them, all fifty, slicing through their outer clothes as though gutting fish. They twisted and squirmed to avoid my blade.

"What're you doing, Book?" Hope asked, but I didn't answer her.

By now, the Hunters were yelling at me. Screaming. Cursing.

"What the hell?" "You can't do that, ya little punk!" "We're going to freeze to death out here!"

I turned to the Man in Orange and met his gaze. "I promise you: that's not how you're going to die."

I thought of Cannon and the other LTs and that initial massacre in the mountains—how the Hunters had tracked them down and been so happy to finish them off. They'd even posed with the LTs' bullet-riddled bodies like big game hunters on safari.

I don't consider myself a vengeful person, but those memories allowed me to do what I did next.

Extending my knife, I swiped the blade across the lead Hunter's stomach—one quick horizontal cut. Not deep enough to kill, just enough to draw blood.

"What do you think you're doing?" the Man in Orange sputtered, writhing and twisting and tugging at his ropes.

I looked into his eyes and said, "What do you *think* I'm doing? I'm feeding the animals."

I sliced a couple of the other Hunters, but not all. There was no need. Libertyville had taught me that the wolves had a taste for human flesh. The scent of just a little human blood would be enough. The other Less Thans and Sisters looked at me with questioning eyes.

"Time to leave," I said.

Flush's eyes widened. "And the wolves are gonna let us?"

"That's what we're about to find out."

No one said anything. It was a crazy, stupid, desperate idea.

"Book's right," Cat said at last. "Let's try it."

Slowly, so as not to startle the circling wolves, everyone rose—all 120-something of us.

At first, the wolves didn't know what to think, and for the longest time they continued their revolutions. Studying. Inspecting. Their whimpers increased, whipped up by the scent of blood and the prospect of an easy meal. Their muzzles pointed toward the sky, sniffing the air. They inched closer, pawing at the ground, their saliva dripping onto snow.

"Follow me," I said, and inched away from the circle.

The others followed single file behind me, sliding through the snow. With each step, we grew closer and closer to the circle of wolves. They eyed us suspiciously. Half of them ogled the helpless Hunters while the other half kept their eyes on us.

"Lower your weapons," I said.

"Then we're as good as dead," Flush said.

"Lower them."

Everyone did, reluctantly dropping spears and bows and arrows to their waists. Still, we gripped them tighter than ever, and in the darkness I could make out the whites of my friends' knuckles. What I couldn't see was how the wolves were reacting.

I was now mere feet from them.

The biggest of the wolves—clearly the alpha male— had edged his way around the circle so that he stood directly in my path. His snout sported a diamond-shaped tuft of white, and the husky growl that rumbled from his throat vibrated through my body.

I came to a halt when I was only a yard away from him.

"There's no need to go for us," I whispered to the wolf. "There's more than enough food right back there. And they're unarmed." I gestured to my weapon as though he could understand.

I can't say he got my words, but he stared me up and

down, his eyes darting from my face to my weapon to the prisoners tied up behind us. After what seemed an eternity, he shuffled to one side. The wolves behind him did as well, creating a narrow passageway for us.

"Go," I said to Flush, who was right behind me. "Lead the others away from here."

"Aren't you coming?"

"In a bit."

I stood there and made sure all the LTs and Sisters got through. I had no more reason to trust the wolves than I did the Hunters, and I needed to see that all of us made it out alive. As Hope passed, her hand accidentally brushed against mine. What surprised me was that even though our lives were in the balance, I felt a shudder of something when her skin touched mine. Recognition? Remembrance? *Pleasure?*

When the last Sister shuffled through, the alpha male and I made eye contact for a final time . . . and then I hurried to catch up with the others. As soon as I moved away from them, the wolves stepped back in place, completing their circle.

"Don't leave us here!" I heard the Man in Orange cry out. *"Please!"*

Shoulda thought of that when you were attacking unarmed Less Thans, I wanted to say.

Maybe what happened next wouldn't have happened in pre-Omega times. But as Frank had told us, wolves were different now. I turned around and watched as they edged closer to the Hunters, who were now yanking at the ropes and crying out in terror. I would have felt compassion for them . . . if I hadn't remembered everything I'd seen them do.

The attack happened in the blink of an eye. Even as the alpha male was in the air, leaping toward the squirming figure of the Man in Orange, the other wolves were right behind. They pounced on the prisoners in a choreography that was both beautiful and awful.

The Hunters' screams filled the night—a haunting sound that pierced my ears. But louder even than their screams were the snarls of wolves feasting on prey. Human bodies being ripped apart, bits of flesh and skin gobbled down. The wolves were desperate for food, and they wasted no time devouring the human meat.

"Keep moving," I whispered to the other LTs, who'd also stopped to look.

We scrambled out of there, slogging through snow in the dead of night, moving faster than we ever had. The sight—and *sound*—of those wolves devouring the Hunters gave us all the incentive we needed. Some of the other LTs and Sisters offered words of congratulations.

"Nice job, Book." "Good thinking back there." "We owe you, man."

Some slapped me on the back; a couple shook my hand.

Hope said absolutely nothing.

So apparently the Man in Orange was right. I was wasting my time.

27.

Hope tries.

As she passes Book on her way out of the circle, she stretches out her hand to touch his. But either he doesn't see her . . . or he doesn't care. In any case, he doesn't respond.

She can't really blame him. Until she can gather the courage to say what she feels, things aren't going to change.

They march through the night and all the next day, and Hope doesn't say a word to anyone. She walks well ahead of the others, not allowing anyone to get close. When they set up camp that next night, they're hungry and exhausted and fall asleep immediately. Except Hope. She takes in her surroundings and dwells on what could be, what could have been.

Hope tiptoes between sleeping bodies, her path lit by the fire's dying embers. When she reaches Book, she takes a deep breath, lowers herself to the ground, and places her hand on his shoulder.

"Book," she says, giving him a gentle shake. "Come on."

His eyes flutter open, surprised to see her. "Where're we going?"

"You'll see."

She rises and strides off. Book stumbles to his feet and follows.

Hope leads the way through the dark forest, pushing aside branches, stepping through thickets. When she comes to a small creek, rimmed in ice, she stops a moment and absently strokes her necklace.

"Where're we going?" Book asks again.

Hope doesn't answer. She jumps the creek and resumes walking.

She walks swiftly now, more confidently. Book has to hurry to keep up. They come to what used to be a dirt road. Even through the snow, it's possible to see the ruts from pre-Omega vehicles. Hope follows the road.

They climb a small hill, halting when they reach the top. They're both breathing heavily. It takes Book a moment to understand why they've come to a stop, but then he sees it. There, nestled in the hollow of the hills, sculpted by moonglow, is a small cabin. It's nearly in ruins—the paint is peeling, one window is shattered, there's a gaping hole in the roof—but Hope inhales sharply at the sight.

"Is this—" Book asks.

She nods. Her former home. Where she grew up. Where her parents rocked her to sleep. Where she and Faith played in the small creek out back. Where her mother was brutally murdered.

They walk down the hill and approach the house, slowly, quietly, reverently. Hope can feel her heart pounding. The porch draws her first. It was where her mother was shot and killed a decade earlier. Hope reaches it and slowly climbs the sagging steps. The wood creaks and groans beneath her weight.

The stain is visible even in the palest moonlight. Kidney shaped and black in color, it represents her mother's dying moments. Hope's eyes travel to the outside wall, and there, scribbled in blood, is one word: *Dekker.* Just as he boasted back at Camp Liberty, the sergeant wrote his name after he murdered Hope's mother.

Hope can't turn away fast enough.

Book places his hand on Hope's elbow and guides her down the stairs. "Come on," he says, and she nods absently.

They leave the porch and reach the flagstone sidewalk. Hope looks around.

"I wonder where . . ."

She sees it then—a small wooden cross embedded in the earth. Her feet take her there like iron fillings to a magnet.

She has never seen her mother's grave before. She knew her father came back here years later and buried her—his wife; Hope and Faith's mother—but he never spoke about it. And Hope and Faith never asked.

There's only the slightest indication that this is a burial plot—just the vaguest hint of borders and edges that mark the grave. A mound of snow atop a mound of earth. It's the cross that gives it away.

Hope bends down and crouches at the marker, rubbing her fingers along its grooved edges. Her index finger traces each of the letters of her mother's name: *Charlotte Patterson Samadi*. The dates of birth and death are there as well, but they mean little to Hope. Just numbers. It's the person she misses.

Hope looks up, only then realizing the grave rests in the shadow of a giant ponderosa pine. It was Hope's mother's favorite tree.

Hope's throat tightens up, and tears press against her eyes. She rises quickly and stumbles away. She doesn't know what she's doing or where she's going. All she knows is that she misses her mother terribly, she needs someone to comfort her, to hold her, to tell her everything's going to be all right. She falls into the outstretched arms of Book—an embrace filled with need and grief and utter longing.

They creep back to camp, silent, and Hope is grateful when they can each return to their beds. The next morning, packing up and setting out, she can barely look Book in the eye. Once more, she volunteers to take the lead position on the trail.

Midway through the afternoon, the group finds itself on a series of rolling hills with hardly a tree in sight. Being so out in the open makes Hope nervous, and she picks up the pace as best she can. When she eventually spies a grove of fir and spruce in the distance, she begins to relax. They can build fires. They can hide themselves in the woods. She ducks her head into the wind and bulldozes through waist-high snow.

Then they hear the howls.

Everyone stops and looks behind them. On a far-off ridge stand dozens of wolves, their faces wreathed in steam. They've been trailing the Sisters and Less Thans this entire time. The incident with the Hunters only slowed them down.

"Come on," Hope says, and they begin to march again. Faster now. Desperate. Hope is no longer leading; they're *all* leading, trying to get to the woods as quickly as they can. There's only one slight dip of land left to go. After a quick descent into a valley, there's a gentle rise leading to the grove of trees. Then they'll be safe. Surrounded by woods. Encircled by fire.

That's when Cat comes to a stop. Then Book, then Hope, then *everyone*. A line of wolves, stretching from side to side like a fortress wall, stands between them and the grove of trees. Even in the swirling snow, Hope can see their gleaming eyes, the dried blood that paints their snouts.

"Spread out and weapons," Cat says. He's can't hide the fact that his voice is trembling.

With teeth bared and bodies lowered, the wolves come slinking forward. Their bellies graze the snow.

The Sisters and Less Thans stretch the line and fumble for arrows, spears, slingshots, *anything*. There may be 120-some of them, but there are easily twice as many wolves.

As the wolves creep closer, Hope can hear their rumbling growls. There's something awful and ominous about the sound, a tornado drifting across the plains, ready to overtake them.

For one of the few times in her life, Hope's legs are shaking. She tries to channel her nervous energy into her spear, gripping it harder than ever, but the hand holding it feels slack and worthless.

Live today, tears tomorrow.

She glances down the line. At the very opposite end is Book. He holds his bowstring taut. Is it her imagination, or does he shoot a look in her direction?

The wolves are two hundred feet away now, and the two groups face off. One final battle. One last stand.

When the pack starts to race forward, it does so as a group, as though someone shouted *Go.* There is an awful beauty in the attack: the sleek motion of legs; paws churning snow; blazing eyes boring through the afternoon gloom like candle flames.

"Draw!" Hope yells at the top of her voice.

"Fire!" she calls out a moment later.

Darts and spears and rocks and arrows whip through air. Many hit their targets. Yelps ring out. Blood splatters snow.

But only a small number of the wolves go down. The rest surge forward, faster now, *angry* now, and Hope cannot just hear their growls, she can feel them, vibrating her feet, radiating up her legs.

"At will!" she cries, and the LTs and Sisters fire as best they can. Arrows soar. Darts zing. Wolves race.

And then it's too late. The wolves are on them, launching themselves through air, soaring through space.

The LTs and Sisters turn and run. Hope keeps stopping to fire off arrows, but it's not enough. The weakest of the LTs have been caught, and even from a distance, she can hear the growling, the snapping of teeth, the rip and snarl as wolves bite into the sick and wounded. The pitiful cries of Less Thans bounce off the wintery sky.

Others stop and fire as best they can: Diana, Book, Cat. Still the wolves come, racing through a nightmare landscape of dead and dying Less Thans, of wounded Sisters. The trees are too far away and there's nowhere to hide.

A flash of movement out of the corner of her eye swings her around: a wolf, the alpha male, sailing through air, lands on Book. Heart pounding, she runs in his direction.

"Book!" she hears herself calling out. *"Book!"*

She readies an arrow as she runs. Not stopping, she lets the bowstring go and the arrow catches the wolf in the back flank. It topples to one side, then just as quickly rights itself, reattaching its bloody teeth to Book's leg. Book is trying to beat it off, but she knows if she doesn't get there fast, he's as good as dead. The thought of it is more than she can take. Her mouth opens wide and she releases a scream that shakes the trees.

She reloads and is about to fire again, but an arrow whizzes by her head. She has to duck. Someone almost hit her. *Idiot.*

Another arrow flies by. And then another after that. Before she knows it, there are hundreds of them. The sky is raining arrows, arcing above the heads of the Sisters and Less Thans and striking the wolves one after the other—*thwack thwack thwack thwack*—dropping them to the ground like birds smashing into windows.

She goes to release her arrow, but the wolf attached to Book's leg lies there motionless. A half dozen arrows jut from its side. She can't believe it. Only a handful of wolves remain, and just like that, they're taken care of as well.

No wolves. All dead.

Hope stands there, stunned. All the Less Thans and Sisters, too. In the course of sixty seconds, the battlefield has turned into a slaughterhouse. Before her lies a field of dead and dying wolves, their lean bodies riddled with arrows, blood staining the snow as far as the eye can see. Rivers of red atop a landscape of white.

Hope looks to the heavens and offers a silent thanks. Then she turns and stares behind her, peering into the falling snow. And out of the mist comes a horde of people, riding horses and covered in hides, wearing the hideous skulls of beasts.

Skull People. Hundreds of them.

The biggest of the bunch—a man with a bushy beard that's spotted with snow—reins his horse to a stop and dismounts into the blood-soaked snow. His thick biceps strain against his buckskin jacket.

"Looks like we got here just in time," he bellows, all smiles. And then he turns his head and spits off to the side. "Well, don't just stand there. Let's build some fires and cook these critters."

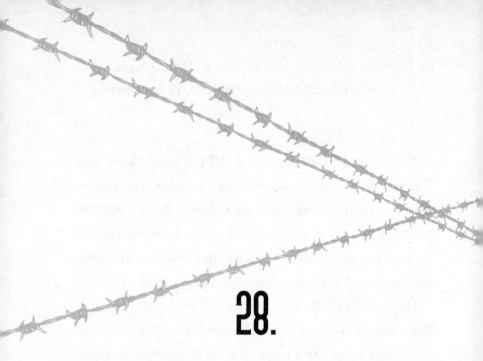

28.

SEVERAL HUNDRED SKULL PEOPLE dismounted from
their horses and began gutting wolves and dressing
meat. Others built fires and set up camp. A final group
began burying our dead.

While Helen ministered to my bloody leg, my eyes
scanned the faces.

"She's not here, Book."

It was Goodman Dougherty. He knelt alongside me,
checking my wound. He'd been my boss back at the
Wheel, and although he was now down to maybe 250
pounds as opposed to the 300 from before, he looked
much the same. His clothes were a combination of torn
denim and faded leather, and his beard was thicker and
bushier than ever.

"Who?" I asked.

"Your grandmother." My eyebrows must have arched in surprised, because he went on to explain. "We heard how you came to their rescue."

"She didn't make it?"

"Passed away not long after you all left."

Maybe it was the wound, maybe it was the thought of my grandmother's final moments, but whatever it was, I felt suddenly dizzy. The blood drained from my face.

Goodman Dougherty placed a thick hand on my shoulder. "You all right there, chief?"

"I'm fine." But of course I wasn't. I wanted—*needed*—her to survive. There was so much I wanted to ask her. Not just about my family. Like why on earth she seemed to think I could save the country.

"And I believe you know this old bat," Dougherty said.

I swiveled my head to see Goodwoman Marciniak. Her hair was whiter than I remembered it, and her wrinkles more pronounced, but her eyes still twinkled with warmth.

She gave Dougherty a slap on one of his beefy arms. "I heard that." Then she turned to me and said, "It's nice to see you again, Book."

She stretched out her arms, and as we hugged, it hit me how grateful I was she had made it out of the Compound. She was now the closest link to my grandmother.

"Come on," she said. "Let's get that wound cleaned up and some food into you all. Then we'll talk."

Sitting around a series of blazing fires and eating grilled wolf, we told the Skull People our stories, and they told us theirs. Those who had survived the ambush of the Crazies had escaped through the very tunnel that was now littered with corpses. When I told them that the Compound was no more, you could see the sorrow etched on their faces.

"How have you been surviving since your escape?" Flush asked.

"Wandering, mostly," Goodman Dougherty answered. "Playing hide-and-seek with the Crazies. Hunting and foraging. Trying to find food to fill our bellies." He slapped his ample stomach. "That's easier for my friends than me."

He turned to the side and hawked up a ball of phlegm. It was as if the cave dust was still embedded in his lungs.

"Where are the Crazies now?" I asked.

"Hard to say. We've ridden through a few towns where they used to live, and we can't find any sign of them. Maybe they're riding out the winter in some cave—who knows? Come spring, I'm sure they'll reappear like the cockroaches that they are. No love lost between the Skullies and the Crazies."

It was true. The Crazies wanted nothing to do with law and order. They'd just as soon everyone followed their own rules.

"So why'd they join forces with the Hunters and ambush you?" I asked.

"Don't know for sure, but it must be that they want guns."

"And the Hunters? What'd they get out of it?"

"That's the million-dollar question, all right. Why? Have you seen 'em recently?"

Dougherty noticed the look I shared with my friends, and I told him about the ambush at Dodge's, the capture on the ice floe, the wolf attack. When I finished, he let out a long, low whistle.

"Gotta hand it to you," he said. "You all knocked off two sets of enemies in one three-day period: first the Hunters, and now the wolves."

"With some help from our friends."

"Sure, but that makes your life a whole lot easier, don't it?"

Yes, I wanted to answer, *but there are still plenty of enemies out there.*

I looked around. Ripples of laughter bounced from one conversation to another, and it was good to see everyone enjoying themselves. The Skull People seemed rejuvenated by the Less Thans and Sisters, and we liked being in the company of elders. Also, it was comforting to finally be around people who weren't trying to kill us.

"So where are you headed?" Goodwoman Marciniak asked.

"To the next territory."

"You're going to the Conclave?"

There was that word again, the one the Man in Orange had refused to explain. My expression must have made it obvious that I had no idea what Marciniak was talking about.

"The Conclave is a series of celebrations," she said. "First and foremost, it's the inauguration of the next president. Plus it's the twenty-first anniversary of Omega. As his final act, President Vasquez wants to bring everyone together. 'Wiping the slate clean,' he calls it. A time for reconciliation."

"And you're going?" I couldn't believe they could be so forgiving after all that had been done to them.

"I know what you're thinking," Goodman Dougherty said. "We may not agree with everything this government does, but hell, we're not getting any younger. And it'll be better to be part of something than against it. And maybe in a future year we can get some of our own people elected."

A sudden anger boiled within me. I wasn't so ready to forgive. Not after being raised in Camp Liberty and having seen my friends slaughtered before my eyes.

I reached into my pocket and pulled out the map of the United States. I unfolded it on the snow.

"Well, well, well," Dougherty said. "What do we have here?"

"A map."

"I can see that. Where'd you get it?"

"I took it from the Compound library."

"You ripped that out of a book?" Goodwoman Marciniak asked, looking mortified.

"Yes, ma'am."

"A *library* book?" It looked like she might pass out.

"Ease up on the boy, Marjorie," Dougherty said. "It's just a couple pages."

Marjorie did not appear the least bit pacified by Goodman Dougherty's words.

I wanted to remind her that the Compound was now just a pile of rubble, and that I actually *saved* these two maps from destruction. But that probably wouldn't have swayed her. A library book was a library book.

Goodman Dougherty leaned over the map, his greasy fingers sliding from one town to the next.

"It's been twenty years since I've seen one of these. Almost forgot what they look like."

Others leaned in to have a look, studying the map with something like reverence. For me, it was like magic, as though this rectangle of paper with its squiggly lines and mysterious place names held vast secrets.

"Near as I can tell, we're about here," Goodman

Dougherty said, pointing to a spot in the middle of nowhere.

"And the Conclave?"

He dragged his finger east to a place where two rivers met. "Should be about here, I'm guessing."

"That's where the inauguration is?"

"Yup. Three weeks from now, that's where they'll be swearing in the new president."

"What's his name, by the way?"

"*Her* name," he corrected me. "A woman by the name of Cynthia Maddox."

Every Less Than and Sister stopped what they were doing. My heart rose in my throat.

"What's the matter?" Dougherty asked. "You all look like you just seen a ghost."

"Cynthia Maddox as in Chancellor Maddox?" I asked.

"That's the one."

"She's going to be the next president?"

"Won by a landslide, apparently."

"Then we can't let the inauguration happen," I said.

Dougherty and Marciniak shared a look. "Why not?"

"Because it'll be the death of every one of us here."

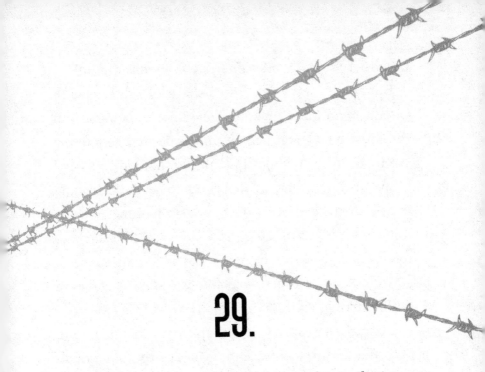

29.

THEY NEED TO GET to the Conclave and stop the inauguration. If Chancellor Maddox becomes president, no territory will ever be safe. Not the Western Federation, not the Heartland, not any of them.

There are eight who head out that next morning: five Less Thans (Cat, Flush, Red, blind Twitch, and Book), two Sisters (Hope and Diana), and one Skully (Goodman Dougherty). Argos, too. Together, they will try to save the country . . . even though the country doesn't know it needs saving.

Before they leave, Hope tells the Skull People what she and Cat discovered: that Chancellor Maddox was stockpiling weapons at the Eagle's Nest.

"I wouldn't read too much into that," Goodman

Dougherty says. "Armies do need weapons, after all."

But then she sees him share a glance with Goodwoman Marciniak, and she knows she's got him thinking. Which is probably why he decided to join the group. He's not convinced Chancellor Maddox is as evil as the LTs and Sisters make her out to be, but he's going to help them get to the Conclave just the same.

"Good-bye again," Hope says to Helen. She starts to remove the good-luck necklace, but Helen stops her.

"You keep it," Helen says. She doesn't state what they're both thinking: *You're going to need it more than me.*

Hope gives Helen a nod of thanks and then turns and goes. She doesn't look back for fear of getting emotional.

The group of eight mount the fastest horses and begin to ride off through the snow. Argos trails them, following their path.

"See you in the next territory!" someone yells after them.

Hope waves back, but she knows it's unlikely she'll see any of them ever again.

They ride half the day without talking. The snow thins, the weather clears. The clouds drift apart, revealing a sky so clear and blue it's almost blinding. Hope's thoughts are interrupted by a distant sound. A kind of squawking.

All eight of them hear it at the same time. They spur their horses forward. The sound grows louder, more insistent. When they reach the edge of a small town, they spy several dozen crows, their ebony wings flapping furiously as they leap, hover, dive. Then the wind shifts and the eight riders smell decay. Rot. *Death.*

Hope whips a bandanna over her face and fights the urge to gag. She breathes through her mouth.

The town isn't much more than a main street with ten or so buildings lining either side. A long-dead stoplight dangles from a cable above an intersection. A window shutter slaps against an outer wall.

The horses nicker, tug at the bridles, toss their heads. As they draw closer, Hope sees why: the crows are feeding on a hundred lifeless human bodies.

The horses come to a stop.

"What is it?" Twitch asks.

Flush describes it as best he can, how the corpses litter the streets and sidewalks like neglected dolls, purplish blood pooling the snow beneath them.

"Who were they, do you think?" Hope asks.

"Crazies, by the looks of it," Goodman Dougherty answers, gesturing to the beards, the rags for clothes, the general disarray of the town itself.

"So who did this?"

"Take your pick. Brown Shirts, Hunters—whoever wants 'em dead."

"Not the Skull People?"

He gives a rueful laugh. "We're just trying to put food in our mouths. We don't have time to attack any others."

They stay there a moment longer, their eyes sweeping across the mass carnage. Bodies, blood, crows.

"Come on," Cat snarls. "Let's get out of here."

He gives his horse a nudge and the eight ride on, relieved to skirt the town and leave the site of festering death behind them.

Soon it's just the wind and the horses' hooves and eight people breathing through their mouths. No one says a word.

30.

THE NEXT DAY, WE came across two more towns where the citizens lay dead and rotting in the streets. Like before, the only activity was that of crows. Lots and lots of crows.

Something about Goodman Dougherty's words rattled around in my head. I supposed he was right—it was probably the work of Brown Shirts or Hunters—but it didn't make sense. The Crazies were just that—crazy— but they didn't bother the government any, and hadn't the Crazies and Hunters worked together when they stormed the Compound? So why would the Brown Shirts or Hunters turn on them?

After two more days of traveling, we came to a resettlement camp created by the Western Federation. *Camp*

Patriot, a rusty sign proclaimed. It dangled from a single hinge and swayed, creaking in the wind. At first glance, Camp Patriot looked an awful lot like Liberty and Freedom: tar-paper barracks, guard towers, mess hall, coils of jagged concertina wire atop the surrounding fences.

But as similar as this camp was to where we'd grown up, there was one significant difference: all the inhabitants lay dead. Boys were sprawled everywhere—on the parade ground, on the steps leading into buildings, even suspended from the barbed-wire fence, as though their last act had been to try and climb it. There wasn't a living soul to be seen.

A couple of us threw up, and the rest couldn't turn away fast enough. There was no question that this was part of Chancellor Maddox's Final Solution. As she herself had said, the sooner we were gone, the better.

We spoke hardly at all the rest of that day. Even when we stopped for the night and set up a meager camp in a stand of pine trees, huddling around a single fire, we did so with the fewest possible words. Just looking into one another's eyes was enough to remind us of what we'd seen . . . and what we wanted to forget.

"You sure you know where this Conclave's at?" Cat asked Goodman Dougherty.

"At the capital, New Washington," he said, biting into some wolf jerky. We were poring over the map—a nightly ritual.

"Yeah, but where's that?"

"It moves around a good deal."

"What do you mean?" Flush asked.

"It doesn't stay in any one place for long." We all stopped eating, and Dougherty realized we were waiting for him to explain.

"After Omega, the president thought it best if we didn't have a permanent capital. That was part of the problem that day—all the leaders were in Washington when the bombs hit."

"So the capital moves?"

"Every couple of weeks." He picked a charred crumb from his beard and tossed it into his mouth. "That way no foreign country can ever drop a bomb on it and wipe everyone out."

"*Are* there foreign countries?"

"Your guess is as good as mine on that one, chief. But if there are and they're trying to bring down our government, they won't know where to look."

It made sense. It sounded like a lot of work, but it made sense.

"So how are we gonna find it if it keeps moving?" I asked.

"The Conclave's different. Since it's the inauguration and the twenty-one-year anniversary, they want as many people there as possible, and they've been putting the word out so people know where to go."

When the conversation faded away, I folded up the

map and said good night to my friends. In no time I was asleep beneath a wash of stars, dreaming of a future where I could live in one place—where I, too, wasn't constantly on the move and trying to evade my enemies.

The next day I slowed my horse so I could ride by Hope's side.

"You okay?" I asked.

So much had happened since she'd taken me to her home, and we hadn't really talked.

"I'm fine," she said, pulling the hoodie tight around her face. "Why wouldn't I be?"

"No reason."

We rode in silence, our horses' hooves clip-clopping atop the frozen ground.

"I'm sorry about your grandmother," she said out of the blue.

Her words surprised me. "Thanks," I said. "It's still hard to believe, you know? I just met her, and then she was gone. Of course, who knows? Maybe she's still around."

Hope gave me a questioning look, and I explained. "I have this weird memory—or maybe it was a dream—of my grandmother once telling me that the dead don't go away. She said each of the stars represents someone who's died, and they're up there, looking down on us."

Hope didn't respond, and I almost wondered if she'd been listening.

Then she asked, "You found her, didn't you?"

"My grandmother? No, like I told them—"

"Not your grandmother. Miranda."

I felt my face go hot. "Yes," I murmured.

"Dead?"

I nodded.

"I'm sorry," she said softly.

"Thanks," I said back.

The horses carried us forward, and we let the subject drop away.

"Where will you go?" I asked. "When this is all over?"

She shrugged. "Get far away from this territory, that's for sure."

"Amen to that. And then?"

"Find someplace where I can live and no one can bother me."

"Doing what?"

"Fishing, hunting, growing a garden." She hesitated. "Maybe learn to knit. I always wanted to do that."

I let out a snort. "*You?* Knit?"

She slapped me on the shoulder. "Don't laugh. I could knit."

"I'm not saying you couldn't, it's just, I never thought of you as the knitting kind."

"I could."

"I'm sure you could."

"I just need someone to teach me."

"Right." I laughed, and she slapped me again. "What?" I said in mock protest. "I didn't say anything."

"You didn't need to."

We rode in companionable silence. It was the first time in forever that she didn't seem angry with me. For the moment, the image of those massacres was far away.

"Where will *you* go?" Hope asked. "When this is over."

"Someplace where I don't have to knit."

"No, seriously."

"Same as you. Find a place where I can live and not be bothered by Brown Shirts—"

"Or Hunters—"

"Or Crazies—"

And in unison we said, "Or wolves."

We shared a glance, then just as quickly looked away.

"Live today," she said under her breath.

"Tears tomorrow," I added softly.

For a moment, our horses were in perfect synchronicity, walking at exactly the same pace, blowing air at the same time. And then Hope spurred hers forward and rode on ahead.

As I watched her ride off, I wondered if she and I would ever say to each other what we really wanted to say. I wondered if either of us had that much courage.

Our horses picked their way east, and although I shouldn't have been, I was surprised when we emerged from the woods the next day into a bare swath of landscape. In the middle of it stood a rusted chain-link fence with coils of razor wire, stretching miles in both directions.

On the other side was the next territory. The Heartland.

"Look familiar?" Goodman Dougherty asked.

"Not this particular section, but yeah," I said. We had been here once before, of course. That seemed like forever ago.

We angled south, not stopping until we reached the town we had seen last summer. Just like before, there were the shops, the houses, the gazebo. The memories of music and food smells came flooding back.

But something was different. There were no people. No hint of human activity at all.

I urged my horse forward, but it nickered and stamped the ground. It didn't want to move. I released the reins and slowly dismounted, walking forward as though in a trance. My fingers curled around the fence and I squinted through the late-afternoon gloom.

That's when I saw it . . . and smelled.

There were corpses everywhere, and the crows were busy pecking, gouging into eyes and ears, stuffing their beaks with food. Maybe it was because we had been here before, had watched the children playing and heard their squeals of delight, but I couldn't bear what I was seeing. I turned away and buried my face in my hands.

"What is it?" Twitch asked.

"Just like the others, cowboy," Goodman Dougherty said soberly. "Another massacre."

We stood there, the only sound the distant flap of wings as crows bounced from one corpse to another. Argos gave a low whimper.

When I allowed myself to look again, I let my eyes travel across the bodies. They were just families—mothers, fathers, children—with no weapons in sight. This was a massacre. Flat-out murder.

I heard a sound and turned. It was Diana—tough Diana—trying to stifle a sob. She was staring at a body sprawled across the gazebo floor. The corpse was a girl from Camp Freedom, one we'd traveled with last summer. When we had made it to this fence, eleven Sisters stayed on the other side, starting their new lives in the Heartland. This girl had been one of them . . . and this was her fate.

As I scanned the ground, I saw more of those Sisters, all dead, all lying piteously on the ground, their swollen bodies pockmarked by crows.

"Come on," a voice said. It was Cat. "Let's get the hell out of here."

I gave a glance to Hope. Her jaw was working back and forth and her eyes were on fire.

I strode back to my horse and we all rode on.

No one was in the mood to talk. For the better part of a year, I'd been dreaming about that town: children playing games, families having picnics, music floating to the skies. There wasn't a one of us who forgot that first encounter; it was our first vision of what the world could be like. *Should* be like. All our choices and actions had been based on getting back.

And now here we were . . . and things were no better on that side of the fence than they were on ours.

We found an opening and crossed into the next territory, finally leaving the Western Federation after a lifetime there. Still, no one said a single word of congratulations. We weren't in the mood.

That evening we huddled around a fire, silent. To get our minds off what we'd seen, I pulled out the map of the world and asked Goodman Dougherty to tell us about the other countries.

"You mean what they're like now?" he asked.

"No, before Omega."

Dougherty did his best, but he found it difficult to concentrate. We all did.

He was about to fold up the map when I suddenly stopped him, my finger pointing at the top of the page.

"Wait," I blurted out. "Who has a copy of the code?"

They all looked at me funny.

"You know," I went on. "The numbers. Who has a copy?"

"I know them by heart," Twitch said. "Four, five, three, nine—"

"Yeah, but can I see it?"

"Sure," he said, shrugging.

He reached into his pocket and pulled out a well-worn slip, handing it to Flush, who handed it to me. I placed it on the map and examined it. We didn't understand the numbers, had no idea what they were code for, but maybe we didn't need to. Maybe we'd been looking at them all wrong.

"What are those numbers?" I asked Goodman Dougherty, pointing to a series of digits at the top of the map.

"Latitude."

"And these?" My finger landed on the side of the page.

"Longitude."

"Tell me about them."

Twitch angled his face in my direction. "They're number coordinates—a way of pinpointing a location."

"A specific place?"

"That's right."

"So what if that's what these numbers are?"

He absently ran his fingers along his jaw while he

considered what I was suggesting. "It's possible, but I thought you said there weren't any spaces between these numbers."

"There aren't, but maybe that's left for us to figure out."

I could tell I had everyone's attention. Goodman Dougherty put down his unfinished dinner. Everyone leaned forward. Even Argos lifted his head and gave a soft whimper.

I began reading off the numbers—"Four, five, three, nine"—and as I did, Dougherty found the coordinates on the world map. Except instead of

4539221103914

it was more like

45 39 22 110 39 14

The map wasn't big enough to allow the kind of precision that we craved, but it gave us a general idea. Our eyes were fixated on Goodman Dougherty's dirt-encrusted finger as it traced the map and landed on the first coordinate that gave us the latitude: a line across the northern hemisphere. That narrowed it down to not just the former United States, but also some countries by the names of France, Italy, the Russian Federation, and many more.

Adding longitude would tell us the exact location. I called out those numbers next—110, 39, 14—and Dougherty swiped his finger to a specific vertical line. As I finished reciting, I was so excited I could barely breathe. But when I looked up, my heart sank. Goodman Dougherty's finger rested on a desolate chunk of land on the other side of the world. Someplace called Mongolia.

"Maybe that's where Omega started," Flush offered.

"Or where it ended," Red added.

"Or the Republic's *real* headquarters."

"Or maybe these numbers aren't latitude and longitude at all," Diana said.

We all sat back, and there was a collective sigh of disappointment. I'd gotten my hopes up for nothing.

"Did you add a minus in front of the longitude?" Twitch asked casually.

"Huh?"

"Prime meridian is zero degrees, and that goes through Greenwich, England, so everything to the west of that—like the Republic—is measured in minus degrees."

Dougherty went back to the map. Sure enough, there was a western 110 as well as an eastern one. He got out the map of the United States and traced the number until he located the coordinate.

"Well?" Twitch asked. Lacking sight, he couldn't see what the rest of us could.

Dougherty sat poised before the map, one hand on it, the other buried in his beard. He turned to me. "You wanna tell him or should I?"

I leaned in to see for myself, and was surprised that his finger had landed on the exact same spot where it had been six days earlier: at the junction of two rivers.

"The Conclave?" I said.

He nodded.

"So not some secret message after all," I said, disappointed. "Just directions to the inauguration."

No one said anything. A piece of wood exploded in the fire and embers flared.

"Then it doesn't mean anything?" Flush asked.

"It means one thing," Dougherty said. "Chancellor Maddox wants everyone and their mother to watch her be sworn in as president. That way we'll all know exactly who's the boss."

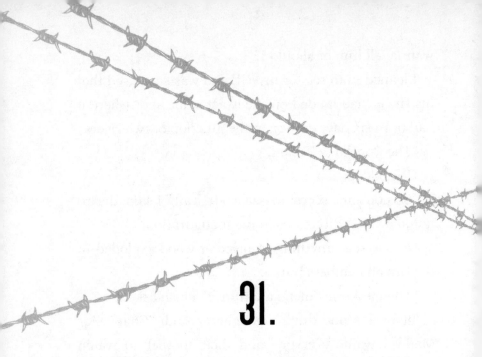

31.

THE NEXT DAY THEY ride on, but Hope speaks to no one. Not to Book, not to Diana, not to anyone. She's not in the mood for talking. It's not just that the woman who came up with the Final Solution will soon be running the country. It's also her father. Why was he considered the Butcher of the West? Was he in some way responsible for all of this?

The landscape flattens and irons itself out. Six days after leaving the others, they ride to the top of a low ridge and draw their horses to a stop. Mud as far as they can see. All the snow has seeped into the prairie, creating an enormous puddle of brownish-black muck, stretching from one horizon to the other. Far to the south is a river snaking through the prairie. Flowing into that is another, smaller river.

Mired in the swampy landscape in the V of these two rivers is a vast array of mud-splattered tents, sprawling from riverbank to riverbank.

"Welcome to New Washington," Goodman Dougherty says. "The capital of the Republic of the True America." He hawks up a ball of phlegm and plants it in the mud.

The sight is utterly dreary. People going about their daily chores, walking through the slop, passing between tents that are smeared top to bottom with mud, mud, and more mud. *This is the capital city of what was once the greatest country on earth?* Hope wonders.

They sit atop their horses and take it all in. Just knowing that Chancellor Maddox is down there somewhere makes Hope's blood run fast.

"What're we waiting for?" she says impatiently. "Let's get going."

"Hold on a sec, Annie Oakley," Dougherty says. "Before we go stormin' in there, guns a-blazin', let's remember we've got two weeks till the inauguration. It might be worth coming up with a strategy."

Hope sighs noisily but knows he's right.

After an hour of conversation and debate, it's decided that she, Book, and Cat will sneak into the capital. The rest will wait out of sight.

"You sure about this?" Dougherty asks. "You might need another hand."

She's insistent that it's just the three of them. "You being a Skully and all, they'd take you for the enemy right off. Besides, less noticeable if there's just a hand-ful of us." What she doesn't say is, *This is my battle. My fight.*

"Any final words of advice?" Book asks Goodman Dougherty.

"Yeah, don't piss anyone off."

As the three ease down the muddy slope, Hope silently promises to sacrifice her own life if that's what it takes to end the lives of Maddox and Gallingham. That realization strikes a chord of emotion.

She runs a hand through her hair and pushes feel-ings to the side. No time for those now.

Live today, tears tomorrow.

Assuming there is a tomorrow.

They creep to the edge of the makeshift city, hid-ing behind tents. If their first impression of New Washington was like looking down at a muddy ocean, now they're in the midst of its swelling seas. There are people everywhere—squishing through the mud, roll-ing carts, selling goods, yelling, trading, bartering. A swarm of humanity going about their daily lives and tramping through the muck like it's the most normal thing in the world.

But there's something else that Hope notices—a quality she's not witnessed before. Despite the mud and dreary appearance, the people project a kind of con-tentment. Like they've survived the worst of it and now they're looking boldly to the future. Hope's never seen that kind of optimism before.

If only the people knew the truth about their new leader.

The trio figure it's in their best interest to remain "invisible," so when they actually enter the city, they walk separately, hands thrust into pockets, each person concealed by the shadows of hats or hoodies.

They pass through the residential section of New Washington, where the people sleep and eat, cooking up their meals atop the small campfires before their tents. Next they come to an enormous field set aside for soldiers. Brown Shirts drill, perform calisthenics, practice with guns—going through the motions of becoming better soldiers.

Finally they reach the business section of town—open-air markets, blacksmiths, laundry services. A chaos of activity. Hope doesn't know what she was expecting when she pictured the nation's capital, but it definitely wasn't this. It seems so temporary. So primitive. So *muddy*.

What they don't see and can't find is the president's headquarters. Their hope is to speak to him, just as Book had a private conversation with the Chief Justice at the Compound. But how do they ask to speak to the leader of the Republic without calling attention to themselves?

Hope notices a tent where an older woman with a

ratty cardigan sells soap. The woman has only one good eye; the other veers off blankly toward the sky.

"Yes?" the woman asks when Hope approaches her. There is a certain wariness in the woman's voice, and Hope can't blame her. The last time Hope encountered soap was months ago, when they all doused themselves with car wash shampoo.

"I'm wondering if you can help me out," Hope says. Even though there's a swarm of humanity just outside the tent, Hope keeps her voice lowered.

"Depends," the woman says.

"I want to know where the president's office is."

"The president?"

"That's right."

"The president of the Republic of the True America?"

"Uh-huh."

"You want to talk to him or somethin'?"

Yes, Hope wants to say. *That's exactly what I want.* Instead, her face burns red and she lowers her eyes.

"If you could just point me in that direction, I'd really appreciate it."

"What is this, a prank?" the woman says.

"No, ma'am."

"You really want to know where the *president* is?"

"I do."

"Well, twenty years ago I wanted to date Channing Tatum, but it wasn't gonna happen." The soap seller breaks into a fit of laughter. "The president," she says. "That's a good one."

Hope realizes there's no point staying there, so she quickly backs out of the tent, even as the soap seller turns to a woman in an adjoining tent.

"This girl wants to talk to the president!"

"Who, *her*?"

And then there are two women laughing, filling the air with their husky cackles.

Hope hurries away, with Book and Cat keeping their distance but trailing behind her. The three zig-zag through the maze of tents until they're far from the one-eyed soap seller. They march to the top of a small knoll and find a scraggly elm tree. Cat has no difficulty climbing it, even with just one good arm. He makes it up several branches and points, taking Hope's gaze to a sprawling collection of adjoining tents, all surrounded by flagpoles.

They start making their way in that direction.

What no one says is how they're going to get access to the president, because no one knows that answer. But the woman's laughter made it obvious: Why will the president agree to see the three of *them*?

32.

FINDING THE PRESIDENT'S HEADQUARTERS was the easy part. Getting inside was another story. Just outside the entrance to the front tent stood four guards armed with automatic weapons. Still more soldiers walked the perimeter, making sure no one got within fifty feet. It became instantly clear that three mud-splattered teens wearing threadbare clothes would never be allowed a private conversation with the president.

How naive could we have been, thinking we could just waltz into town and speak to the ruler of the Republic?

We kept on walking until we reached the woods. There, we sat on stumps and picked the mud from our clothes. None of us bothered to hide our disappointment.

"Now what?" Hope asked.

Her question hung in the air like the layer of wood

smoke that hovered above the city. We'd come all this way, but we weren't allowed to share what we knew with the one person who could do something about it.

"Maybe we don't need to see the president," I suggested. "Maybe there's someone else we could talk to."

"The problem's the same," Cat said. "Look at us."

He tugged at his T-shirt, which was more holes than fabric. His jeans were encrusted with mud, blackened from campfires. We looked like something you'd scrape off the bottom of a boot.

"So maybe instead of trying to cover up what we look like, we take advantage of it," I said.

"What're you thinking?"

I didn't have a definite answer to that, but I did have one idea.

We staked out the president's headquarters, sitting in the shadow of a shoe repair tent, pretending to wait for our boots to be fixed. A number of people came and went to see the president—but not, thank goodness, Chancellor Maddox. We had yet to lay eyes on her. It was possible she hadn't yet arrived.

Our attention went to a middle-aged black gentleman with white hair and matching white goatee. He entered and exited the headquarters several times a day, and the fact that he was always accompanied by two Brown Shirts convinced us he was someone important.

One morning, three days after we'd been in New

Washington, Cat ventured out into the street, leaning on a walking stick. As the man approached the headquarters, the stick slipped and Cat fell headfirst into the slop. His artificial arm went flying.

"I got him, mister," I said, running forward. The older man stopped in the middle of the road, not knowing what to make of a mud-soaked, one-armed Cat lying in the muck.

"Are you all right, son?" he asked.

"Fine," Cat said with a grimace, taking all the time in the world to raise himself to a standing position. "Just can't seem to get the hang of this thing." He swiped angrily at the prosthetic.

"I can imagine it would take time. Well, if you're all right—"

"Course, some of my fellow soldiers have it worse."

The man studied Cat as though he hadn't really seen him before. "You were in the service?"

"Yes, sir. Western Federation."

"You're young."

"Twenty," he lied. "But never too young to fight the Crazies. They're the ones who did this." He slapped the stump of his arm.

"Yes, well," the man said, "thank you for your service."

He turned and started to go. I had no choice but to blurt out, "We sure would like to talk to the president. Thank him for everything he's done."

The man's smile was kind but tight-lipped. "I wish

that were possible. He's a very busy man, what with the Conclave and all. Why don't you write him a letter and I'll see that he gets it?"

He started to pivot away, but before he did, I thrust out my hand. A grimy envelope dangled between my fingers. "I already have; it's right here."

The man studied me, studied the envelope, then reluctantly plucked it from my hand. "I'll see that he gets it," he said.

"We're staying down at the stables if he'd like to talk to us."

He grunted and was gone, slipping past the guards and behind the flaps of the presidential headquarters, his bodyguards right behind him.

Cat and I returned to the stables, where we joined back up with Hope.

"You really think it'll work?" she asked.

"It better," I said.

"What's Plan B?"

"That's just it. We don't have one."

Inside the envelope was a letter detailing all the murderous acts we'd seen Chancellor Maddox commit the last year. For good measure, we threw in the pictures of Faith and Hope when they'd first been admitted to Camp Freedom, shaved and tattooed. If that didn't get the president's attention, we didn't know what would.

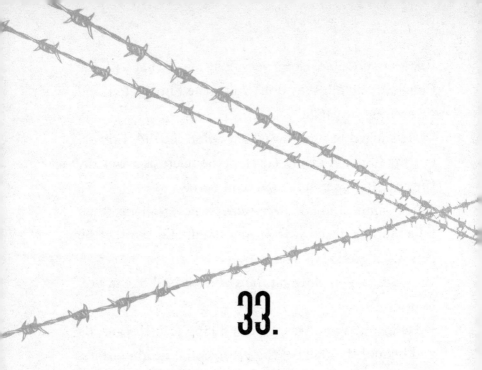

33.

WHILE THEY WAIT, THEY work for food—grooming horses in exchange for a loaf of bread, chopping wood for a bowl of soup—but one of the three always remains at the stables. Just in case someone from the president's office should pop by for a visit.

No one does.

Which means either no one read the letter, or they did but didn't believe it, or the president is too busy planning the Conclave to focus on anything else. And each day that passes is another day closer to Chancellor Maddox's inauguration.

On the third afternoon after delivering the letter, as Hope is returning to the stables, she notices the townspeople are nearly ecstatic as they prepare for the upcoming inauguration. Shops seem to be doing record business, people stop and talk and laugh, and in the distance, music plays: some combination of banjos and fiddles. Celebrations both planned and spontaneous pop up everywhere.

Their joy only increases Hope's frustration. She and Cat and Book know what Chancellor Maddox is capable of, and yet no one wants to listen to what they have to say.

She veers away from the main avenue and loses herself in the backstreets of New Washington, walking with her head lowered, her hoodie pulled tight, her thoughts swirling. She passes a massive tent that is so large, it's less a tent and more a warehouse. She is nearly beyond it when something draws her back. She retraces her steps until she can read the simple, unadorned sign out front.

RTA Dept. of Records

She stands there a moment, thinking.

Instead of returning to the stables, she finds a spot between two tents just across the road and studies the warehouse-like tent, taking note of people entering and exiting through a security check.

Darkness can't come soon enough.

Stars pop from a velvet sky. After timing the guards all afternoon, Hope knows just the right moment to make her move. She tiptoes across the road and down a muddy alley. Taking out her knife, she slices through the thick canvas, creating a small flap in the side of the tent. She slips inside.

Not so difficult, but then again, who would want to break into here? It's just files and records. Dusty archives.

She fumbles for a match, strikes it, and then spies a hurricane lantern. When she lights it, she can make out her surroundings. The place is huge—a vast cavern of metal shelving stacked floor to ceiling with cardboard boxes. Needles in haystacks are more easily found than what she's looking for.

The milky light from the lantern leads her forward. The floor is a series of wobbly boards placed atop the mud. She glides down the length of the building, noting the markers at the ends of aisles. Things like *Historical Archives* and *Congressional Records* and *Presidential Papers*. And one that reads *Government Employees*. That's the row she chooses to explore.

She works her way down the long aisle, trailing through the alphabet until she reaches Sa–Sc. She pulls out a damp cardboard box and rifles through its contents. Buried in the very middle is a file with a label that makes her heart leap.

Samadi, Uzair.

She removes the thick folder and places it in her lap.

Her fingers tremble as they peel away the top sheets. She begins to read.

Biography. Terms of Employment. RTA Contract. Past Employment Record. All of it.

Hope reads quickly, greedily, hungrily. Some of this she knows; some she has never heard before. Like the fact that her father grew up in Chicago and went to a school called Yale and was employed by an organization called the Mayo Clinic. That's all new to her. After Omega happened, things get vague.

She flips quickly through the pages, looking for something else, *anything*.

One page grabs her attention most—a Letter of Agreement between Dr. Uzair Samadi and Dr. Joseph Gallingham, signed by Chancellor Cynthia Maddox. Hope is both eager and afraid to read it. She forces herself to go through it, slowly, carefully.

Among other things, it lists her father's title—research scientist—but at the bottom of the document there's a space marked *Duties*, and it's been left blank. There's nothing there that tells her what he actually did. She is about to turn the page when something catches her eye. Hope brings the lantern closer . . . and she sees the space wasn't always blank. There used to be text there. Someone, for some reason, marked over it with a kind of white glop. All that's left is a faint indication of typed letters—a gauzy dream of alphabet.

But what was it that it said? And who covered it up?

She places the document in front of the lantern to study it further when the sound of a scraping foot stops her cold. She hastily stuffs the paper in a pocket and extinguishes the lantern's flame. Her fingers wrap themselves around the handle of her knife, and her breath goes short, even as the footsteps grow closer and closer.

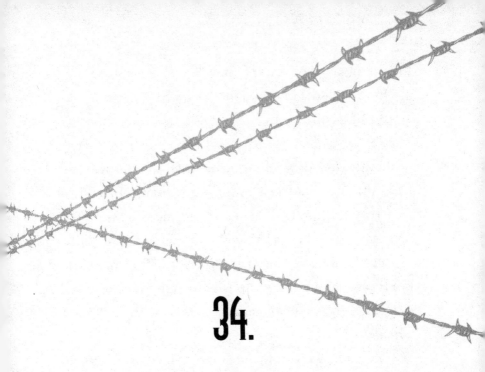

34.

THE GLOW OF LANTERN beams startled us awake.

"You the boys who wrote the note?" a voice asked.

"Yes," I said, shielding my eyes from the sudden brightness.

"We'd like to talk with you."

I was sitting up now. Cat, too. For some reason, Hope's bed was empty.

A figure emerged, stepping forward until he stood directly between the soldiers and us. Lantern light silhouetted his body from behind.

"My name is James Heywood," he said. "I'm one of President Vasquez's aides. We spoke the other day."

"I remember."

"The president read your letter and asked that we

talk with you. Are you free now?"

"In the middle of the night?" I asked.

"If that's convenient."

"Uh, sure."

It was kind of a silly question. Of course we were free; the man had just found us sleeping. Besides, it didn't really matter if it was convenient or not. This was why we had traveled here—to talk to the president of the Republic of the True America. Still, this man's kindness was just the opposite of our overseers back in Camp Liberty, who usually woke us with a shriek of whistles.

"We could wait until morning," Heywood went on, "but based on everything you wrote, I imagine you would prefer to speak sooner rather than later."

"Yes, sir. That's right."

"Good—that's what we think, too. Then we'll let you get dressed and you can join us outside."

Cat and I threw on clothes, exited the stables, and joined Heywood and his soldiers. They led us through the dark and empty streets to the presidential compound, a dizzying array of tents in various heights and configurations. When we reached the entrance, the guards gestured for us to spread our arms and legs.

"Sorry," Heywood said. "Merely a precaution."

The soldiers frisked us and discovered our knives. "We'll hold them here," one soldier said, removing them from our scabbards and placing them in a box. "You'll get them back when you leave."

We followed Heywood through the checkpoint. Much to our surprise, the first person we laid eyes on was Hope, sitting on a bench, elbows resting on knees.

"What're you doing here?" I asked.

"Same thing as you," she answered. "Finally getting the chance to tell our story."

35.

HOPE AND THE TWO Less Thans are led down a series of hallways, passing from one official-looking tent to another. Although there are soldiers everywhere, there's a difference between these Brown Shirts and the ones from her past. They may brandish the same weapons, but these soldiers seem somehow less vindictive. A couple of them actually smile.

The trio is taken to a waiting room and asked to sit on benches.

"Where were you?" Book asks Hope, when Heywood and the soldiers disappear.

"At the Department of Records."

"The Department of Records? Doing what?"

"Digging," she says, and her tone makes it clear she

won't explain any more than that.

The three of them wait for nearly an hour, hearing the muffled conversations that drift through canvas. Hope has nearly dozed off by the time a Brown Shirt sticks his head through one of the flaps.

"All right," he says. "Follow me."

The three are ushered through a final series of tunnels and tents, reaching a chamber that's the most elaborately furnished of them all. Ornate rugs line the floor, and wingback chairs are spread around like chess pieces on a board.

Behind a large wooden desk sits an older woman wearing a dark suit, a cream-colored blouse, and a plain necklace. She has short, reddish-brown hair. Although it's the dead of night, she pores over a series of documents like it's the middle of a workday. Hope feels a pang of disappointment. This isn't President Vasquez.

The woman finishes writing, leans back in her chair, and makes a steeple of her fingertips. She smiles warmly, but Hope notices the deep bags under her eyes. She looks as tired as Hope feels.

"My name is Jocelyn Perrella," she says. "I'm overseeing the transition from President Vasquez to President-Elect Maddox. I know you wanted to meet personally with the president, but I'm sure you can appreciate how busy he is, what with the inauguration and commemoration. He sends his regrets and asked if I would meet with you instead. Are we all fine with that?"

It seems less a question than a statement.

"Yes, ma'am," the three say in unison.

"Good." She nods first toward James Heywood and then to a woman sitting in the corner, scribbling furiously. "You've already met James, and I've asked one of the staff to take notes, so we have a clear record of your statements."

"Thank you," Hope says.

"No, thank *you*," Perrella says. "Your letter was eye-opening, to say the least, and I'm sure what you're about to tell us will be a big help to the Republic as we move forward."

Hope, Book, and Cat start with basic introductions, and when they draw up their sleeves to show their tattoos, it's easy to note the shared glance of concern between Perrella and Heywood.

"What camps were you at?" Perrella asks.

"Liberty and Freedom," Hope explains.

"So you're orphans."

"Now, yes," Hope says.

"Been there how long?"

"Pretty much my whole life," Book says.

"Less than a year for me," Hope says.

"Same," Cat adds.

Jocelyn Perrella studies them a moment. Her

fingertips dance on the envelope sitting on the corner of her desk.

"I read your letter. Saw those pictures. But for the benefit of this hearing, would you mind telling me, in your own words, everything that's happened to you?"

Hope and Book take turns describing all that they've experienced, starting with the discovery of Cat outside Camp Liberty and going through each of the atrocities they witnessed—which are many. Hope watches the woman's face as Book explains. On more than one occasion, she shows genuine surprise. For Hope, it feels good to finally share this story with someone willing to listen.

When they finish, the older woman removes her glasses, lays them carefully on the table, and rubs the bridge of her nose with her thumb and index finger. It's almost as if she's hoping to massage away this situation.

She turns to Hope. "Why'd you break into the Department of Records earlier this evening?"

"I was looking for something," Hope answers.

"Did you find it?"

"Only partially."

"I see. Well, next time, you should go through the proper channels and not damage government property."

"Yes, ma'am," Hope murmurs. Her face burns.

"When the soldiers discovered you, you were examining the folder of Dr. Uzair Samadi. Why?"

She hesitates before saying, "He was my father."

"Dr. Samadi was your father?" Hope nods, and the woman shares another glance with James Heywood. "Is that why you came here? To read about your father?"

"No. We came here to warn you about Chancellor Maddox. But when I saw the Department of Records—"

"You just figured you would break in and find your father's file."

"Something like that, yes."

"And did you find anything interesting?"

Hope starts to answer but then stops herself. She could be mistaken, but the tone of the conversation feels suddenly different. Hope gives her head a shake.

"So you don't care to share what you discovered?" the woman prompts.

"No, ma'am."

Jocelyn Perrella nods grimly. "And all three of you are convinced Chancellor Maddox is up to no good?"

"That's right."

"Based on what?"

Was the woman not listening? "Based on everything Book and I just told you," Hope says impatiently. "Based on everything she did. The people she tortured, the people she *killed*. The weapons she's stockpiling at the Eagle's Nest. Stuff we saw with our own eyes."

"I see," Perrella says, and sighs. "And what do you want me to do about it?"

Hope can't believe what she's hearing. "What do you mean, what do we want you to do about it?" she sputters. "We want you to stop her!"

"You realize you're talking about the next president of the Republic of the True America."

"Not if the current president prevents her from taking over—"

"It's not a matter of President Vasquez preventing her from *taking over*. The election is done. The people voted. This is a democracy."

"Yeah, but if the people knew—"

"What? How she's revived the Western Federation? How its unemployment numbers are the lowest in the country? How it has the fewest reported cases of unrest?"

Hope feels like she's in a bad dream. This can't be happening. The woman can't possibly be saying this.

"I don't know anything about those statistics," Hope says, "or whether they're true or not—"

"Trust me, they're true."

"—but they don't alter the fact that Chancellor Maddox is a cold-blooded killer."

Jocelyn Perrella smiles grimly.

"I have an idea," she says, giving one of the Brown Shirts a nod. "Why don't we find out the truth so we can end this game of speculation?"

Hope doesn't understand what the woman is getting

211

at, even when the Brown Shirt disappears from the room and reappears a moment later . . . with Chancellor Maddox at his side. The chancellor's blond hair is as perfect as ever. A beauty-queen smile plasters her face. Her ankle-length coat drapes across her shoulders.

"Yes, these are the ones," Maddox says with a self-satisfied air. "These are the terrorists who are trying to bring down the country."

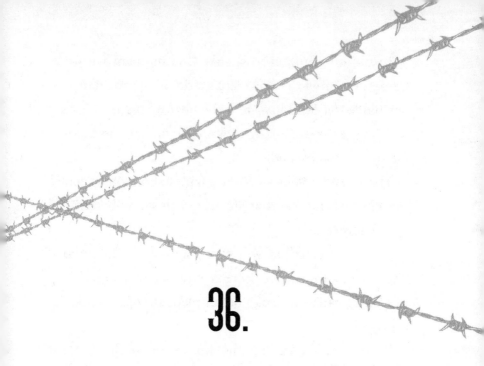

36.

FOR THE LONGEST TIME, no one spoke. Chancellor Maddox was calling *us* terrorists? Here all this time I thought we were the good guys.

"Which crime would you like to answer to first?" Maddox said. "Running away from your resettlement camp? Burning down an infirmary? Killing soldiers of the Republic? Oh, and let's not forget your little stunt with the avalanche. Thank goodness Dr. Gallingham and I had just left camp."

She took a step forward until she stood next to Jocelyn Perrella's desk. Her eyes blazed. "Did you really think I wouldn't find out what you were saying about me? I'm the next president of the Republic, you little turds!"

I was too stunned to speak. One moment we were heroes, warning the president's aides about the dangers of Chancellor Maddox—and the next we were traitors.

"How do you explain those weapons at the launch facility?" Hope asked.

The president-elect actually laughed, a condescending kind of chuckle that suggested this was better left to the adults.

"I don't doubt that you saw a launch facility, and I don't doubt that there were a number of rifles there. Frankly, I can't think of a better place to store weapons. Can you?"

"Then why were you moving them to the Eagle's Nest?"

"First of all, there's nothing unusual about moving arms and ammunition from one site to another—that's standard military procedure. Especially in a time of rebellion," she added pointedly. "And secondly, I've never heard of this Eagle's Nest and doubt that it even exists."

"What're you talking about?" Hope sputtered. "Of course it exists. It's your headquarters."

"Now I know you're lying. Everybody knows I'm stationed at Camp Freedom." She turned her head to share a smile with Jocelyn Perrella.

"But I saw it," Hope said. "I was there!"

"I see. And my soldiers just let you into this fictional place?"

"I broke in."

"So you broke into 'my headquarters,' where you mistakenly thought I would be, even though you'd allegedly seen firsthand how I treated so many of your friends? Why is your story not making much sense to me?" She sent a condescending smirk in Perrella's direction.

Hope looked at me and I looked at Heywood, appealing for understanding. He stared back at me with cold, indifferent eyes.

"How about Camp Freedom?" I asked desperately.

"How about it?" Maddox replied.

"It was a concentration camp. Twins were experimented on there, tortured, *killed*. Girls died because the doctors injected poison into their veins. Hope's sister was murdered right before her eyes."

"Yes, I saw the pictures you gave to Mr. Heywood. But how do we know when they were taken? Or what they really represent? As far as I can tell, they show some girls with bruises and sad expressions."

"But it's all true!" Hope blurted. "It was my own sister. Dr. Gallingham dunked us in the freezing water! I survived, but Faith didn't! And then you did this to me!" She angled her cheeks to the president-elect.

"You honestly think I would carve up a girl's face?"

"Yes, because you did!"

Hope was hyperventilating so much that I was afraid she might pass out.

Maddox gave a nod to Jocelyn Perrella, and the head

of the presidential transition team slid open a desk drawer and pulled out a large manila envelope. She slowly removed its contents: a thin stack of eight-by-ten photographs. She arranged them neatly on her desk.

"Take a look," Maddox said.

We leaned forward. They were pictures of Camp Freedom.

But they weren't the Camp Freedom that we knew. This was like some dream Camp Freedom from the past, where all the buildings were freshly painted and there were flower beds and manicured lawns. Signs on the buildings read *Rec Room, Swimming Pool, Library*. Even stranger were the groups of smiling, giggling children. A far cry from the Camp Freedom we had experienced.

"I don't know about you," Jocelyn Perrella said, "but this doesn't look so bad to me."

"Maybe this is how it used to be," I said. "Way back when. But it's not that way now."

"You sure about that?"

"Positive."

"Funny," Perrella said, "because Chancellor Maddox invited us there just two weeks ago, and that's when we took these pictures. It's exactly how it looked."

Air left me. What was going on? It was like we'd stepped through a portal into some universe I didn't recognize.

"And perhaps you can tell me this," Chancellor

Maddox said sweetly. "Why are the graduates of Camp Freedom so happy?"

"What're you talking about?" Hope said in disbelief. "They're not happy. The ones who manage to survive are the most tortured people alive."

"The reports claim otherwise. The girls graduating from Camp Freedom are consistently the most well-adjusted, the brightest, the happiest of all our young people. They're the ones we need most in leadership positions. So you see, it's not a *concentration camp*, but rather the very model of how *all* resettlement camps should be." With her long, elegant fingers, she gestured to the pictures on the desk. "It might be that you're just jealous."

My mouth hung open dumbly. This was all some kind of massive conspiracy, but there was no way for us to prove it. That's when I noticed that a half dozen Brown Shirts had slipped into the tent and were now standing directly behind us.

"One last thing," Chancellor Maddox said, removing a piece of paper from an inner pocket of her coat. She placed the paper on the desk, then rotated it so we could read it. It was a short typed letter, addressed to *My Fellow Inmates of Camp Liberty.*

It's up to us, the letter read, *to bring this government down—now. Whatever it takes, these leaders must be destroyed.*

The signature below the sentences was familiar. It was mine.

217

"Where did you—"

"Apparently soldiers found it in your bunk after your escape from Camp Liberty," Maddox said. "Do you deny writing it?"

"Yes, I deny writing it!"

"And yet that's your signature, is it not?"

I wanted to say no, but one look told me it was absolutely my signature. I didn't know how they'd forged it—maybe they'd taken it from the report I'd filed after we first found Cat—but it was definitely mine.

When I didn't answer, President-Elect Maddox turned to one of the Brown Shirts.

"Sergeant, take these three terrorists away and lock them up. President Vasquez asked that I give them a trial, and I just did. They're guilty of high treason. A week from tomorrow we'll hang them, right before the inauguration. A little present for the new Congress—to show what we do to terrorists."

Before we had a chance to respond, the soldiers stepped forward, grabbed our arms, and roughly pushed us out of the room.

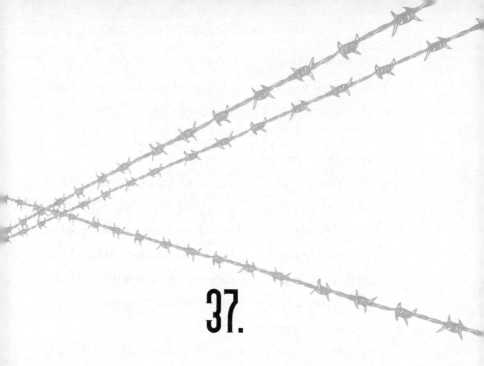

37.

THEY'RE WHISKED AWAY DOWN a long, dark passage, led outdoors, then marched across town to a large canvas tent. Inside it is an enormous steel cage—the New Washington jail. The guards toss the three of them into it, slam the door shut, and lock it with a key.

Hope, Book, and Cat stand there a moment. Then Hope goes to one of the cots and begins stripping blankets and throwing them to the floor, preparing her bed. No one says anything. They've been outwitted by a former beauty queen. Their private audience with the authorities only made things worse. Now they're going to be hanged.

"Did you notice?" Cat says out of the blue.

"Notice what?" Hope asks.

219

"The Brown Shirts."

Hope gives a glance to the flap in the tent, where armed soldiers stand on the other side. "What about them?"

"No badges," he says.

Cat's right. Hope's father always told her those three inverted triangles weren't a symbol of patriotism as much as they were one of hatred, and her entire life she's feared them. They represented an attitude: *I belong and you don't.* But here in the capital, there are none. *Why?*

"Maybe they've come up with something new," Book says. "New president, new symbol."

"Maybe," Cat says. But she can tell he doesn't think so. She doesn't either.

When she finally drifts off to sleep, it's not triangles or even her upcoming execution that occupies her thoughts. It's one simple nagging question. *What is Chancellor Maddox really up to?*

The sad thing is that she'll never find out. Her body will be dangling from a rope in downtown New Washington before Maddox's true intentions are revealed.

Days pass and the Conclave nears, and with the passage of time there's an increase of excitement in the capital city. Through a crack in the canvas at the back of their tent, Hope watches as people hurry to and fro in preparation for the festivities. It's easy to see their anticipation for the big events: the inauguration, the commemoration . . . the hanging.

Cutting through the noise is the persistent sound of hammers, and Hope can't help but wonder if it's from workers building an execution scaffolding. If so, each nail pounded in feels like it's going straight into their coffins.

"You think they'll let us speak?" Book says one evening. All three lie on their beds, staring up through the steel bars at the tent's ceiling.

"What're you talking about?" Hope asks.

"Before they hang us. It's customary for a prisoner facing execution to get to say some final words."

"I doubt it," Hope says. "The last thing Chancellor Maddox wants is three *terrorists* speaking publicly."

"Yeah, but if she's not president yet, who says we can't? So what if?"

Cat rolls his eyes. "You and words. Me, I don't plan on saying anything. I came into this world not speaking, and I plan to exit the same."

Book can't help but smile. Typical Cat.

He turns to Hope. "How about you?"

She thinks a moment. "I guess I'd tell Chancellor Maddox that she can carve up my outer world, but not my inner one."

"Now you're talking."

"And that she's not half the person my father was."

"Good."

"And that if she wants to be a real leader, she should bring people together instead of splitting them apart. Anyone can be divisive, but it takes someone special to unite people."

"I like it."

They're quiet a moment. Hope didn't mean to say so much, but now that she has, she's glad.

"How about you, Book?" Hope asks. "Lemme guess: some famous quote?"

"I've thought about that. At the end of *A Tale of Two Cities*, right before Sydney Carton goes to the guillotine, he thinks, 'It is a far, far better thing that I do, than I have ever done; it is a far, far better rest that I go to than I have ever known.'"

"That's not bad."

"But then there's Nathan Hale, who was hanged in the Revolutionary War. His final words were 'I only regret that I have but one life to lose for my country.'"

"So which one are you gonna go with?" Hope asks.

"Neither. I think I'll say, 'Sticks and stones may break my bones, but calling me a Less Than will never hurt me.'"

At first, Cat and Hope are too stunned to react, but when they see a smile spreading across Book's face, they can't help but smile, too.

"I would *pay* to hear you say that," Cat says.

"Me too," Hope adds. "The smartest of the bunch choosing a children's rhyme. It's just what Maddox wouldn't expect."

"So maybe we should all do it," Book says. "'I know you are, but what am I?'"

"'I'm tellin', you're smellin',"' Hope says.

"'You think you're hot shit, but you're really just cold diarrhea,'" Cat chimes in.

"'Yo mamma.'"

"'Yo daddy.'"

"'Your bald-headed granny!'"

They're giggling hysterically now, barely able to catch their breaths.

"Is this what they mean by 'gallows humor'?" Hope asks.

"I guess so," Book says. "Never really experienced it before."

"That's 'cause we've never been hanged before," Cat points out, and that makes them laugh all the harder.

When the laughter dies and a silence settles on them, they hear the hammers pounding nails.

"We tried, you know," Book says. "We escaped the camps, we rescued a lot of people. . . ."

"We didn't finish," Hope says.

"No, but not bad considering we're a bunch of out-casts. It's just a shame we couldn't prevent what

223

happened in those towns. All those deaths."

The thought of it clenches Hope's stomach. It's not just what happened—it's what will continue to happen once President Maddox takes over.

A similar thought must be going through the minds of Book and Cat, because the conversation comes to a dead stop. They lie there, three prisoners about to be hanged.

Maybe it's the dark, maybe it's because of what's about to happen to them, but Hope finds a sudden courage.

"Did you love her?" she asks Book.

"Who?"

"Miranda."

The echo of Miranda's name dissipates into air before Book answers.

"No," he says, softly.

"You can tell me the truth, you know."

"No," he says again. "I liked her. She was fun. But no."

Hope is surprised by a rush of emotion surging through her—how his simple answer prompts something raw and powerful in her.

"And you're sure it was her? In the Compound?"

Book nods in the dark. "She looked different, but yeah, it was her. No question."

"How was she killed?"

Book opens his mouth to answer, then just as quickly shuts it.

"Those towns," he says, almost to himself.

There's something about his tone that startles Hope. "Which towns?"

"The ones we rode through. Tell me about them."

She swivels her head and looks at him funny. "What're you talking about?"

"Tell me what we saw," he says.

"You were there like the rest of us."

"I know, but what'd we see?"

Hope shrugs. "Bodies. Blood. Crows picking at corpses."

"Yeah, but how'd they die?" He suddenly sits up, swinging his feet to the floor.

"What's this have to do with anything, Book?"

"Yeah, where're you going with this?" Cat adds.

"*How* were the towns wiped out?" Book asks.

Hope shares a look with Cat. "Shot, of course."

"Were there bullet holes?"

"There was blood."

"Were there bullet holes?"

At that precise moment, Hope knows that Book is onto something.

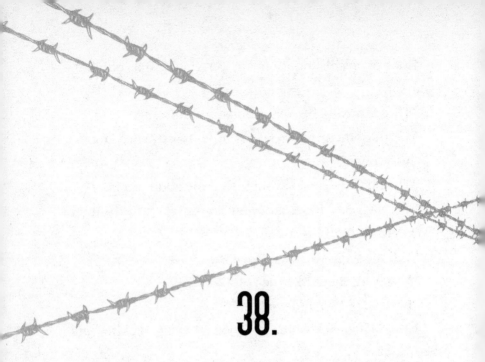

38.

NEITHER HOPE NOR CAT knew what I was thinking—and frankly, I wasn't entirely sure myself—but ever since we'd ridden through those towns, something had gnawed at me.

My sudden memory of Miranda only confirmed those suspicions.

"Did you see bullet holes?" I asked Cat.

"No. . . ."

And then I turned to Hope.

"No, I just assumed—"

"Exactly!" I said. "We all just assumed. We saw the crows and the bodies and the blood, and we just figured they'd been shot, because that's what we've seen before. But what if they were massacred some other way?"

"Like how?" Hope asked.

I hesitated before saying, "Like chemicals."

Hope and Cat regarded me a long moment.

"Go on," Cat said.

"We saw blood, but people who die from poisoning bleed, too—from the mouth, the nose, any number of places. So of course there was blood, but maybe it wasn't caused by bullets." These were the thoughts that had been swirling inside my head. I'd just never been able to make sense of them before.

"When Red and Flush and I went to the Compound, it was the same thing. Hundreds of corpses, but no bullet holes. No indication of how they died."

"So then . . . how?" Hope asked.

I met her eyes. "Tell me about those crates you saw at the missile silo."

"Huh?"

"Those crates. Tell me about 'em."

She shot a glance to Cat. "They were just a bunch of wooden crates containing weapons."

"What kind of weapons?"

"The usual Republic guns: M4s, M16s, AK-47s."

"How do you know?"

"Because it was stenciled on the sides."

"Did you *see* the weapons?"

"You mean did we open the crates?"

"Exactly."

227

"No, but I'm sure—"

"So you didn't actually *see* them?"

"Well, no, but—"

"How do you know for sure what was inside if you didn't see?"

"What're you getting at, Book?" Cat asked.

"What if it's all related?" Even if I wasn't exactly sure where I was going with this, the words began to flow. The floodgates were opened and the waters went rushing through. "Think back to Camp Freedom. Those experiments that were done on you and Faith and the other Sisters—maybe Dr. Gallingham wasn't looking for cures. Maybe he was looking for *poisons*. He wasn't trying to save people, he was trying to kill them."

"Chemicals that could wipe out entire towns," Cat said.

"Right. And maybe that's what he's been giving Chancellor Maddox when they meet. That's what we saw on the country road that night."

Cat and Hope were speechless, remembering the gleaming steel box and the vials.

"But why go to the trouble of labeling them as guns?" Cat asked.

"Because of exactly what happened: people spying. You saw the crates, but you had no interest in those weapons, so you didn't open them up."

"I doubt they went to all that trouble just because of us."

"You're right. They didn't go to that trouble because of us."

"Then . . . why?"

"They went to that trouble because of everyone else. Because of the other territories. Because of President Vasquez."

Hope and Cat were both sitting up now. We were all leaning forward, elbows on knees. Our voices were hushed.

"That might even explain what that Brown Shirt told us," Cat said. "He claimed his gun jammed in the silo, that that's why he didn't fire at me. But maybe he was afraid if he shot and hit one of those crates, it'd activate a poison and kill us all."

"Why President Vasquez?" Hope asked. "Why would the chancellor keep all this from him?"

"Because he has no idea what Maddox is up to, and that's the way she likes it," I said. "Think about it. That's why she painted over Camp Freedom—to fool him and that Perrella woman. And she tested those chemicals on those towns in the middle of nowhere because she could get away with it there. She has no use for Crazies one way or the other. They're just lab rats. That's also why she hired the Hunters, who hired the Crazies to kill the Skull People. Her hands are clean. The president will never find out about it."

"But why is she developing these weapons in the first place?"

"It's the greatest trump card of all time. Once she becomes president, she can restructure the government however she wants, because she can wipe out anyone who disagrees with her. She has the ultimate power."

There was a long moment of stunned silence as we all seemed to realize the same thing at the same time: Chancellor Maddox had fooled us—had fooled *everyone*. And with missiles and chemical weapons on her side, there was no one left in the world who had even a remote chance of stopping her.

That next evening, two guards brought us dinner. One was thin with a goatee. The other was barrel-chested and clean-shaven, his face nicked in a dozen places from his razor. The floor shook a little with each of his steps.

"Eat up," Barrel Chest called out. "Slop time!"

He slid a tray of food under the cell bars, then moved back to let the other guard slide his trays forward. The goateed guard was kneeling on the floor when Barrel Chest whipped out a pistol and placed it to the other guard's temple.

"Don't move, pardner. And if you so much as break wind, I'll send your head flying to the moon."

My mouth gaped open. And then I realized what I was seeing. The heavyset soldier was none other than Goodman Dougherty, minus facial hair.

"Hope you all realize the sacrifice I made," he said, as he tied up the prisoner and put a gag in his mouth. "Took me fifteen years to get my beard all perfect like that."

"How'd you find us?" I asked.

"That dog of yours led me right to you a couple days ago. That thing's got a snout that could sniff out a petunia in a bed of daisies."

Argos. Once more coming to our rescue.

"Getting a soldier's uniform was the hard part," Dougherty went on. "At least, one that fit." Even now, his chest and belly strained against the buttons.

He unlocked the cell door and eased it open. Before we exited, he turned back around and met our eyes.

"By the way, I thought I told you all not to piss anyone off," he said.

"Guess we didn't listen," Hope said.

"Yeah, I guess you didn't. Come on. We don't have much time."

The four of us tiptoed forward. Dougherty pried open the flap of the tent, then led the three of us outside.

"Best we keep to the shadows," he said. "This place is jumpier than a three-legged cat in a rocking-chair factory."

Even though we slid through back alleys, I saw what Dougherty was talking about. Everyone was tense, on edge, short-tempered. There weren't the smiles and sense of fun we saw when we first came to town.

When we stopped to catch our breath, I asked, "What's going on?"

"Hard to say," Dougherty answered. "All sorts of rumors flyin' about—like maybe Maddox doesn't want to be president after all."

"Are you kidding?" Hope said. "The woman's in love with power. Why wouldn't she want to be president?"

"Your guess is as good as mine, but something's up. The inauguration's in four days and she's no longer here."

"*She's gone?*" I asked.

"Left town in the middle of the night, and no one knows why."

I couldn't believe it. None of us could.

We heard a clomping of boots and watched as a platoon of soldiers marched by. For the first time, I realized they were everywhere—soldiers, Humvees, tanks—moving through the muddy streets with a sense of urgency. Like they knew something the rest of us didn't.

A military vehicle revved by, engine growling, splashing mud. It was a large camouflaged truck with a series of enormous cylinders in the bed.

"What're those?" Hope asked.

"Multiple rocket launchers," Dougherty said. "The only missiles left after Omega. Apparently, they go everywhere the president goes."

It was no wonder Chancellor Maddox was so cocky. How could a bunch of slingshot-wielding Less Thans possibly take her down? Especially when she was about to inherit those weapons.

"And all the military's here?" Hope asked.

"Just about," Dougherty said. "It's not just the Conclave but the first public inauguration ceremony since pre-Omega."

We started up again, stopping when we came to the gallows. It was all lit up as workers were putting in the finishing touches, installing the trapdoors our bodies were intended to drop through. The sight of it made my hair stand up. We hurried on until we were out of town.

We were marching through an abandoned field when Hope sidled up to Dougherty. "Tell me about those multiple rocket launchers," she said.

He shrugged. "Not as precise as the silo missiles, of course, but they're mobile. Can be moved anywhere. Plus they deliver a whole slew of rockets all at once."

"Why would Chancellor Maddox have them up at the Eagle's Nest?"

Dougherty shook his head. "I doubt she does."

"What if I told you I saw them there?"

The four of us came to an abrupt halt.

"When I snuck into the Eagle's Nest," she explained, "there were a million things going on, but mainly they were working on trucks. A couple dozen of them. Welding and hammering and creating flatbeds—"

"That doesn't mean anything."

"—and off to the side were those cylinders. Missiles."

"Maybe, but she can't have enough to do any serious damage."

"Unless she has a different type of weapon," I said. "Like chemicals."

Goodman Dougherty's mouth dropped open, and we told him our suspicions. Even in the darkness, I could see his freshly shaved cheeks go pale.

"Could they arm those missiles with chemical weapons?" I asked.

"Sure," he said, "but it doesn't make any sense. She's gonna be the new president. She's going to be inaugurated in a few days."

"Not if she wipes out New Washington first."

39.

"Just because Chancellor Maddox may or may not be developing chemical weapons," Goodman Dougherty says, "that doesn't mean she intends to use 'em on her own people."

"It would explain why she's no longer here," Hope says. "And the latitude and longitude numbers—they weren't to let people know how to get to the Conclave, they were to tell her soldiers where to stay away from."

"But she was just elected president. Why would she wipe out the capital?"

"It's not just the capital she's wiping out. It's most of the military and every other leader in the Republic. With no Congress, she becomes the supreme ruler."

"Even if it means killing thousands of people in the process?"

"It's never bothered her in the past."

Hope knows they're all remembering the same thing. The towns. The corpses. The crows. They've seen for themselves what the chemicals do.

"Could she really get away with it?" Dougherty asks.

"Hitler did," Book says. "When the Reichstag was set on fire, he blamed it on the Communists. It gave him all the power he needed."

The thought sinks in. What they're envisioning would be the ultimate act of evil. Which is why Hope is convinced it's exactly what Maddox intends.

"So what do we do?" Dougherty asks.

Hope turns to the former Skull Person. "I know it won't be easy, but somehow you have to see the president. Explain everything: the chemical weapons, the multiple rocket launchers, all of it. Convince him to evacuate the city."

"You didn't have any luck reaching him. Why would he listen to me?"

"I don't know, but somehow you're going to have to." It's less a request and more an outright challenge.

"Okay," he says warily. "And you?"

"We need to stop Maddox."

"I hate to break it to you, but she's long gone, and probably not coming back."

"So then we go to her."

236

40.

Hope's words took us by surprise.

"If Maddox has gone back to the Eagle's Nest," Hope said, "then I'll just go there too."

"One against an army?" Goodman Dougherty asked. "Good luck even getting up there."

"I did it before. No reason I can't again."

"And this time there'll be two of us," I added.

Hope gave me an *I can do this on my own* look.

"It'll be easier with some company," I said.

She opened her mouth to protest but realized there was no point. I was coming along, whether she wanted me to or not. Still, there was something in her eyes I couldn't read. Something she wasn't saying.

"How're you gonna get there in time?" Cat asked.

"I don't know," Hope said. "But we've gotta try."

Goodman Dougherty tugged at the place where his beard once was. "Might be that I can be of some assistance with that."

He led us to the hollow where we'd first stopped, and as we neared, Flush, Red, Diana, and Twitch rushed from the aspen grove and greeted us. Of course, none was faster than Argos, who burrowed his head in my arms.

As everyone exchanged hugs and handshakes, Goodman Dougherty went to a pile of tree limbs and began flinging them to one side. Buried beneath the branches was a military Humvee.

"How'd you get that?" I asked.

"Guess I just look trustworthy, now that I'm all clean cut." He rubbed his bare, razor-nicked face. "That and the fact I stole it when no one was looking."

He reached into his pocket and pulled out the map of the United States we'd been passing back and forth. He spread it out on the vehicle's hood.

"You'll want to follow these roads. They aren't great, but they're the most passable ones." His finger snaked along a series of thin blue and red lines.

Hope and I studied the map. "Is there enough gas?" she asked.

"I put some spare cans in the back. Should be enough to get you there. I can't promise about the return."

Hope didn't respond—it was like she didn't care about that small detail—and Dougherty went on.

"I picked up some more weapons, too—knives, bows and arrows, slingshots. Figured we'd be needing 'em." He glanced at his watch. "I'm not kicking you out or anything, but if you hope to stop her in time, you better get going."

There was an awkward moment as the eight of us looked at one another. Here we'd just reunited and now we were splitting up again.

Once more, we exchanged handshakes and hugs, but this time ones of farewell. When I went to shake Cat's hand, he waved me off.

"I'll see you again," he growled.

We'd had our share of good-byes before, but this one felt different—maybe even permanent.

As Hope, Argos, and I climbed into the Humvee, Dougherty said, "I never asked. Do you know how to drive one of these things?"

Hope shrugged. "If Brown Shirts can do it, how difficult can it be?"

She put her foot on the gas and we peeled out, flinging mud. I glanced out the side window and saw the other six standing in the shadow of the ridge, waving good-bye. I had a feeling I would never see them again.

PART THREE
RELEASE

We have it in our power to begin the world over again.

—THOMAS PAINE

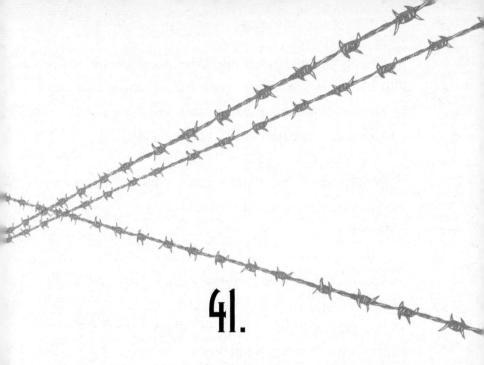

41.

WE TOOK TURNS DRIVING, one catching z's when the other was at the wheel. Occasionally we passed other Humvees, but no one gave us a second glance. We were just one more military vehicle keeping the RTA safe from harm.

We drove through the night, all the next day, into the next night and day as well. We knew our timeline. The inauguration was just days away, and the math was pretty simple: either we got to Chancellor Maddox before then . . . or it wouldn't matter.

The farther north we drove, the more snow we saw. Up there in the foothills of Skeleton Ridge, it was still late winter, the earth frozen.

Once, when we stopped, I caught Hope looking up at the millions of stars pressing down on us. She extended her hand, fooling herself into thinking she could actually touch one. When she saw me watching her, she blushed and tightened the hoodie around her face.

"Come on," she muttered. "Let's get going."

We got back in the car and drove on.

"You think we'll see him again?" I asked. She was at the wheel, I was riding shotgun.

"Who?"

"Cat."

"Course we'll see him. Nothing can destroy that guy."

"It's not him I'm worried about."

Hope didn't speak. Her gaze followed the headlight beams until they faded into black.

"You're not planning on coming back, are you?" I asked.

At first, I wasn't sure she'd heard me. The tires hissed. Argos snored softly from the backseat.

"One way or the other, Chancellor Maddox was responsible for the death of every single person in my family," she said, "and I'm going to end her life if it's the last thing I do."

"Don't say that."

"Whether I live or die is irrelevant. In fact, it's probably better if I die. Less hurt that way."

"Not for me."

She offered a weak smile, and her hand fumbled for mine in the dark. "Oh, Book. You and me, we could never make it. We're too different."

"You mean because I like to read and you don't? So I'll read enough for both of us."

"It's not that. . . ."

"Don't tell me you're going to bring up those silly scars again."

"They're anything but silly. I may not be the most feminine girl, but I still care, and I don't think I could ever forget that I'm damaged goods."

I actually laughed.

"What's so funny?"

"Believe me," I said, "of the two of us, you're the one who's got it together."

She didn't answer, and the road hummed beneath us.

"So that's it? End of story? You and me are no more?"

"You figure it out, Book. There can't very well be a you and me if one of us doesn't make it."

What could I say? Hope was as stubborn and head-strong as any person I'd ever met. When she set her mind to something, she did it. On her terms. And woe to whoever stood in her way.

But that didn't change one simple fact: I was in love with her.

I pulled my hand away and pressed my forehead against the glass, only vaguely aware of the haunted reflection staring back at me.

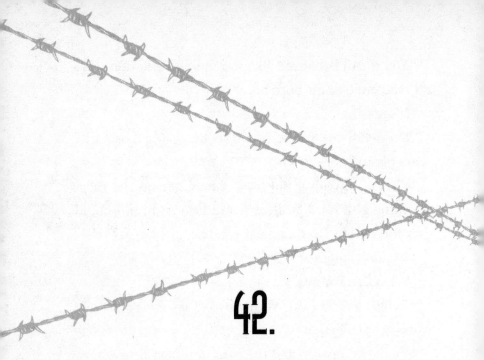

42.

IT'S THE MIDDLE OF the night when Book and Hope reach the foothills of Skeleton Ridge. The Humvee's headlights show that the road up the mountain is still buried in snow. By their calculations, they have about thirty hours before the inauguration, which means thirty hours before Chancellor Maddox fires off her chemical-laced missiles. Hope suggests they lie low for the day and ride the tram sometime that night; there will be fewer guards then. Less chance of getting caught.

There's a deserted barn just south of town, and they stash the Humvee there. Book swings the barn doors shut so that passing vehicles can't spy them. They're safe for a while. The calm before the storm.

Hope lights a match and it flares to life. She finds a kerosene lantern and coaxes the small flame. A yellow pool of light encases them like a soap bubble.

"Where should we sleep?" she asks.

There isn't much space on the main floor that isn't covered in fossilized animal dung.

"How about the hayloft?" Book says.

"Sure."

Argos curls himself contentedly in a corner while Hope and Book climb the rickety ladder to the top. As they do, Hope is reminded of the first time they met. That was in a hayloft, too, back in Camp Freedom. Despite all the months that have passed since then, Hope can still feel the warmth of Book's hand from that day.

She shakes away the thoughts.

They form a pile out of what little hay there is, and from that they create a mattress. They lie there, burying themselves as best they can. It's cold and breezy and the wind whistles as it slides between the planks. Hope rotates the knob until the lantern goes off.

Even in darkness, Book sees that Hope is shaking.

"Come here," he says.

They scooch sideways so that their bodies touch. Hope rolls over on her side and Book spoons her—his chest pressed against her back, his arms enveloping her.

For the longest time they lie there, neither saying a word. Hope feels the steady pulse of Book's exhalations on her neck. In the coal-black darkness, the world goes floating by, and her body gives an involuntary shiver as she thinks back to all the occasions that he's held her. And now this, the final time.

She rolls over until their faces are inches apart. Her eyes have adjusted to the dark and she can make out Book's expression. It's like he's remembering the same things that she is. He opens his mouth to speak, but before he can say anything, Hope leans forward and kisses him. Soft. Tentative. Inviting. Her lips are warm and he kisses her in return . . . and then he pulls away.

"Sorry," he says, rubbing his face.

"It's okay. I kissed you first."

"But if we're not going to be a couple, I can't do this. Sorry. It's not what I want."

"What *do* you want?"

"What you said earlier: Book and Hope together."

"Oh, Book . . ."

"It's not worth it otherwise. I'll just fall more in love with you than I already am, and then you'll go and get yourself killed, and where will that leave me?"

Hope inhales sharply at his words. She no longer feels cold; on the contrary, she's burning up.

"But Book—"

"I mean it. I can't pretend I don't have feelings for you. And if we kiss now, well . . ."

He doesn't finish the sentence. The blood is pounding in Hope's ears, and she feels a sudden need to get away, to lose herself in darkness. She pushes herself to her feet.

"Where're you going?"

She doesn't answer. She scrambles down the ladder, then rushes outside where the stars are blinding and the winter night soothes her like a bucket of cold water cooling a scalding iron.

She doesn't know how long she's out there. Long enough to feel the effects of cold and to know the stars are limitless. With a clarity that surprises her, she recalls the deaths of her mom, her dad, her sister Faith.

Book is right, of course. Without the hope of a future, kisses are just kisses. He's right to put an end to it. She's the one who has always said it's not going to happen, that they can't be together. So why did she feel the sudden desire to kiss him, to hold him, to have him hold her? Is it because she's afraid? And if so, of what?

She edges back through the barn door, her breath frosting in front of her. Argos looks up, gives a whimper, then returns to sleep. Easing up the ladder, Hope tries to quiet the creaks of the old wood. She slides into their makeshift bed and watches Book sleep, the gentle rise and fall of his chest. Time passes. An owl calls out from the trees.

She leans forward and presses her lips against his.

Book's eyes flutter open. "Hope," he says groggily, "I told you—"

"I know. And you're right." She kisses him again, more firmly.

Book is awake now, and she shushes him with a finger. He pushes himself up on his elbow and leans forward to kiss her, but not on the lips. First on her right cheek, and then on her left. On the two scars left by Chancellor Maddox.

A smile stretches Hope's face and she tucks her head, embarrassed.

Book places a finger on her chin and raises her face until their eyes lock. He extends his hands and caresses both her cheeks. He brings her into him and kisses her fully on the lips. There is a gentle firmness in how he holds her.

His hands slide to her arms, her sides, her lower back. He pulls her into him and she pulls him just as strongly into her. She can feel the heat buzzing from his hands, an electric current that makes her arms and legs tingle.

They slide into the hay, their hungry kisses exploring the other, their arms wrapped around each other. Two bodies mingled as one. Hope and Book. Book and Hope.

Together.

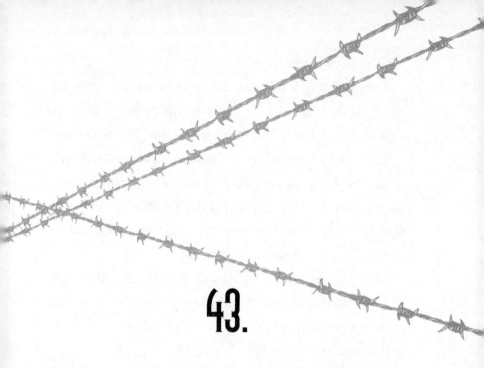

43.

GRAY SUNLIGHT EDGED THE oaken planks. The morning was cold and crisp, and I was convinced I'd never slept more soundly in my life. A smile crept on my face as I remembered why.

Hope.

I went to give a morning stretch . . . but couldn't. Odd. I tried again, but with the same result. I looked around and discovered why: My wrists were bound together with a piece of rope—and they were tied to a joist that stretched from loft to ceiling.

"What the . . ."

Someone had snuck in during the night and tied us up. But who? A Brown Shirt? One of Chancellor Maddox's thugs? How had they gotten past Argos? And

251

why had they left us here?

I turned to Hope and the bottom of my stomach dropped out. Her side of the bed was empty, and there was only a vague indentation in the hay. She was gone.

Even as I struggled to free myself, I racked my brain, seeing if there was anything I could remember about getting tied to a barn pole in the middle of the night. Outside of the good memories—and there were plenty of those—I could think of nothing.

That's when I noticed the symbol on the other side of me. The hay had been swept away and someone had etched a giant heart in the dust, with the letters HBT in the middle. Hope and Book Together.

"Hope!" I called out, my voice echoing off the rafters. "Little help up here."

Argos barked from down below, but that was the only response.

"Very funny, Hope. You got me. Now would you mind untying me?"

Still no response. I yanked and tugged until the hemp bit my skin and turned my wrists raw.

When I rolled over to my side, my face landed on a crack and I was able to see to the ground floor below. There was Argos, sitting on his haunches and looking back up at me. Next to him was where we'd parked the Humvee. Only now the space was empty.

Hope was gone.

I called out her name a few times more, but I knew there was no point. She had driven off sometime during the night, wanting to stop Chancellor Maddox on her own.

That's when I realized there was no way I could save Hope—I would never see her again.

44.

Hope didn't want to leave Book behind. It's just that she knows him . . . and she knows he will try to stop her.

By the time he frees himself—she tied the knots in such a way that he *will* eventually be able to free himself, just not right away—her mission will be complete. Chancellor Maddox and Dr. Gallingham will be no more.

She parks the Humvee behind an abandoned home on the far side of town. She spends the day foraging for food and clothing, slipping on a black T-shirt, a black hoodie, a pair of black pants. She charcoals her face so she will blend in with the night.

Darkness falls and she waits. Finally, when it nears midnight, Hope races through the deserted streets. Her breath frosts before her, puffs of white in an otherwise inky universe.

The town is eerily silent. Even the makeshift saloons and restaurants are all closed up, as though everyone's at the Conclave. Or up at the Eagle's Nest, getting ready to fire their missiles *at* the Conclave.

Hope's gaze lands on the highest tip of the mountain, where there's a yellow glow. She can imagine the swarm of activity as soldiers ready weapons and prepare to attack the Republic of the True America. In just under ten hours, Chancellor Maddox will unleash a barrage of chemical weapons on New Washington, wiping out the capital and every high-ranking official in the land.

By this time tomorrow, the country might very well be called "Maddox America" or "The Republic of Maddox" or even "The United States of Cynthia." Who's going to stop her?

From shadows, Hope spies a lone soldier guarding the tram. For a long time she studies his movements. She sneaks up on him just as he's switching his automatic rifle from one shoulder to the other. Her knife against his neck persuades him to drop it.

Less than sixty seconds after she's stowed the gagged and bound soldier, the tram jerks to life. Hope runs from the booth and leaps in through the open door. The tram swings drunkenly from side to side, but she's in, ascending the mountain, hovering above a forest of snow-covered spruces.

One step closer.

The downward-heading tram is in sight, and she cowers beneath the window. The two trams slide by each other, and she waits for the other tram to be well below her before she unfolds herself.

A glance up the mountain shows her the yellow glow is brighter now. It looks like every light is on. She can just make out the tram stop now, and as she nears it, she sees the Brown Shirts. There must be a dozen of them, facing the tram, their guns pointing in her direction like a firing squad.

She can't jump to the rocky mountainside like she did before, not in the middle of the night. She's got to find some other way to avoid the soldiers. But what that is, she doesn't yet know.

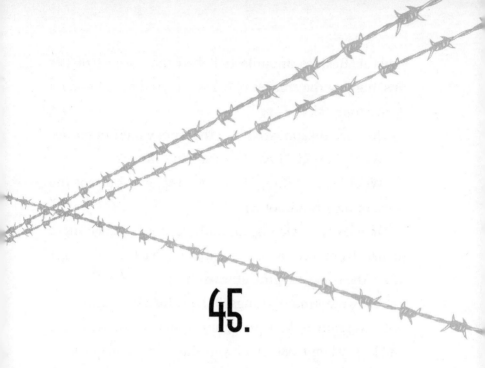

45.

IN MY DREAMS, SHE was there again: the woman with the long black hair. My grandmother. It was the first time I'd dreamed of her since I'd met her in the Compound, all those months ago. Ever since then—ever since I realized she was the stuff of memories and not just dreams—she no longer visited me in my sleep.

But there she was like always, leading me through a smoke-filled prairie, dodging bullets, my tiny child hand clasped firmly in her aged one. Bullets sang, the air reeked of gunpowder, explosions rocked the ground. She pulled me close and looked into my eyes.

"This is you, Book," she said, her message as cryptic as ever.

I knew better than to waste my breath asking her to

explain. Besides, a smile twitched the corners of her lips, tugging the creases of her weathered face. I had no desire to break the spell.

Then she disappeared into the smoky haze of battle.

"Wait," I cried. "I need to ask you things!"

"What kind of things?" a voice replied—but not the voice of my grandmother.

My eyes struggled open, and there was a face mere inches from my own. I scrambled backward to get away, the ropes tugging at my wrists.

"Ask what kind of things?" the voice asked again.

I was ready to kick, to fight off this person with feet and legs, when I saw that it was Cat. I shook my head to make sure I wasn't dreaming.

"What're you doing here?" I asked. "How'd you even find me?"

"Saw the tracks leading off the highway. Not that many Humvees headed in and out of barns."

"Yeah, but why're you here?"

He shrugged nonchalantly. "Figured the guy who talked me into rejoining the human race might not be out of the woods just yet. And I managed to hop a ride." His eyes landed on the rope handcuffs. "Who did this? Brown Shirts?"

"Hope."

His eyebrows arched. "Kinky."

"It's not what you think."

"Hey, what you do in your spare time—"

"*It's not what you think.*"

"Did I say anything?"

"You didn't have to."

He tried—and failed—to conceal a smile. "Let's get out of here before someone else pulls up. You'll have plenty of time to tell me the details later."

"It's not like that—" I stopped, realizing there was someone else in the hayloft with us. James Heywood—the president's aide—stood just behind Cat.

"What's he doing here?" I asked. The last time I'd seen him, he'd been with Jocelyn Perrella and Chancellor Maddox as they sentenced us to hanging.

"He's the one who brought me."

"Huh?"

"Extend your hands."

I absently did as he commanded, and Cat began slicing the ropes with a knife.

"You believe us?" I asked Heywood.

His eyes traveled between Cat and me. "It's not that I believe you, but after the last twenty years, I know enough not to *dis*believe you."

"Thanks, I think. So where's the army? Are they on their way up the mountain?"

This time he shared a look with Cat alone.

"What?" I said.

"*I* may think you're onto something," Heywood said,

259

"but that doesn't mean anyone else does."

"Wait. Are you saying—"

"Your friend Dougherty was able to convince the president to give us some troops, but not nearly enough. They should reach the Eagle's Nest sometime tomorrow."

"But the inauguration's at ten. That's when Maddox'll fire the missiles."

"I know. The troops are hurrying, but—"

"And the capital?"

"Not evacuated, if that's what you're asking."

"But they're all going to die."

"That's what we're hoping to prevent." He glanced at his watch. "Assuming there's time."

The knife cut through the last of the ropes, and I rubbed my wrists. After being tied up all day I was grateful to be free, but it was tempered by the fact that the president didn't really believe our warnings, and all the citizens of New Washington were in harm's way.

"There's a vehicle downstairs," Heywood said. "I can get you to town. From there, you're on your own—until backup arrives."

The cold, harsh reality sank in. The soldiers might very well be too late. It was up to Cat and me—and Hope, if she was still alive.

"Thank you for believing," I said.

"Don't thank me. Just be right."

260

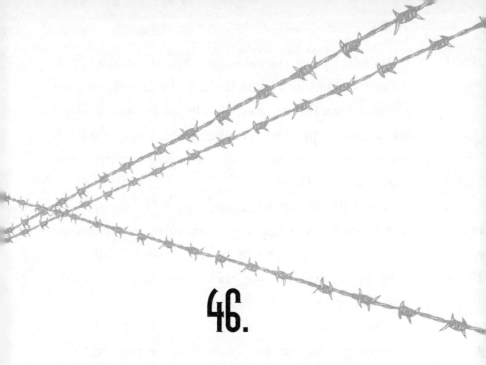

46.

THE BROWN SHIRTS TRAIN their weapons on the tram as it nears the mountaintop, and once it jolts to a stop, the soldiers swarm it from every angle. One looks inside the tram. Two climb to the top and search the roof. One soldier even checks beneath it.

Nothing. No one.

The commanding officer, a short, grizzled man with a plug of tobacco in his cheek, runs a hand through his thinning hair.

"Still nothing from below?"

A soldier stands with a walkie-talkie pressed to his ear. "No, sir. No one's answering."

The officer shoots the wad of tobacco into the snow, then squints into the dark.

Dangling from the cable forty feet down the mountain, Hope sees and hears it all. At the last minute, she squeezed out the window, clambered to the top of the tram, then jumped to the other cable. It was a miracle she found it in the dark—and an even greater one that she's able to hold on.

When the officer turns and speaks to his soldiers, she begins to work her way up the cable, one hand over the other. When he turns back, she stops. Talking to soldiers—climb. Turning back—stop. This could take a while.

The cable is icy and cuts into her fingers. Blood oozes from her palms and trickles down her wrists. But when she thinks she can't hold on another second, the smug smile of Chancellor Maddox flashes in her mind . . . and she moves again.

Fifteen feet from the station she stops, realizing her next movements will bring her into a pool of light. She dangles above the snow. The commanding officer takes most of the soldiers with him and they go marching off. That leaves two . . . which is still two too many. They both wield automatic rifles.

Hope begins to count.

On three, she releases her right hand so that she's only hanging on by her left. Her free hand races to her neck and fumbles for the necklace—the good-luck charm with the photographs of her parents. She yanks it off, and then her hand lunges for the cable, the necklace pressed inside the palm. The cable sways. She breathes heavily.

Don't let go, she tells herself. *Hang on.*

Once more she counts, and on three she drops the right hand and tosses the necklace. It sails above the soldiers' heads and clatters against the back wall of the tram stop. Both soldiers turn and raise their weapons.

Hope inches up the cable—right hand, left hand, right hand, left hand—until she's nearly to the platform. With trembling arms, she repositions herself, takes a breath, then lifts her legs and extends them forward until they wrap around the neck of the nearest soldier. She squeezes her thighs together until they go tight around his throat. The Brown Shirt's face purples as he struggles for air. He drops his gun and reaches for her legs, trying to pry them off.

The other soldier hears the commotion and turns. Hope kicks the strangled soldier in his direction and they both go toppling down. She leaps onto the platform, whips out her knife, and presses it against the second soldier's neck.

"Don't even think about it," she hisses. He has no choice but to drop his gun.

As she gags and binds them, her mind races. She's made it up the mountain. She's gotten past the soldier at the bottom and these two up here. But there are still many Brown Shirts left, and the clock continues to tick.

▪ ▪ ▪

The tunnel stretching from the tram stop to the elevator is long and dark . . . but not dark enough. She removes a slingshot from her back pocket and deftly takes out the few remaining lightbulbs. *Smash, smash, smash.*

The tunnel is now completely black. If she should pass any soldiers, she'll be nothing more than a dark shape moving in the gloom.

All goes according to plan until the elevator doors slide open and a rectangle of light falls on the stone. A Brown Shirt emerges and takes one look at the darkened tunnel.

"Doesn't anyone change lightbulbs around here?"

"Tell me about it," Hope mutters, lowering her head.

She tries to walk past him, but there's enough glow from the elevator to illuminate her.

"Hey, wait a minute—"

Hope sends an elbow smashing into his windpipe. He grabs his throat and buckles over, and she finishes him off with a well-placed kick to the groin. He collapses in a heap on the stone.

She drags him out of sight, realizing that the last time she was up here, she wore a uniform and cap. But this soldier's clothes are way too small. So she'll need to avoid the light if she wants to reach Chancellor Maddox. She lets the elevator doors whisper closed without stepping in . . . and then heads for the lone door tucked in the corner. She gives it a yank and sticks her head inside.

It's a steep stairwell—a series of metal steps that switchback up four hundred-some feet to the top. Hope realizes she'd have to be crazy to climb all these stairs. Or desperate. She takes a deep breath and begins.

The stairway is lit, and there are no exit doors. If someone were to enter from the top, she'd have to turn around and scamper back to the bottom. The sooner she can get out of here, the better.

Hope is in good shape, but there are over seven hundred steps. She's winded before she reaches the halfway point. Her heart is slamming against her chest, like some wild animal trying frantically to escape a cage. She wants to rest but then remembers her parents and her sister—and the woman responsible for their deaths.

She keeps walking.

Despite the damp cool of the stairwell, sweat runs down her jaw, her sides, the small of her back. *Keep going,* she wills herself. *Don't stop now.*

When she finally nears the top, her hand tightens around the knife handle. She presses her ear against the door, listens, then eases it open. She is shocked by what she sees.

She figured the fortress would be on high alert, but she didn't expect to see so many Brown Shirts. They're *everywhere,* in battle gear and fully armed. Locked and loaded and ready for what comes next.

But there's something else she picks up on, too. Although they move with soldierly efficiency, it almost seems like they carry a sense of dread. As though they're not all that enthusiastic about unleashing a fatal dose of chemical weapons on New Washington and its citizens.

Hope glances at her watch. One forty-five a.m. The inauguration starts at ten. Just over eight hours to prevent the slaughter of thousands of innocent people.

Four soldiers go running past, and Hope tucks herself in the shadows. She waits for the echo of their footsteps to evaporate before easing back out. Her gaze lands on the enormous structure that looms above the fortress: the towering white cylinder. She is convinced that's where Maddox is.

Which is why Hope turns around and promptly walks the other way.

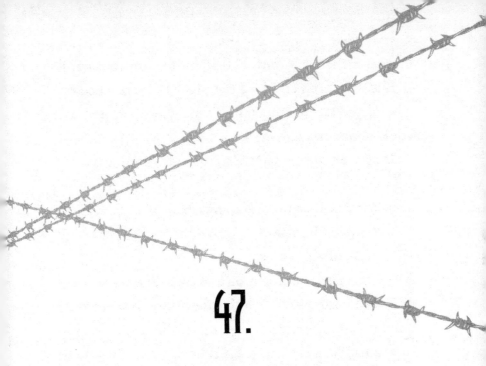

47.

ONE LOOK AT THE empty tram booth told us everything.

"Hope," Cat and I said in unison.

We followed the footprints in the snow and found a soldier, bound and gagged in a back alley.

"Definitely Hope," we said.

Our gazes reached up to the distant yellow glow atop the mountain. If she was up there, would our joining her help or hinder? We didn't want to do anything to mess up her plans.

"I don't know that we can pull this one off, Book."

It was one of the few times Cat thought a problem was bigger than a solution. And on the surface of things, I agreed. It was downright foolish to think we could waltz into an enemy fortress, stop the missiles, and rescue Hope. Utterly ridiculous to even consider it.

But then I remembered the night Hope reached out a hand and tried to touch the stars. There was no way I could abandon that person.

"I have an idea," I said, and took off running.

The barrel of the gun poked my ribs.

"Okay, I get it," I said.

"Hey, I gotta practice."

Cat wore the uniform of a Brown Shirt—courtesy of the soldier now lying in the alley—and it was creepy how authentic he looked. Of course, if he hadn't escaped the Young Officers Camp when he did, these would be his daily clothes.

"You sure about this?" he asked.

"Can you think of any other way?"

We stepped into the tram, and when it jolted to a start, I realized there was no turning back. We were headed up the mountain—a lone tram carrying two Less Thans. Below us, the snow sparkled in moonlight.

For the longest time neither of us spoke. Maybe it was nerves. Maybe it was the thought that there was really no good way we could get out of this.

"What do you think it's like?" Cat asked, breaking the silence.

"The Eagle's Nest?"

"No. Heaven. Hell."

I'm sure my eyes widened in surprise. It wasn't like Cat to suddenly start philosophizing.

"I'm serious," he said. "What do you think it's like?"

"Well," I said, "I see it like a road. A long, dusty road in the middle of nowhere. And on this road are other people who've died before, and they walk with you."

He shook his head. "That's not how I see it."

"How do you see it then? Angels and stuff?"

"Not hardly."

"Well then?"

He didn't answer at first. When he did speak, his voice was barely a whisper. "Frank's place."

He turned to me. His blue eyes were piercing.

"That's how I see heaven—like Frank's place. A tiny oasis in the middle of nowhere. In the mountains. On a lake with fish. Plenty of game nearby. A garden. A wife. Everything he needed, all right there."

I was surprised. I didn't know Cat had a soft side. Here I figured he considered Frank's cabin just another stop on the way. A resting place with a roof. I had no idea it meant more to him than that.

"There's a library in there," I said.

"I know."

"Would you keep it?"

He shrugged. "In heaven, I might start to read. Stranger things have happened."

What could I say? It seemed like Cat was turning

over a new leaf. But then I realized: What did it matter? Because there was the Eagle's Nest right there, and the closer we got, the more helpless we were. We might as well have put our heads on a silver platter.

The cables shrieked and groaned as the tram slowed to a stop.

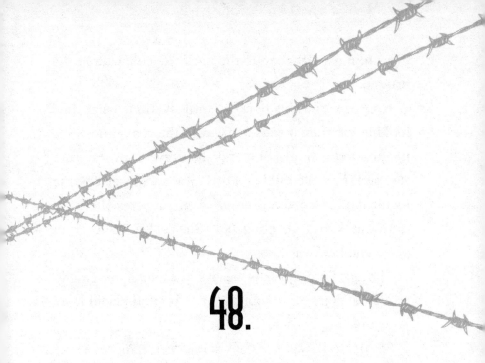

48.

HOPE DOES A QUICK tour of the Eagle's Nest, not stopping until she locates the rocket launchers. They're positioned at the southern edge of the fortress, snuggled against the castle walls. There's no way in the world Hope can get anywhere near them; soldiers are everywhere.

She notices the crates, the ones she saw back at the launch facility. They lie scattered across the ground, their contents now armed into the missiles.

She hurries back the other way, finding the garage she saw that first day. There's only a lone Brown Shirt keeping guard, half asleep. He takes deep drags from a cigarette, his face cocooned in a chaos of smoke. She reaches him just as he's stubbing out his cigarette and gives him a swift chop to the neck. He collapses to the ground.

Hope searches his pockets until she finds what she's looking for, then makes her way to the gas pumps. The metal handle is icy cold, and she draws it as far from the pump as the rubber hose allows. She places the metal handle on the ground, then squeezes the lever until gas starts gurgling out. She locks the lever in place and backs away.

The gasoline spreads across the stone pavement, reflecting stars and moon like a calm and placid lake. The pungent odor wrinkles her nose.

She opens the soldier's box of matches, removes a lone match, and strikes it against the side. It flares. When she tosses it forward—*whoompf!*—night is turned to day and the ground crawls with the jagged crowns of blue flame. Hope turns and runs, her shadow dancing on the walls.

49.

THE CLOSER THE TRAM got to the platform, the harder Cat jammed the pistol into my ribs. The tram jolted to a stop, and we swayed a moment, waiting for soldiers to whip open the door.

No one did.

We stood there, unsure of what to do. Finally, Cat stepped around me and slid open the door.

There was no one there. The platform was empty.

"What's going on?" I mouthed.

Cat shrugged and gave his head a shake.

We stepped out onto the platform, and that's when we heard the sirens. Loud, screeching klaxons emanating from the fortress above us. We shared a look. *Hope.*

"Come on," Cat said, and we hurried toward the tunnel.

Water dripped from the ceiling as our footsteps echoed against the stone walls. Our feet crunched on broken glass—a shattered lightbulb by the sounds of it. We didn't say a word, fearing a Brown Shirt would appear at any moment. When we reached the elevator, we looked down the black tunnel behind us. Still no one in sight.

Cat pressed the brass button, and when the doors slid open, a rectangle of yellow light fell at our feet . . . and a soldier stood by the control panel.

"What do we have here?" he asked. A sweep of blond hair covered half his forehead.

"Less Than," Cat said, disgusted. "Caught him down below."

The Brown Shirt's face hardened. "Why'd you bring him here? You know the directive. No more prisoners, especially tonight."

"Thought Dr. Gallingham could try out some of his new medicines," Cat said. "One final time."

Judging from the Brown Shirt's smile, it seemed he liked the idea. "Come on in. I'll take you up top."

Cat gave me a rough push and I stumbled forward, slamming into the elevator's back wall. The operator laughed.

The doors whisked shut, and the elevator jerked upward.

"Probably wondering why you got an operator," the Brown Shirt said.

"Crossed my mind," Cat said.

"Something's going on up top. Big fire by the garage. The president-elect put the place on lockdown. Everyone's a little jumpy."

"Yeah, the guy at the bottom said people were on edge."

We were silent. The elevator hummed upward.

"The sentry at the bottom of the mountain told you that?" the soldier asked, absently sweeping a hand through his hair.

"That's right."

"Funny, 'cause he's not answering his phone."

"Probably dozing. The guy was half asleep when we talked to him."

"*We?*"

"I," Cat corrected himself.

More silence. Even with my jacket on, I could sense the tension from Cat's muscles spilling into the gun, which in turn pressed into me.

"What'd you say your name was again?" the soldier asked.

"I didn't."

"Didn't think you did, but it says right there, doesn't it?" He pointed at the badge on Cat's chest. "Dawkins, huh?"

"That's right."

"I always thought Dawkins was taller. Heavier, too."

"Went on a diet the first of the year. Musta done the trick."

"Yeah. Musta."

The elevator inched skyward. I kept my head bowed, not daring to make eye contact with either the Brown Shirt or Cat. Which was why I heard but did not see the soldier whipping his pistol from its holster and training it on Cat. At the same time, Cat swung his own gun around until the two faced off: pistol against pistol.

"Now why don't we cut the bullshit and you tell me who you really are," the soldier said.

Cat's jaw clenched. He didn't speak.

"Nothing? All right. But we'll be up top in another couple of seconds, and I'm sure my CO would love to hear your explanation. And if you try to shoot me before then, you know damn well I'll pull my trigger at the exact same time."

I believed him. I didn't know about Cat, but I sure did.

The elevator slowed. In another second, the doors would slide open and we'd be marched straight to the soldier's commanding officer. And who knew what would happen then?

So I did the one thing I could do: I lowered my shoulder and rammed it into the Brown Shirt. His gun went off—*wham!*—and a bullet lodged in the ceiling. The explosion was deafening, the sound waves bouncing off the elevator walls like a rubber ball. I turned myself around and pressed the red Emergency button; the elevator jolted to a stop.

At the same time, Cat took the butt of his gun and cracked it across the soldier's chin. The Brown Shirt went stumbling into the far wall, out cold.

Cat turned to me. "You okay?" he asked.

"I can't hear, if that's what you asked. But yeah, I'm okay."

Cat released the Emergency button, and we shuddered upward.

When the doors rattled open, we pushed the button for the bottom floor and stepped out as quickly as we could. The doors shut behind us and the elevator descended.

We had made it to the top of the mountain, but one glance told us we'd stepped into a hornet's nest. Sirens sounded, klaxons clanged, and the glow of an inferno lit the sky. Soldiers ran in every possible direction— some with hoses, some with buckets of water, all with automatic rifles. How could we possibly find Hope in all this chaos?

Or were we too late? Had she already sacrificed her life to kill Chancellor Maddox? The mere thought of it sent the blood rushing from my head and nearly brought me to my knees.

50.

Sirens wail and soldiers race. The same recorded announcement plays over and over from speakers mounted on tall poles: "Warning: Breach! Warning: Breach!"

Hope stays hidden, waiting for the right moment to emerge from the shadows. She walks purposefully toward the white tower, head lowered. Two guards stand sentry, looking tense—one involuntary jerk away from pulling triggers.

When she's thirty feet from the entrance, Hope pulls back her hood, revealing her charcoaled face. She raises her hands above her head.

"Don't shoot," she says, affecting a thick accent.

The two soldiers train their rifles on her. Their faces are clouded with indecision. How is it that someone other than a Brown Shirt has managed to gain entry into the Eagle's Nest?

"Who are you?" one of them asks, squinting. Hope has positioned herself so the fire is behind her, the backlight obscuring her features.

"Unarmed," she says, continuing to glide forward. The trick—as she remembers her father once explaining it—is for the predator to approach without the prey knowing.

"Don't come any closer," one of the guards warns.

"No gun," she says, her accent thicker. She waves her empty hands.

"Okay, but stop right there."

Hope takes two more steps and does as he says. She's twenty feet from them. She'd like to be closer, but she can make this work.

"No gun," she repeats. "Unarmed."

One of the guards steps forward. When he's within five feet, he asks, "Who are you? What're you doing here?"

"Unarmed. No gun." Her accent is thicker each time she opens her mouth. She can see down the long, black tunnel of his rifle barrel.

The Brown Shirt sighs impatiently and takes another step forward, about to frisk her. As his hands reach her waist, Hope lowers her arm and jabs an elbow into his face. Blood spurts from his nose. He tumbles backward. Even before he reaches the ground, she releases a knife hidden on her forearm, clutches the handle, and sends it spinning through the air. It lands squarely in the other guard's chest. He collapses without firing a shot.

Hope kneels by the first soldier—who's squirming, bleeding, crying out in pain—and gives him a swift chop to the neck. He's out cold. She rushes to the other guard, removes the knife from his chest, and slips through the unguarded entrance.

The interior is a large, empty atrium, modern and sleek and bathed in white. It reeks of clean. Hope wonders if this was what the world was like pre-Omega.

A shiny plaque on the wall lists the office numbers of people and departments. Her finger traces down the column until she finds who she's looking for. She avoids the elevator and scrambles up the staircase to the fifth floor.

The sirens here are muted, but red emergency lights flash on, off, on, off. There is no sign of personnel, and Hope wonders if they've been evacuated. Has she missed her opportunity? Was her fire *too* effective?

She makes her way down the hall, stopping when she reaches a sign posted on a door.

RESEARCH LABORATORY

There's another door farther down the hall that seems to open into the same room, and she chooses that one. Less conspicuous. She grabs hold of the doorknob and eases inside. Stainless-steel tables are laid out in a series of precise rows, and gleaming white cabinets line the walls. The counters and tables are covered with all kinds of science equipment: flasks, beakers, burners, tubes.

There is one person present.

It's been weeks since Hope last laid eyes on Dr. Gallingham, but he is exactly how she remembered him, wearing his black suit and dabbing at the corners of his eyes with a damp hanky. Even though his back is to her as he sits hunched over a microscope, she would recognize him anywhere.

She tiptoes forward, dagger extended. Before she reaches him, his voice calls out, "Well well, look who the cat dragged in."

She stops in her tracks. Gallingham pulls back from the microscope, swivels on his stool, and turns to look at her, a smug expression on his face.

"You forget. You Sisters always did have a distinctive smell. No, not so much a smell—more like a *stench*." He motions toward her charcoaled face. "I like what you've done with your makeup. Far more flattering. By the way, it's Hope, isn't it? Or is it Faith? In any case, the greatest of these—"

"It's an old joke."

"Old jokes are the best jokes, my dear. Don't you know that?"

She doesn't answer him. Instead, she says, "Tell me about my father."

His eyes widen. *"That's* why you're here? We're about to unleash the next Omega and you want to know about *your father?"* He sighs. "Like father, like daughter."

"Tell me about him."

"You haven't lost faith in him, have you? Oh, wait a minute, you already lost Faith." He snickers.

"Tell me about my father," she says through gritted teeth.

"It's so interesting. From names alone, you would think Faith would have been the stronger of the two. It implies a certain power. But Hope . . . well, that just sounds desperate."

Hope steps forward and smacks Gallingham across the face.

He forces a smile even as a red flush blooms on his cheek.

"I told you months ago," he says. "Your father was a doctor. Taught me everything I know. So good with a scalpel. He knew just how to inflict the most pain and yet keep a patient alive. Not an easy balance. You've never heard screaming until you watched Dr. Samadi at work."

"Don't lie to me."

"Why would I lie? I have nothing to hide."

"Give me specifics."

"About the Butcher of the West? Well, he loved a good torture. Said it made him feel whole. And you don't just earn a nickname like that for nothing."

Hope's face goes hot. She's so angry she has difficulty breathing.

With her free hand, she fumbles inside her coat, removing the piece of paper she took from the folder back in New Washington—the one from the Department of Records. She thrusts the crumpled sheet before Dr. Gallingham's eyes.

"What was written there?"

He squints and leans into the paper. "Looks like someone had a little fun with Wite-Out."

"What'd it say? What'd they white out?"

"How should I know? I'm not a clerk."

She places her knife against his neck. "No, but something tells me you know about this."

"Wish I could help you. I forget things as the years pass. Old age, you know."

"So let's help you remember." The knife blade kisses his skin, drawing the first pearls of blood. Gallingham's expression darkens.

"Are there personnel files here?" she asks.

"Here? Of course not. Why would there be?"

Something in how quickly he answers makes her think otherwise.

"Where are they?"

"I just told you—"

"*Where are they?*"

She presses the knife into the fleshy folds of his neck. A drop of blood snakes its way down the blade. "I'll ask you one more time: are there personnel files here or not?"

He gives the slightest of nods.

"In this building?"

Another nod.

"Take me there."

"You can look for yourself," he snarls. "Or is it that you don't think you can find it? I guess without your sister, you only do *half* the thinking."

Hope lifts the knife from his neck and swipes the edge across the bottom of his ear. A chunk of flesh plops to the ground.

"You little bitch!" he cries, reaching for the wound. Blood dribbles between his fingers.

"Take me there," she hisses, "or I'll cut off something other than your ear."

Cradling the side of his head, he lurches to his feet. They're nearly to the door when Hope races back to Gallingham's work station. There's something there that interests her. She returns to the doctor, places her knifepoint in his back, and they step into the hall. The doctor is heading to the elevator when Hope stops him.

"Where're we going?" she asks.

"Two floors up."

"We take the stairs."

"It's two floors up," he complains.

"*Stairs.*"

He lets out an exaggerated sigh and they make their way to the stairwell. He's winded after the first few steps. A slick coating of blood covers his hand and dribbles down his wrist.

"Quit stalling," she says.

They exit through the seventh-floor door, then shuffle down the long hallway until they reach a door marked *Records*. He waddles to a stop.

"Can I go now? I need medical attention."

"Open it," she says.

He jangles the knob. "It's locked."

"Something tells me you have a key." The knife finds an opening between his ribs.

The doctor flinches, then reaches for a key card. He swipes it on a panel and the door clicks open. He leads her inside and she flicks on a light.

The room is massive—far larger than the laboratory downstairs. Nearly as daunting as the Department of Records back in New Washington.

"Love us or hate us," Gallingham says smugly, "but you have to admit: we are meticulous record keepers."

"As proof of your cruelty?"

"Proof of how to build a functioning civilization."

Hope grunts and looks around. It's overwhelming, the rows and rows of filing cabinets.

"Any hints where I should look?" she asks.

"I've never stepped in here before."

Hope knows he's lying, but there's no point pressing the issue. Her eyes give the room a once-over, landing on a dangling sign marked *Personnel*.

Hope throws Gallingham into a chair, where he lands with a heavy plop. "Move and you die," she says.

She can hear Brown Shirts running in the hall. There's not much time.

Her feet pull her forward. As she nears the cabinets, she can't help but wonder: Does she really want to do this? Does she really want to discover the *truth*?

The *S*'s are tucked in the far corner of the room. Hope's fingers tremble as they wade atop the file folders, stopping when they reach the name she's looking for: *Samadi, Uzair*. Pinching the thick folder free, she removes it from the cabinet and takes it to a nearby table.

"Did you find it under *S* for 'Sellout' or *T* for 'Traitor'?" Gallingham asks from across the room. He uses his handkerchief to try and stanch the flow of blood. The once-white hanky is now crimson.

Hope opens the folder and examines its contents, realizing she's barely breathing.

It's all here: her father's upbringing, the names of

his parents and siblings, the marriage to Charlotte Patterson. The next page provides more biography still—the birth of twin girls, the disappearance of the Samadi family, the death of Hope's mom by "natural causes." So that's how the Republic classifies a murder in cold blood.

Hope zips through the file—page after page of biographical information. It's far more than what she found in New Washington.

It's the final document that grabs her attention most—the Letter of Agreement between Dr. Uzair Samadi and Dr. Joseph Gallingham, signed by Chancellor Cynthia Maddox. A carbon copy of the document she saw back in New Washington.

Hope is both eager and afraid to read it. She forces herself to examine it slowly.

It lists Dr. Uzair Samadi's title as research scientist, and when she comes to the space marked *Duties*—the space blotted out in the New Washington version—she sees writing. Typed words. No mysterious Wite-Out blurring the letters.

But instead of listing his job, it gives a short series of directions. "Refuses to cooperate. Relieve of all duties, then confiscate the twin daughters and terminate at will."

Hope's breath leaves her. It's a death order. But what's just as powerful is what *isn't* there—no mention of her father's experimenting on others or developing chemical weapons.

She flips frantically through the pages.

"I don't get it," she says. "This says he was a scientist, but nothing about what he actually did."

Even with the blood dripping down his hand and wrist, Dr. Gallingham manages to shrug innocently.

"You know something," Hope goes on. "What is it?"

"Who says I know anything?" A smile oozes across his face. "I'm just a scientist like your father was. Making the Republic a better place for the next generation."

"But you know details. You wouldn't be so smug, otherwise."

"Smug? *Moi?*"

Hope lunges for him, grabbing him by the shoulders and giving him a shake. "Tell me what you know! What does it mean when it says 'Refuses to cooperate'?"

"It means exactly what it says. He refused to cooperate."

"In what way exactly?"

Instead of answering, Gallingham begins to hum.

"Tell me!"

Dr. Gallingham stops long enough to meet her eyes. "You're so smart," he whispers. "What do you think it means?"

Hope stares at him . . . and then her eyes go wide and her hand flies to her mouth. "Oh my God," she says, her legs suddenly weak.

"You believed it, didn't you? This whole time."

"Oh my God . . ."

"Everyone did. It was our only way of ensuring that no one would let him into their homes. He would be an outcast for the rest of his life. Call someone by a name and people believe it, especially if they hear it over and over again. It doesn't matter if it's true or not, as long as you say it with conviction. I learned that from the politicians."

"How could you?"

"We had no choice. Your father left us, and with everything he knew about our chemical weapons program, we couldn't let him get away with that. So we had to make him the enemy. We fabricated that whole Butcher of the West stuff . . . and people believed it. *You* believed it."

More than anything, Hope wants to cover her ears, to block out everything Gallingham is saying. Because everything he's saying is true. She genuinely believed her father was collaborating with the enemy. All this time, she's been duped.

"You had no right," she says.

"We had every right. Your father put his own self-interest above the good of the Republic. In my book, that's the definition of a traitor. He deserved everything we said about him, whether it was true or not. And if you believed it, well, shame on you."

Hope feels light-headed, dizzy. The world is spinning

and she stumbles away. To think she could have doubted her father, the man who rescued her after her mother's murder, who took care of her and Faith for ten years while on the run. How could she have turned on his memory like that?

Dr. Gallingham is still talking.

"... hated for your mother to suffer like that, but she brought that on herself, didn't she?"

Hope looks at him blankly. "My mother?" she repeats.

"Why she chose your father for a husband, I'll never know." He begins to hum again. "Come, Thou Fount of Every Blessing." Hope's mother's favorite hymn.

Hope stares at him a moment . . . and then something clicks. "You knew her," she says without breath.

Gallingham's eyes flick away.

"You knew my mother. *Liked* my mother."

"Frankly, I don't know why she chose him. I had more job security, better prospects, a better salary, even *before* Omega."

"You killed my parents for personal reasons."

"I don't know what you're—"

"You killed my parents because you were *jealous*?"

"She rejected me! Spurned my advances. Said she wanted nothing to do with me. Well, fine. If that's your choice, then get ready to pay the consequences."

Hope can't believe it. All these years of running from the Brown Shirts was in large part because *her mother had the good sense to turn down Dr. Gallingham?*

"Yes, we made up those lies about your father. And what was remarkable was how easy it was to get inside your head. We'd started the rumor years earlier, of course, ever since Dr. Samadi left us, and when we captured you and your sister, I didn't think for a second you'd buy it. But you did. All of it. Just shows how little faith you had in him. Pun intended."

Hope can't hear any more. She has had enough of Dr. Gallingham, his lies, his smug behavior. She draws her knife and takes a step forward, ready to end his life once and for all. No more will he inflict his sordid practices on the rest of the world.

A click of metal stops her cold. In the doctor's non-bloody hand is a pistol . . . trained on Hope.

"In the future, you should really check your prisoner for weapons. That is to say, if you *had* a future."

Hope can't believe it. How could she have been so stupid? How? *How?*

"Yes, it's loaded," Gallingham goes on. "And yes, I intend to use it. Finish off all the Samadis once and for all."

Hope's shoulders sag at her own stupidity, even as a part of her can't help but feel she deserves this. It's what she gets for doubting her father in the first place.

"I imagine you could kill yourself for being so thoughtless," Gallingham says. "But don't worry. I'm going to take care of that for you."

He raises his gun, and although Hope's mind races, there is no way out. Not this time. The gun is pointed at her forehead, and unless it miraculously misfires, the man who killed Faith Samadi is about to end Hope's life as well.

What surprises her is that in this final moment of living, a weight lifts from her shoulders. Her father was a good and decent man who did his best for his wife and daughters. There is comfort in that, just as there is comfort in the lessons he passed on.

Live today, tears tomorrow.

But when her thoughts go to Book, something stabs at her—the sad realization that she never told him how she felt. Although she's lived a life without fear or hesitation, she's always stalled when it comes to sharing feelings. Never has she truly revealed the contents of her heart. *In my next life,* she vows, *I won't let this happen.*

She closes her eyes—there's no way in the world she will allow her final image to be that of Dr. Gallingham—and pictures Book. The bang of the pistol shatters the stuffy silence.

51.

I POINTED TO THE round tower. If Hope had made it this far, there was no question in my mind that she'd be in the very center of the enemy's headquarters.

If she was still alive, that is.

Cat's pistol pressed against my ribs as we made our way across the square, dodging squads of running soldiers. They were so preoccupied, they barely gave us a glance.

We noticed two sentries lying at the building entrance. One was out cold; the other had a knife wound to his chest.

Hope.

We entered the building, stepping into an empty lobby. What we *thought* was an empty lobby. We were

293

headed for the stairwell when we heard a voice bark out.

"Stop!"

A Brown Shirt came strolling over, checking us out every step of the way.

"What're you doing here with a prisoner?" he asked Cat.

"Delivery," Cat mumbled. "Dr. Gallingham."

"In the middle of the night?"

"Just following orders."

The Brown Shirt squinted and looked us up and down. "Papers," he said.

"Huh?"

"Papers," the soldier repeated. Even though he was young, not much older than us, his uniform had sergeant's stripes. "I can't let you up the tower without proper ID."

"Right."

Cat made a show of patting his pockets, looking for a set of papers that didn't exist. His hands lowered, then neared his waist, and I knew he was reaching for his pistol—the one he'd taken from the Brown Shirt at the bottom of the mountain.

The sergeant was no dummy. He yanked Cat's pistol from its holster before Cat had a chance. He leveled the gun at Cat, then at me, than back at Cat.

"Can't find those papers?" he asked.

"Can't seem to," Cat answered.

"Huh." His jaw tightened and untightened as his eyes fixed on the name on Cat's uniform. "Then, *Private Dawkins*, why don't you tell me where you got this Less Than."

"Given to me. I was told to bring him up here."

"By who?"

"Some captain. Reese, Reynolds, Ramirez—something."

"You don't know this captain?"

"No, sir."

"You just do what you're told?"

"That's the Republic way."

The muscles in the Brown Shirt's jaw went crazy. "Then why don't we just head upstairs and get some new orders. You good with that?"

"Sounds like a plan."

The sergeant motioned us to the elevator. I wanted to shoot a glance at Cat, but I didn't dare. I was a prisoner.

We were *both* prisoners. Although we had made it into the tower—and I was convinced Hope was here somewhere—it felt like every step we took was one step farther away from her.

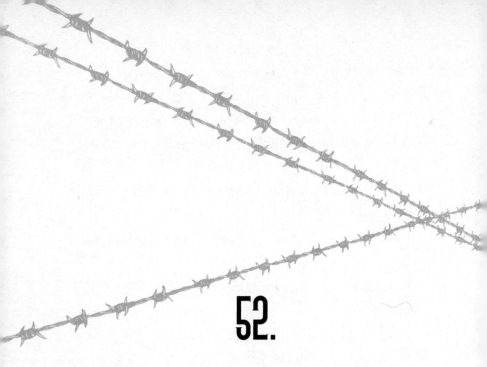

52.

In Hope's final moments on this earth, she is overwhelmed by senses. Bang of the pistol. Acrid scent of gunpowder. Spreading warmth of blood. Blackness.

But when she opens her eyes . . . she's still standing, and the spreading warmth is blood flowing *through* her veins, not outside them.

Her hands flounder against her body. There's no wound.

At her feet, Dr. Gallingham lies motionless, a single bullet hole in the side of his head. A thin trickle of moisture dribbles from an eye.

Hope tries to make sense of it all, and when her gaze finally shifts to the doorway, she is surprised to see someone else in the room.

Scylla.

There's a gun in her hand; smoke curls from its barrel.

"I heard the sirens and guessed it was you," Scylla says. "Took me forever to figure out where you were."

Hope is speechless. Not just that she is still alive and was spared from death at the last possible moment, but that Scylla *talked*. For the first time since Hope has known her, words have come from Scylla's mouth.

"Scylla . . ."

"I know," she says, her voice raspy and unpracticed. "Surprised me too."

There is no time to figure it out, and Hope rushes to her friend and gives her a grateful hug.

When they pull apart, Hope says, "You survived the avalanche."

"Barely. I tried to get back to you, but Maddox found me first."

"And they've held you prisoner here?"

Scylla nods.

"How'd you get free?"

"Once the alarms went off, the guards stopped paying attention. I was able to sneak up on one. That's where I got this." She holds up the gun. They hear footsteps outside the door. "We better get going. There's a service elevator that'll get us back down."

She turns to go and is nearly to the door when she notices Hope hasn't moved. Scylla looks at her a moment . . . and then understands. "Chancellor Maddox?"

Hope nods.

"It won't be easy," Scylla says.

"It never is."

Before they go, Hope takes one last look at Dr. Gallingham, knowing she will never have to see his face again, never have to hear his grating voice. Whatever else happens tonight, there is that small bit of comfort.

They slip out of the Records room, and Scylla leads Hope to a far staircase. They scurry up until they reach the top floor, the fifteenth. Scylla presses her ear against the door.

"Brown Shirts," she mouths.

They grip their knives and Scylla whips open the door.

There are four soldiers keeping guard. By the time they register the presence of the two Sisters, Hope has kicked one in the groin and disarmed another. Scylla sweeps her knife across the throats of the other two.

All four lie scattered on the floor.

"You okay?" Hope asks.

Scylla nods, then takes two pistols from the soldiers, handing one to Hope. Hope is no fan of guns, but something tells her they might come in handy. They race down the hall toward the very last door. After a shared look, they step through it.

Chancellor Maddox stands on the far side of the room, facing them. Her hair is as long and blond as ever, and as perfectly combed. The calm expression on her face seems to indicate that she's been expecting Hope. The beauty-pageant queen ever ready for the next event.

"Come in," she says, smiling pleasantly. "Don't just stand there."

Hope and Scylla take several steps in, their pistols trained on the chancellor. A long oval table sits in the center of the room, surrounded by thick leather chairs. On one wall is a series of maps, tattooed with symbols. The opposite wall is glass, looking out past the Eagle's Nest and into the black night. Hope is able to make out the rocket launchers at the far edge of the fortress.

"I wondered when you'd be showing up," the chancellor says.

Hope has no good response. She can't get over the fact that the chancellor's tone is so pleasant. Something's not right. Hope and Scylla have snuck into the headquarters, gotten past the guards, have their guns pointed at the chancellor, and yet Maddox acts like she's happy to see them.

"You're just in time to watch," the chancellor says.

"Not if we stop the launch before it happens."

"Oh, I'm sorry—I wasn't making myself clear. I'm not talking about the attack, I'm talking about the execution."

Hope doesn't understand, and even when Chancellor Maddox raises her hand and reveals a small pistol, Hope still doesn't get it. After all, she and Scylla have weapons too. But instead of aiming the gun at Hope or Scylla, the chancellor points it to a far corner of the room . . . where Book and Cat stand bathed in shadows, their hands tied behind their backs.

Hope's heart does a flutter at the sight of them. She is awash in emotions.

"What're you doing here?" she asks.

"Trying to help," Book says.

"Maybe I don't need your help."

"Now now, children," the chancellor interrupts. "Let's play nice. Especially on this momentous day."

Hope turns to the former beauty queen. "You can stop with the pretending," she says. "We know what you intend to do."

"Oh?"

"The chemical weapons, the rocket launchers. You're going to murder thousands of innocent civilians and every government official there is."

"Correction: every government official but one."

If Chancellor Maddox is impressed that Hope has figured out her plans, she doesn't show it.

"You were even going to kill the Hunters," Hope goes on, "if the wolves hadn't done it first."

"You know what they say. 'Keep your friends close, and your enemies closer.'" She smiles innocently. "Now why don't you and your little mute friend put down those guns before your boyfriends get hurt."

"Don't do it," Book says to Hope.

Hope glances at him. She knows he's right—this is the moment she's been waiting for. But it's *her* life she's willing to give up, not someone else's. As much as she wants to pull the trigger, she can't. It's not fair to sacrifice Book and Cat when she's the one who wants revenge.

She places her weapon on the oval table and slides it forward across the varnished surface. Scylla does the same.

"So tell me," Chancellor Maddox says, waving the pistol between the prisoners. "Should I shoot you now, or would you like to witness the second Omega and *then* be shot? I can't make any promises about the fireworks, but I can guarantee that this time we'll get it right."

For the longest time, no one speaks. They barely even breathe. There's no good answer to the chancellor's question, and no possible way to save their lives.

It's Book who breaks the silence.

"It was you, wasn't it?"

Something about his words—and the tone behind them—sends a shudder down Hope's spine.

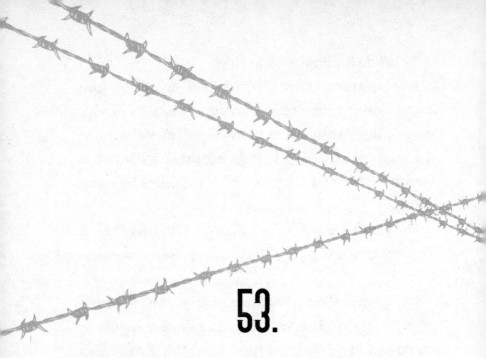

53.

FOR THE FIRST TIME, it all made sense. It was too late to do anything about it, but I finally understood.

"What are you jabbering about?" Chancellor Maddox asked.

"Omega," I said. "It didn't happen the way we were told."

"I don't know what you were told, so I have no idea what you're talking about."

"I think you do. The Brown Shirts always said some country on the other side of the world started it. They fired off the first missiles and our country had no choice but to retaliate." I was talking slowly, forming my thoughts even as I spoke the words. "But that wasn't it at all, was it? There wasn't any other country

302

attacking us. *You* fired the first missiles. *You* made Omega happen."

Chancellor Maddox smiled her condescending beauty-queen smile, all white teeth and perky dimples. "Don't be silly. Why would you even think that?"

"Because you just said, 'and this time we'll get it right.'"

"So what? That doesn't mean—"

"You gave the order. You started a nuclear holocaust just so you could have more power."

"Oh please, this is nonsense—"

"I don't know how you did it, but somehow—"

"I have no idea what you're talking ab—"

"—you persuaded the generals or whoever had access to the missiles to go along, to fire them when and where you wanted. Here we're all horrified about what you're going to do to New Washington, but you've done this before, haven't you?"

I could feel the stares of my three friends, their eyes darting between me and the chancellor. Maddox, too, studied me a long time before speaking.

"I didn't build the bombs, if that's what you're saying," she finally said. "And if you think I have regrets, I don't. It was the smartest thing I ever did."

I was at a loss for words. We all were. Over the course of the last many months, I thought I'd witnessed every possible kind of evil. But to think Omega was planned

303

by a single individual—*a lone member of Congress*—was more than I could comprehend.

"How'd you survive?" I asked.

"Easy. I just *happened* to be away from Washington that day. In an underground bunker. Unfortunately, the vice president was on a campaign trip to Iowa and also survived; I hadn't counted on that."

"You assumed you'd be the highest ranking member of Congress left—maybe the only one. You didn't think you'd have to wait twenty years to become president."

A brittle smile scarred the chancellor's face—a crack in a plaster wall. "All good things come to those who wait."

I had a sudden flash of the mother I never knew—the woman who was doused with so much radiation, she gave birth to my deformity, then died shortly thereafter. I thought of all the Less Thans who'd died over the years from acute radiation syndrome. All because of this one vain, vile, power-hungry woman.

"Why?" I managed.

Chancellor Maddox looked at me as though the answer was so obvious it didn't need to be voiced. "It was in our best interests."

"To destroy the world?"

"To *save* the world. Everything that was great about us was slipping away. And if I hadn't done it, if I hadn't done *something*, we were doomed to failure."

"You killed billions of people."

"'The tree of liberty must be refreshed from time to time with the blood of patriots and tyrants.' Thomas Jefferson."

"'The first thing we do, let's kill all the chancellors.' William Shakespeare."

She smiled smugly. "Nice try. Don't you mean 'lawyers'?"

"Not in this case."

Chancellor Maddox made a *tsk, tsk* sound and shook her head. "Oh, I get it. The young people are up in arms. They would've known the *right thing* to do. They would've acted properly. But let me tell you something. The world was on its last legs. Overpopulation, climate change, terrorists. The Middle East alone was one giant cesspool. It took someone with vision—with courage— to say, 'Let's start over. Let's go back to square one and make this a decent world to live in.' No different than God creating the flood. The world has me to thank for saving it."

"Not the Less Thans," I said.

"Or the Sisters," Hope added.

Maddox shrugged. "'Can't please all the people all the time.'"

She said it with such giggly innocence—like it was just another beauty-pageant answer—that the life went out of me. Nothing we said or did had any effect. The

305

woman was incapable of reason.

She grabbed a walkie-talkie from the oval table and positioned her thumb over the orange button.

"How close are we?" she asked into it.

"Whenever you're ready, Madame President-Elect," a staticky voice replied. "Just say the word."

She gave us a look like *You see? There's nothing you can do.*

My friends and I exchanged a horrified look. "I thought you weren't going to launch the missiles until the same time as the inauguration."

"That was the original plan, but you know what they say: It's a woman's prerogative to change her mind. And I'm in the mood to get this over with now."

She was in the process of bringing the walkie-talkie to her mouth when Cat blurted out, "Wait!"

Chancellor Maddox looked at him expectantly.

"You gave us the option," Cat said. "You said we could choose whether we were executed before or after the attack. Right?"

"That's right."

"Well, I choose before. I don't want to watch another Omega."

The smile that adorned the chancellor's face was bright enough to light the room.

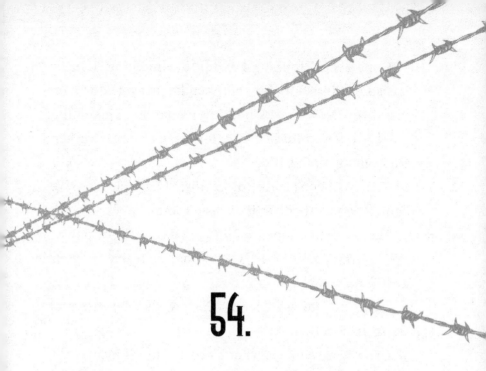

54.

"Any other takers?" Chancellor Maddox asks the other three.

Hope can't believe that Cat is giving in so easily.

"Fine," Maddox says. "Then we'll do one now, and the rest of you after we fire the missiles." Her tone is utterly casual, as if she's asking for volunteers in class.

She waves her pistol and motions for Cat to come forward. "Slowly," she says. In her other hand is the walkie-talkie.

Cat can barely meet his friends' eyes. "Sorry, guys," he says, and shuffles away from the corner. His hands are bound tightly behind his back.

After a half dozen steps, Chancellor Maddox holds up her hand.

"Kneel," she commands.

Hope keeps thinking he's up to something, that he has some kind of a plan, but then he just gets down on his knees. Now there's nothing he can do. He's still a good five feet from her—too far away to lunge for her. He is giving up his life.

"Cat, you don't have to do this," Hope pleads. "We can all go together. We'll die as a group."

The chancellor looks at him, waiting for his response. "Well?" she asks. "Are you going to listen to your girlfriend?"

"She's not my girlfriend," Cat growls. "Let her and Book die together."

His words send a rush of blood to Hope's face.

"So there we have it," Maddox says with icy pleasure. "The crux of the matter."

She places the walkie-talkie on the table, then checks the chamber of the gun. She levels it at Cat's forehead. Her index finger hovers against the trigger. The second she pulls, Cat's life will end for good.

Hope wonders what he's thinking. Does Cat really not want to witness the missile attack? Or does it have to do with her and Book?

For a long moment that feels like forever, Cat kneels there, and Chancellor Maddox readies the pistol. Hope, Scylla, and Book watch helplessly.

"Any final words?" the chancellor asks.

"No," he snaps.

"Would you like a blindfold?"

"No way. I want my eyes open."

"And why is that?"

"So I can see your reaction."

"My reaction?" Her face twists in confusion. "My reaction to what?"

Cat's right arm whips around his body. At the end of it is his prosthetic left arm, still tied to his right hand. By releasing the prosthetic from his shoulder, he's managed to create an improvised whip of real arm and fake arm, and in one blindingly fast move, he cracks it forward. The end of his prosthetic arm snaps against the gun. Two bullets explode before the pistol goes cartwheeling through the air. Chancellor Maddox's eyes go wide and she stumbles backward and the gun goes clattering to the floor. Smoke curls from its barrel.

The silence that follows is overwhelming. No one moves. The air is thick with the scent of gunpowder.

Hope feels a sharp pain in her leg like a wasp sting. When she looks down, she sees blood spilling from her right thigh. She caught one of the bullets from the chancellor's gun. She starts to examine the wound when she sees Cat.

He lies on his back, blood gurgling from his chest like a spring. He took the other bullet.

"Stay with me!" Book yells to Cat, already hovering over his friend.

Hope limps forward and unties Book's hands, and she watches as he works with silent fury, *desperation*, as if Cat's life is *his* life. He rips off his outer shirt and bunches it into a ball, pressing it against the blood. Within seconds, his shirt is a soggy mess.

"You're going to be okay," Book says, not giving up. "Stay with me here."

That's the moment Hope realizes how wrong she was—way back when—to ever think Book would abandon Cat. Not a chance. It was Book and Cat together from the very beginning. Friends to the bitter end.

The sound of Chancellor Maddox's voice whips Hope's head around.

"Now," the chancellor is saying into the walkie-talkie. *"Launch the missiles now!"*

In the confusion following the gunshots, everyone forgot about her, but now Hope sees her, frantically stabbing the orange button with her thumb and placing her mouth close to the walkie-talkie.

"Launch the missiles now!" she says again.

At first, the only answer she gets is static. Everyone holds their breath, waiting to hear the confirmation of the launch, the beginning of Omega II, missiles erupting from the Eagle's Nest and arcing through the sky.

But the static continues, only gradually replaced by another sound—muffled gunfire—not from the walkie-talkie but from outside the windows. An explosion rocks the building.

Chancellor Maddox shoots a daggered look at Hope. "What's going on?"

Hope honestly doesn't know, but Book answers without looking up. "The president's soldiers," he says. "They've arrived."

The chancellor's face burns red, twisting into an expression of rage and fury. Her lips part, revealing bared teeth. Her jaw is entirely too tense to allow the formation of words. She sputters a string of unintelligible words, then turns and races out of the room. The door slams behind her.

Book's eyes don't leave Cat. "Go," he says aloud.

At first, Hope doesn't understand. Then she realizes he's talking to her—and the need to stop Chancellor Maddox.

For a long moment, Hope is unable to move, torn between Cat's fatal wounds, Book's grief, and Chancellor Maddox getting away. She's paralyzed.

"Go!" Book screams.

She takes a final look at Cat and then rushes out the door.

Even as she staggers after Chancellor Maddox, it occurs to her that Cat knew exactly what he was doing. He knew he would be shot, but he knew it was the only way to prevent the next Omega. For perhaps the last time, Cat has saved the lives of others—even if it meant giving up his own in the process.

Hope vows that if it comes to it, she will gladly do the same. Blood streams down her leg as she limps through the hall.

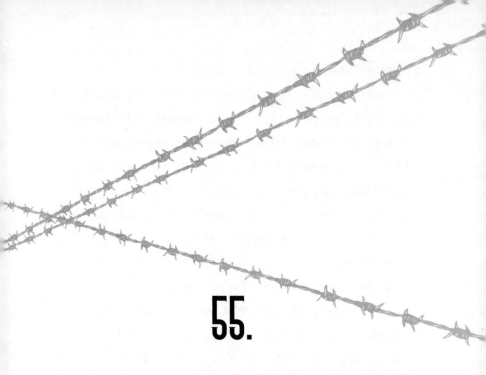

55.

CAT GREW PALER BY the second, and in no time at all, his face was the color of chalk. He was slipping away.

I heard Hope faltering down the hallway. I hoped she could catch up with Chancellor Maddox, but at that particular moment I almost didn't care. What I cared about was Cat, my friend Cat, who I'd discovered dying in the desert and who'd taught me more about myself than anyone I'd ever known.

And now he was dying before my eyes. As Scylla helped put pressure on the wound, I began to babble.

"Remember that day?" I said to Cat. "We found you fried like an egg, wearing that black T-shirt. That's what we called you at first: Black T-Shirt. Later we realized Cat was a better name."

313

Blood flowed from Cat's chest.

"And then you kept saving us. The wolves and that shot at the propane tank and that time you got Sergeant Dekker with your arrow when we went back to Camp Liberty. Remember? You even lost your arm, but you came back stronger than ever. And this'll be the same. We'll get some doctors and they'll fix you up and you'll be the same old Cat, better than ever."

His eyes told me he didn't believe me. Our fingers clutched when his hand flailed forward.

"You're going to recover," I said, still talking nonstop, my throat suddenly tight. "And we're going to do all those things we said we'd do: eat all kinds of good food and you're going to teach me how to hunt and we're not going worry about Brown Shirts anymore."

His eyes fluttered closed.

"And maybe I'll even get you to read. You'll probably love it once you start—it's just getting started that's sometimes tough. And I'm guessing you'll really like Jack London and Jules Verne and who knows what else."

His chest struggled to rise. When he exhaled, there was a bubbling sound.

"Okay, you rest," I said. "When you wake up, you'll see. The doctors will have you patched up and we'll get a bunch of us and rebuild that cabin at Frank's place. And we'll fish and hunt and we'll plant a garden and no one'll bother us and we'll start our own community, far away from all the politicians and the soldiers and the Chancellor Maddoxes of the world. And we'll build another library, just like Frank's, and it'll be perfect. Life'll be perfect."

Cat's mouth parted, and I realized he was trying to say something. I leaned in to hear and I remembered: this was exactly how we'd met back in the No Water, him struggling to talk and me placing my ear against his cracked and bleeding lips. Just like then, he mumbled something, but I couldn't tell what.

"What's that, Cat? I didn't get what you said."

His lips moved slowly, as though putting every last effort into producing sound. When he spoke, it was the vaguest of whispers, all sandpapery and rough—but I understood.

"Book . . . and Hope . . . together."

I slowly drew back and looked at him. Was it my imagination, or was there a smile on his face? If it existed, it was brief and fleeting. A moment later, his head lolled to the side, his chest stopped rising, the blood stopped spilling out.

He was still.

Cat—my friend Cat—who told us what was really going on in the world and who showed us how to live our lives, was dead.

I buried my face in his chest and sobbed.

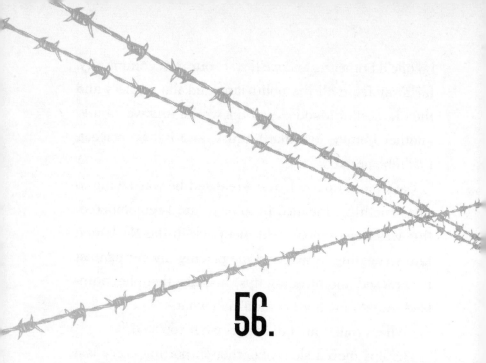

56.

HOPE EMERGES FROM THE headquarters and steps into chaos. Several platoons of President Vasquez's Brown Shirts have plowed their way to the top of the mountain and are battling it out with Chancellor Maddox's soldiers. It's Brown Shirt against Brown Shirt—inverted triangles versus no triangles. The rattle of bullets fills the night.

Hope bends at the waist, putting her hands on her knees. The pain from her thigh shoots down her leg, numbing her foot and her toes. Blood pools in her shoe. She looks around and catches a glimpse of Chancellor Maddox's ankle-length coat, trailing her as she races away.

Hope pushes herself to a standing position and gives

chase, knowing exactly where Maddox is headed: the elevator.

Soldiers from both sides close in, and Hope has to take a sweeping arc to avoid their gunfire. Her lower pant leg is soaked in blood, and at one point she stops and uses her belt to tie a tourniquet around her upper thigh.

By the time she reaches the elevator, it doesn't work. Hope can press the button all night long, but it's not lighting up. Maddox has somehow disabled the thing— it's stuck at the very bottom. Hope has no choice but to take the stairs, all seven hundred of them. At least this time she's going down.

She limps and shuffles down the metal steps, feet clanging, the sound echoing off the cement walls. The loss of blood and all the switchbacking back and forth makes her dizzy. Her face goes clammy. She hugs the railing, wondering how far ahead the chancellor's going to be.

By the time she reaches the bottom of the stairwell, her head swims. She opens the door and steps into the blackened tunnel, stumbling the length of the passage-way. Only when she emerges from the tunnel and sees the stars does she regain her balance. The fresh air is a welcome slap to the face.

She hurries to the tram stop, but when she reaches it, her heart sinks. The tram is halfway down the mountain, and in the distant window, growing ever smaller, is the silhouette of Chancellor Maddox.

"Damn it!" Hope curses.

She'll have to wait for it to reach the bottom and the other tram to reach the top. Then again, something tells her that Maddox might very well disable the tram, just as she disabled the elevator. *So how will I get down the mountain?* she wonders.

That's when the possibility occurs to her. It's dangerous, it's foolhardy, it's downright stupid. But it's the only solution she can think of.

There's a small wooden hut by the tram stop, and she makes a beeline for it. It's locked, of course, but nothing she can't open after a couple of well-placed kicks, even with only one good leg. It's a storage shed, filled floor to ceiling with tools, cleaning supplies . . . and ski equipment.

She finds a pair of skis that seem long enough, grabs some gloves and goggles, and lugs them to the tram stop. As she slips on the equipment, her eyes take in the steep mountainside below. It slopes downward in a hurry, and she can only guess the angle. Forty-five degrees. Maybe fifty. Maybe more.

When her father taught her how to ski, he explained how in pre-Omega days, ski runs were categorized. Green Circle for easiest, Blue Square for intermediate, Black Diamond for advanced, and Double Black

Diamond for expert only. She would rank this slope as Double Double Black Diamond—Trapezoid of Death.

She has strapped on the skis and slipped the goggles over her eyes. She grimaces as she stands, puts weight on her leg . . . and pushes off.

She falls almost immediately. Even when she gets up, it takes her a long moment to get used to the skis, to find her balance, to adjust to the fresh powder. The angle is steep—steeper even than she guessed—and she falls twice more in quick succession, stopping only when she rolls into a tree. Her right leg can barely support her weight. She tries again, slowly finding her rhythm. The skis' edges bite into the snow, sending a wave of powder into the air. A trail of blood follows her down the mountain like fairy-tale bread crumbs.

Her only illumination is the moon, casting a pale-blue light on the gleaming white of the snow. The snow-shrouded pines and firs are mere shadows—absences of light in a dark night. Things to avoid.

She finds herself in a clearing where she can see all the way to the bottom of the hill. The tram is coming to a stop, and a yellow rectangle of light falls on the snow as the door opens and a figure emerges. Chancellor Maddox has reached the town; Hope is still halfway up the mountain.

She has no choice but to ski faster.

She straightens out her path, doesn't zigzag quite

so far to either side. Her speed increases, and the icy wind numbs her cheeks, her nose, her lips. She hurtles down the mountainside, clipping branches, scraping rocks. On more than one occasion she face-plants into the snow, then hurries to extract herself. Her right leg burns with pain.

Still, it all comes down to this: she can't let Maddox get away. *Live today, tears tomorrow.*

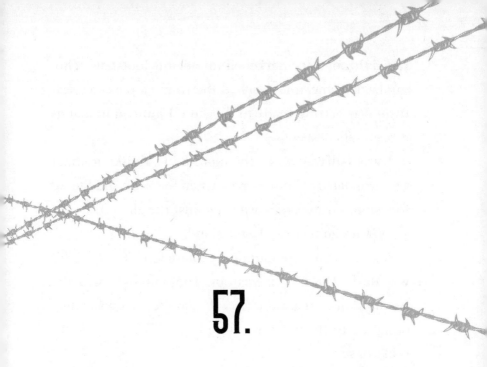

57.

CAT WAS DEAD.

Although I wanted to stay there and mourn his death, there was work to do. And Hope was out there on her own.

I felt a hand on my shoulder.

"Go," Scylla said—the first time I'd ever heard her speak. I wiped away my tears and hauled myself to my feet.

The lights blinked off and on as I hurried through the hallways. The gunfire was louder now—President Vasquez's army was drawing close.

I rode the elevator down to the lobby, dashed outside, then hurried to the main elevator. It didn't work, so I was forced to run down the hundreds of stairs. I raced through the darkened tunnel, my footsteps echoing back at me, and reached the tram stop as the next tram was getting ready to descend. I jumped in just as it began its descent.

I was halfway down the mountain—thinking about Cat, wondering about Hope—when the tram shuddered to a stop. I tumbled forward against the glass.

"What's going on?" I said aloud.

A glance up the mountain explained it. The fortress was dark. The power was out. The only light was the fading flames from the fire. Which meant I was stuck dangling in the air, a good half mile from the mountain's base.

The tram began to sway in the wind, rocking this way and that. My breathing grew rapid, and I had a sudden need to get out.

With trembling fingers I slid open the door. An icy wind rushed inside and chilled me to the bone. I dared to stick my head out and peer to the ground below. Pale moonlight bounced off the snowy, rock-strewn landscape far below me. I was way too high to jump. The snow might cushion my fall—the granite boulders wouldn't.

I slid the door shut and tried to think of a plan. The tram continued to rock in the howling wind. My heart slammed against my chest.

As I was trying to figure out what to do, I felt a

strange vibration. Different from the wind. Different from the tram in motion. This vibration rattled the windowpanes and radiated up my feet. My teeth began to chatter, and not from cold.

"What's going on?" I repeated.

The vibration increased. The tram buzzed with streaking currents of electricity. Except it wasn't electricity, it was something else. Something from the cable.

The tram lurched, plunging a couple of feet downward. The descent was so quick that I fell to the floor. The tram rocked and swayed. The vibration increased.

That's when I realized what was happening—someone was trying to cut the cable, chopping it with an ax. And with each whack, the tram lurched downward. It was only a matter of time before the metal ropes would fray and I would go plunging to the rocky mountainside below.

I whipped off my belt and doubled it back on itself, then jammed it between my teeth. If I somehow survived the fall—which seemed unlikely—I didn't want my jaw to snap open and shut so hard that I'd lose my teeth. I'd read about that somewhere.

The vibration ceased, and I wondered if maybe I was overreacting. Like this was all my imagination.

And then I heard a distant *whack* and the tram plunged downward.

Wind whistled through the tram as it sailed through air like a missile. Falling, falling, *falling*. My stomach rose to my throat, and all I could do was bite into the belt and throw out my hands and hope I could somehow cushion the fall.

One moment I was trying to protect myself, and the next the tram slammed into the mountainside. There was the muffled crunch of metal pounding into snow and granite. I went flying, bounced hard against the floor, ricocheted off all four walls. The windows shattered. Glass exploded everywhere, and I felt the jagged edges slice into my skin.

The tram bounced atop the ground, once, twice, and then began to slide. It picked up speed. In no time it was rocketing down the mountain like a runaway sled. It slammed against boulders, the impact jarring my insides, and the air whooshed by with a howl that was a ghostly wail. I folded my body into a tiny ball, waiting for the moment of impact—the screaming meteor slamming into earth.

Nothing could have prepared me for the sheer force of it. It banged into something immovable with such a jarring collision that my body was hurled forward and my head whiplashed back. The side of my face slammed into the metal wall and I felt the blood oozing. My teeth rattled. The sound of the crash bounced off the mountains and seemed to take forever before the echo fully disappeared.

I lay there a moment, assessing injuries. Bleeding, yes. Sore, definitely. But I hadn't broken bones. My heart was racing faster than it ever had.

I managed to squeeze through an open window and collapsed into the snow. Every bone and muscle screamed. When I finally lifted my head and looked around, I saw that the tram had slid a good quarter of a mile down the mountain before running into an enormous pine, wrapping itself around the tree's trunk like a flattened tin can. The door was crumpled. It had shrunk to half its size. It was a miracle I was alive.

I ran my sleeve across my cheek, wiped away the blood, and staggered to my feet. I began limping down the mountain, wading through drifts, knowing I had to push myself if I was going to save Hope. Not just from Chancellor Maddox, but from herself.

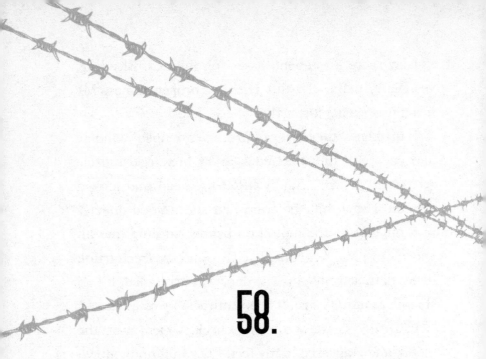

58.

Hope reaches the base of the mountain and tumbles to the ground. She untangles herself from her skis.

The tiny town is ablaze with activity. A convoy of New Washington soldiers snakes its way through the main street, heading up the mountain.

But where is Chancellor Maddox?

With all these soldiers here—the *president's* soldiers— the chancellor has no choice but to stick to back alleys. Hope does the same. She limps through town, searching for any sign of the woman who just shot her. Who scarred her face. Who ordered the deaths of billions of innocent people.

She reaches the endless prairie at the edge of town, and her spirits drop. There's no sign of the chancellor anywhere. She's gotten away. Hope is about to turn around and head back when she spies a small figure stumbling across the snow-covered grasslands. The figure has blond hair and wears an ankle-length coat.

Hope wonders where she's going. Why run blindly across a frozen field? What good will that do?

Then Hope spies a vehicle on the far side of a ridge. A Humvee, just waiting to take the president-elect wherever she wants to go. Hope can't let the chancellor get inside that vehicle.

Hope gives chase as best she can but grows winded quickly, the horizon tilting wildly. Her right pant leg clings to her skin, and blood squishes in her shoe.

As she limps along, her eyes scan the snow-stubbled field. For all the effort Hope is putting into the chase, the chancellor is getting farther and farther away.

Hope comes to a stop, defeated. She could maybe return to town and try to persuade some soldier to drive her across the field, but by the time she could even hope to make that happen, Chancellor Maddox will be long gone. Disappeared for good.

Hope crumples to the ground—not just from loss of blood but from bone-racking despair. Her unfinished business will remain just that—unfinished.

She slips into a deep sleep.

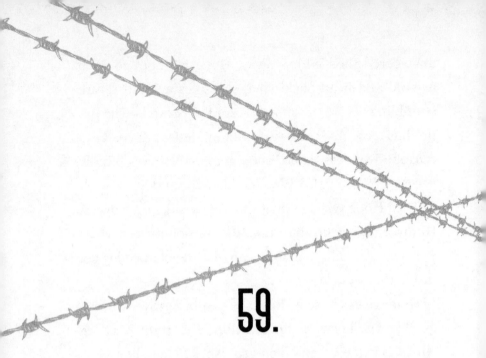

59.

EVEN IN MOONLIGHT, THE blood was easy to spot. I crouched down and examined the red droplets on the white snow. They were fresh enough to convince me of their source: Hope.

I got up and followed the trail.

It led me through the back alleys of the small town, and I expected to round a corner at any moment and come face-to-face with her, standing victorious over a slain Chancellor Maddox.

But somewhere in the middle of town I lost the trail, and when the buildings abruptly ended, I found myself on the edge of the prairie. No Hope. No Chancellor Maddox. No indication of where they'd gone.

"Where are you, Hope?" I whispered, my eyes

sweeping the vast expanse of rolling hills. Behind me, all the way up to the Eagle's Nest, I could hear the clatter of gunfire as soldiers battled soldiers. Every so often, an explosion shook the ground.

I retraced my steps until I came to a convoy of Humvees waiting to ascend the mountain. I began running from vehicle to vehicle.

"Excuse me! Do any of you know James Heywood? Have you seen him anywhere?"

If I could find him, he could talk a soldier into driving us in search of Hope. But no one responded. The few soldiers who met my eye either shook their heads or looked in another direction.

"Anyone?!" I called out.

The Humvees rumbled past.

I was running out of time. There was no other option but to return to where I'd been. Racing through the back alleys, I reached the far edge of town, my eyes once more sweeping across rolling hills and endless prairie.

I scoured the ground and found what I'd missed before: the trail of blood. The droplets were as purple—and fresh—as ever. I followed them. I was so focused on the perfect circles of red on white that I nearly tripped over the object at my feet.

It was Hope, curled in a fetal position. With her black clothing and makeup, she blended in with the darkness. I crouched down beside her and shook her shoulder.

"Hope, can you hear me?"

She didn't budge.

"Hope," I cried again. "Please wake up."

Relief surged through me when her eyes fluttered open.

"Book," she said groggily, trying to focus. When she attempted to get up, I reached out my hands to her. She slapped them away. "Don't stop me, Book. I need to get to Chancellor Maddox." Her words were slurred and hard to understand.

"I know—"

"I've been waiting for this—"

"I know—"

"I need to do this one thing."

Even in her weakened condition, she looked at me with eyes blazing, spoiling for a fight.

"I'm not stopping you, Hope," I said. "I'm going to help you."

Her eyes pinched close together, studying me.

"Yes?" she asked.

"Yes," I said.

I raised her to her feet, and only then did she realize I wasn't kidding. Of course, I knew that I was putting her life in danger—that by going after Maddox she was basically sacrificing her life. But I also knew she wouldn't allow someone else to finish her job; no gunshot to the leg was going to stop her.

330

My eyes fell on her tourniquet. I reached my hands to her thigh and placed them there.

"May I?" I asked.

She nodded, and I cinched the belt tighter. When I stood up, our eyes locked.

"Do you know where Maddox is?" I asked.

She pointed to the sweeping prairie. In the far distance was a Humvee.

"You think you can make it?"

She nodded.

"You sure?"

Another nod.

"Then let's get going," I said.

She draped an arm around my shoulder and we took off, hurrying as best we could. We were both in awful shape: bruised, bleeding, exhausted. As sore as I was from my sleigh ride down the mountain, Hope had it worse. Even with the tightened belt, she was losing blood at an alarming rate.

She suddenly withdrew her arm and began to run.

"Are you sure?" I said. "I don't think—"

She didn't respond, just took my hand and squeezed it, and soon we were both racing across the plains together.

And that's when it hit me.

It was like I was in the very place from my dreams— surrounded by rolling hills and desolate prairie. It was the stench of gunpowder, the whine of bullets, the pop of guns. But instead of my grandmother's hand clutching mine, it was Hope's.

Was that it? I wondered. *Was that why I had this dream for all those years—to prepare me for this moment?*

But the sad reality was that we weren't fast enough. We could spy Chancellor Maddox in the distance . . . and she was nearly to the vehicle. Our wounds were too crippling. I could feel Hope straining against her leg— her limp more severe than ever—and when I looked, I saw that her face was covered in a clammy sheen of perspiration. There was no way we were going to catch up in time.

"I could go on ahead," I suggested, but Hope wouldn't hear of it. She gritted her teeth and we pressed on.

At the same time we realized we weren't going to reach the chancellor before she reached the Humvee. Hope's chest was heaving up and down, and her hair was damp from sweat. But most telling of all was the look of defeat in her eyes. It was an expression I'd rarely seen from her.

"It's okay," I said. But I knew it wasn't.

Catching Chancellor Maddox wasn't just a game; it mattered. For the country. For the Sisters and Less Thans. For Hope.

"Maybe we should return to town," I suggested. "Convince some soldiers to go after her." *And get a doctor to look at that leg,* I wanted to add.

Hope gave a blank nod. She seemed a million miles away, and I could only imagine the thoughts swirling through her head—things having to do with her mom and her dad and her sister, Faith. We turned to go.

And that's when the most remarkable thing happened.

Just as Chancellor Maddox was about to be free and clear of us—a small speck on the far horizon reaching a waiting vehicle—a series of forms appeared out of the smoke. Just one or two at first, but then more. And then more after that. They rose from the far hills, wreathed by mist, and at first I couldn't make out who or what they were. All I knew was that there was a line of them. Dozens at first, then scores, then *hundreds*. They straddled a distant ridge and advanced, hand in hand, as they approached Chancellor Maddox.

The chancellor stopped, saw them on one side of her, and Hope and me on the other.

"Come on," I said, and Hope and I limped forward.

For reasons we couldn't understand, this group had mysteriously appeared. It was a miracle. A barricade of people springing up from nowhere, preventing the president-elect from reaching her vehicle.

Only as we got closer, and pale moonlight caught the faces of the people forming the line, did I realize: it wasn't a miracle. It was an act of friendship.

For standing there was Flush. And Red. And Helen

and Twitch and Diana and *all* the Less Thans and Sisters we'd rescued along the way. And not just them, but the Skull People, too. Hundreds of people standing hand in hand, shoulder to shoulder along the ridge, blocking any escape for Maddox. They'd followed us, come all this way to help. Argos was there, too, scarred and limping from all the injuries he'd endured these many months.

As we approached, the chancellor yelled at Hope and me. "Tell your friends to get out of the way! I need to get to that car."

We said nothing.

Our friends weren't the perfectly built soldiers who made up the ranks of the Brown Shirts. They were the flawed, scarred, damaged human beings who the Western Federation Territory wanted nothing to do with. They were blind and missing limbs and blotched from radiation. They had witnessed the deaths of their sisters and the slaughter of their friends. They were Sisters and they were Less Thans. They were Skull People, who had committed no crime other than having a different belief system from the government. Every single person standing there had gone through the fire—and was now hardened and stronger because of it.

They were the outcasts. The throwaways. Less Thans, every one.

They had no business being alive, making it these twenty years when so many wanted them dead. But by standing there that night, they proved they hadn't just survived—they had prevailed.

They continued to advance, and the ends of the line slowly arced inward until they'd formed an enormous circle—a circle with Chancellor Maddox in the very middle of it like a bull's-eye. Then some of them stepped forward, as though they'd choreographed this all before, and formed a smaller circler. It grew tighter and tighter, until, finally, Chancellor Maddox had nowhere to go. That's when they stopped.

The chancellor was like a trapped animal, running from person to person, trying to break through: pushing, slapping, spitting, yelling.

"You can't do this!" she screamed. "I'm the president-elect of the Republic of the True America! You have to let me through!"

Our friends didn't fight back, didn't say a word. They just linked arms, suffering her blows and insults. Their faces were without expression.

Chancellor Maddox ran faster and faster around the circle, trying to squeeze through, trying to wedge her way between Less Thans and Sisters. Spit flew from her mouth. Her eyes were wide, her nostrils flared with desperation, like some dying, desperate horse. The Less Thans and Sisters just stood there.

When Hope and I arrived, a section of the circle pulled apart and formed an aisle. We limped down it toward the defiant former leader. Once we were inside, the circle closed back up. I looked at the Sisters and Less Thans, at all the friends we'd traipsed across the country with. Others, too. Goodman Dougherty. Goodwoman Marciniak. All standing there, arms linked, holding firm.

Chancellor Maddox had fallen to the ground and was writhing on the snow and dirt. Mud plastered her knees, smudged her face and hands. She looked up at us with a sneer.

"Is this what you wanted?" she shrieked. "You want to carve up my cheeks so we're even? Is that it?" She was yelling. More spittle flew.

"So get it over with! I'm here, aren't I? Carve any damn thing you want. Carve your initials for all I care." She angled her face upward, waiting for Hope to tattoo her face.

Hope said nothing.

I studied Hope for the longest time. Despite all the sleepless nights and battles, I'd never seen her so spent before. It was utter exhaustion. Not just physically, but emotionally as well. After everything we'd seen the past year, how could Hope—how could *any of us*—not be wiped out? It was too much to take in, what human beings had been doing to other human beings, and at that moment, I was sure Hope realized that. That was why she just stood there, arms hanging limply by her side.

Finally, after a long moment, she reached into the folds of her hoodie and pulled something out. Not a knife or a gun, but a syringe. The clear liquid in the plastic tube caught the moonlight and prismed outward.

Chancellor Maddox recognized it immediately.

"Where'd you get that?" she snapped.

"Dr. Gallingham's lab," Hope said flatly. "I didn't think he'd mind if I borrowed it."

"You can't use that. You have no idea what it does."

"Actually, I do. I've seen. We've all seen."

The other Sisters and Less Thans nodded.

"Then please, I beg you—don't do it!" Like a cornered animal, Chancellor Maddox began to back away on hands and knees.

"Don't worry," Hope said. "I'm not like you. I'm not going to do that." Maddox's face relaxed, and then Hope added, "But you are."

Hope took a step toward the cowering chancellor. She extended her hand, the syringe squarely in her palm. That was when Maddox began to scream.

"Shoot me! Knife me. Anything but that!"

Hope didn't respond, didn't say a word, and the chancellor rose to her knees and began to beg. Her long, slender fingers were clenched tightly in prayer.

"Please. Don't do this. I beg you."

Hope still said nothing.

"For the love of God, show some mercy."

"Funny," Hope said. "I don't remember mercy being something you showed my friends and family." She inched her hand forward.

When Chancellor Maddox realized Hope wasn't backing down, wasn't changing her mind, she reached a tentative hand forward and plucked the syringe from Hope's hand.

"This is what you want?" she asked.

"It's what I want," Hope answered.

Chancellor Maddox studied the needle: its razor tip, its clear liquid in the plastic capsule, its lethal contents.

"I didn't mean any harm," she said. Tears and snot stained her face. "I was just trying to make the world a better place."

Neither Hope nor I dignified her comment with a response.

"But you're fooling yourself if you think the Final Solution will die with me," Maddox said. "The movement will go on, and won't stop until all of you are utterly wiped out."

Hope gave her head a shake. "The movement's over. Now that Gallingham's dead, you're the last one who still believes in it."

It was impossible to read the chancellor's expression. The only emotions I could see were desperation and seething anger. She took the syringe and slowly raised it. She placed its tip against her arm and readied her thumb. Her hand trembled.

"Do I have to?" she asked.

"You have to," Hope answered.

"Then if I go, you go with me."

Chancellor Maddox leaped to her feet and lunged for Hope. The needle flashed through air, and those of us watching couldn't help but gasp. The world seemed to come to a crawl as the poison tip sliced through night and made its way toward Hope.

But Hope was ready—had been anticipating the attack, it seemed. She shuffled to one side, extended her arms, grabbed Chancellor Maddox by the wrist, and stopped the chancellor's hand midstrike. Hope turned the syringe around. For a brief moment, the needle was directly between the two, a compass point stuck between directions. Then Hope turned the icy tip and plunged it into the chancellor's neck. She thumbed the evil contents from the plunger straight into Maddox's blood.

The chancellor's eyes grew large, even as Hope ripped out the syringe and flung it to the ground. The former leader of the Western Federation Territory sat there a moment, breathing heavily, panting like a thirsty dog. Then, slowly, she pushed herself to her feet and unfolded her body.

"It didn't work," she crowed triumphantly, addressing

everyone who circled her. "You think it's that easy to bring me down? I'm Chancellor Cynthia Maddox, president-elect of the Republic of the True America! You can't just—"

A leg went slack, and she plopped to the ground. She tried hauling herself to her feet, but she was limping badly, walking in an aimless circle.

"You think . . . a bunch of Sisters and Less Thans . . . can topple . . . ?"

Foam bubbled from her mouth, running down her chin. Blood erupted from her nose and ears. She had the crazed look of a rabid dog, unable to comprehend what was happening. Her words became gibberish.

"There's no . . . you can't . . . *me!*"

She tripped over her feet, bouncing against the wall of Less Thans who pushed her back into the circle. When she fell splat into the slush, her body twitched, the milky foam erupting from her mouth like lava. Her eyes bolted left and right, unable to focus. Only at the last, when her arms and legs went into one final convulsive fit, did her eyes fix on a single person.

Hope Samadi.

Chancellor Maddox's mouth opened as though trying to cry for mercy, but no words came, not even sound, and when life left her with a blubbering sigh, it was with that final look of horror painted across her face.

We stared at the chancellor a long moment, and then

I looked at Hope. There was no joy in her expression, no self-righteous satisfaction, no taunting pleasure. She turned, briefly met my eyes and walked back the way we'd come. The aisle opened up and the others let her pass.

Chancellor Maddox was dead, and we could finally get on with our lives.

60.

THEY TAKE CAT'S BODY back to Libertyville. A group
of Brown Shirts—President Vasquez's Brown Shirts,
whose goal is to protect and serve its citizens—take
them there on horseback and in wagons. These soldiers
never met Chancellor Maddox, nor followed a single
one of her orders. They have no desire to implement
any Final Solution.

They return to the small cemetery at the edge of the
No Water, not so very far from the mesquite bush where
Book first found Cat all those months ago. And there,
one week after Cat's death, they bury him next to Major
Karsten—his dad.

The ceremony is brief and informal—just how Cat
would like it—but many of the LTs say a word or two. It

wouldn't be right not to. They talk about the wolf attack up on Skeleton Ridge, the propane blast, his skill with a bow, how he was always making arrows and firing them *accurately*, even with only one arm. War stories.

Book speaks the longest, reciting not Cat's accomplishments but rather something from a play by Shakespeare.

> *When he shall die,*
> *Take him and cut him out in little stars,*
> *And he will make the face of heaven so fine*
> *That all the world will be in love with night*
> *And pay no worship to the garish sun.*

As he speaks, he and Hope hold hands, their fingers intertwined. This is their final day together, and it's important they make each moment count.

Hope looks around; the life of every Sister and Less Than present was saved by Cat at one time or another. He came to their rescue on multiple occasions, and now he is a memory. A treasured place within their hearts.

When the mourners ease away from the cemetery, shuffling through sand and sage, there isn't a dry eye among them. Only Hope and Book remain at the graveside. She leans to one side, still favoring her leg.

"What did he say to you?" she asks Book.

"When?"

343

"There at the end."

Book opens his mouth to speak, then changes his mind. "Nothing," he says. "He asked me to take his hand."

"Nothing more?"

Book gives his head a shake.

A spring wind stirs the dust, bringing with it the clean smell of desert and pine and mountains. It's an intoxicating perfume.

"Was he afraid, do you think?" Hope asks.

"Of death? No way. If I was death, I'd be afraid of *him*."

Hope smiles at that. Heaven had better make sure the rules up there make sense; otherwise, Cat will see to it that things change in a hurry. He might see to it anyway.

"What now?" she asks. Even though they've talked about it a hundred times, it's become a ritual: sharing the details of their future. Now that President Vasquez understands what's been happening in the Western Federation all these years, the world is suddenly different. They're no longer prey. They get to make actual choices.

"Go back up to Frank's place," Book says. "Rebuild the cabin."

"With a library?"

"Already collecting books to take up there."

Hope smiles. She knows Book won't be happy unless he's surrounded by his namesake.

"You?" he asks.

"Heywood offered me a job with the presidential guard. Who woulda thought I'd be working for the government?"

"I know, right?" Then Book asks, "Is it permanent?"

"As permanent as I want it to be."

Book grunts but says nothing.

She turns to him. "What?"

"Nothing."

"Were you going to say—"

"No."

Hope's heart falls. It's been an odd time, the last few days. Here she accomplished what she set out to do—exacting her revenge on the people who tortured and killed her family—and yet, surprisingly, she feels remarkably unsatisfied. No, that's not the word. *Incomplete.* She's excited by the future and the promise of working for people who value her skills. But at the same time, she knows there's something missing. It's like there's an enormous hole in her heart.

"Tonight?" she asks.

"Tonight," Book says.

They separate, Book walking back to the former shantytown, Hope toward the foothills. When she's off alone, far away from the eyes and ears of others, tears begin to flow. Although she swipes them angrily with her fingertips, her hands can't keep up. The tears are far too many and come much too fast and eventually she just gives in. She leans against an aspen tree until her shoulders ache from sobbing. At one point, she lifts her head back and cries out in a scream that is primal and painful and comes from someplace deep within. An appeal to the heavens, soaring to the blue sky above.

And then she collapses to the ground.

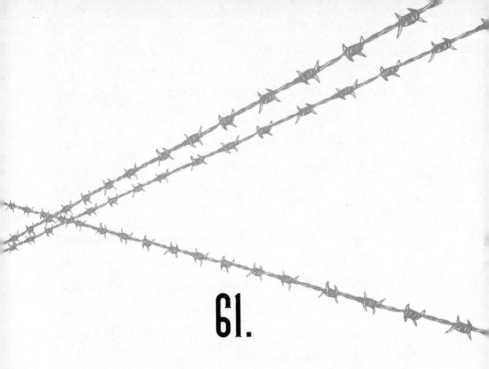

61.

I ALWAYS SAID IT started the day we found Cat in the desert, dying from dehydration. He told us things we didn't know, and after a year of battles and captures, of victories and disappointments, of friends and enemies and love and life and death, the world was changed.

We were changed.

"She would've been proud, you know," Goodwoman Marciniak said to me that evening as we sat around a campfire. I knew without asking she was talking about my grandmother.

"Maybe."

"No 'maybe' about it, she would've been." Then she whispered, "There's something else."

Her tone was serious, and a part of me wasn't sure I

wanted to hear what she was about to say.

"There's one thing you might want to know before we say good-bye tomorrow."

"What's that?" I asked.

"Your real name."

My eyes widened. "You know?"

"She told me once."

I couldn't believe it. It was something I'd been dreaming about for years—my true identity. I had even fantasized about it, imagining the acquisition of a new name the way one dreams about receiving a gift. I nodded eagerly, about to learn—for the first time—what my parents had called me.

Goodwoman Marciniak leaned in to tell me . . . and I suddenly leaned back.

"No," I said, changing my mind. "It's better this way."

She gave me a questioning look. "You don't want to know?"

"No."

"You're sure?"

"Positive."

The fact was that I already knew. I was a Less Than. I was *Book* the Less Than, and Flush was Flush and Twitch was Twitch . . . and Cat was Cat. Finding out my given name might just make me turn my back on who I really was, and I didn't want that.

I thanked Goodwoman Marciniak and walked away from the fire.

Hope and I spent our final night together in my hut. A dozen or so candles spread an amber glow, and we lay on our sides, my arms wrapped around her, my chest pressed against her back. It was as though all the emotions we'd ever experienced—the sorrows, joys, frustrations, *downright longing*—were channeled into one night. I never let her go—not once.

In the morning, when sunlight flooded through the hut's cracks, we held each other awkwardly, kissed briefly, then shuffled off to get ready for our departures. I made the rounds and said good-bye to my friends. The new government was thrilled with this sudden infusion of young people and had promised to enroll them in a new school they were starting. Some, like Red and Flush, promised to come visit when they got vacation time. Others, like Scylla, I had a feeling I'd never see again. I would miss her. I would miss all of them.

Then it was time for Hope and me to say good-bye. We had already said it once that morning, and we were in no mood to repeat it. One farewell was enough. Too many, in fact.

We kind of looked at each other, kind of didn't. Like there were things we wanted to say but didn't know how. Even if we could find the words, I'm not sure we were capable of putting them together. My mouth and tongue felt oddly clumsy, as if I was chewing on a bag of rocks.

"Hope," I said, stalling. I didn't know how to say what

I wanted to say, and Hope cut me off before I had the chance.

"Don't," she said, and we just looked at each other for a long time. Then she broke the silence and said, "I'd better get going."

"Yeah, I guess you'd better."

We locked eyes a moment more, and then she strode off to join the others. Those were our final words.

Everyone saddled and mounted their horses. A group of soldiers was set to lead the column of riders back to the capital in its new—and perhaps permanent—position. I was the only one staying behind.

Even though she was still recovering from a gunshot wound, Hope climbed atop her horse as effortlessly as rising from a chair. She gave a backward glance, then quickly turned around. When everyone was in line and ready to move out, the horses started forward.

"Bye, Book!" Flush yelled.

"See you l-l-later," Red called.

I waved good-bye but said nothing. My throat was way too tight to allow the passage of words. Shielding my eyes from the morning sun, I watched them depart, a line of horses and riders snaking east, heading for the river and the next territory and the new capital. No more Western Federation for them. Argos gave a soft whimper and leaned into me. I scratched his head.

The others rode on, the horses' hooves printing

themselves in the damp earth. Because Hope was last in line, she was the easiest to follow, her black hair shimmering in morning light. I stood there frozen, watching her get smaller and smaller until she was the tiniest speck on the horizon, a final star evaporating into the day's blue sky.

And then she was gone, and once more I was alone.

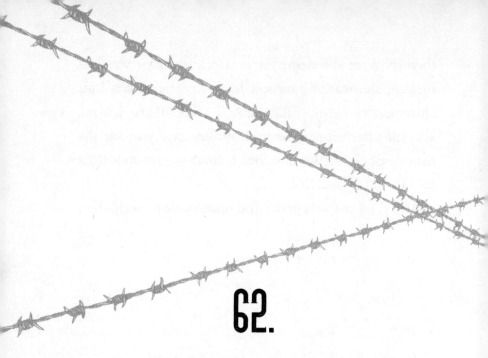

62.

THEY RIDE ALL DAY, the miles disappearing beneath the horses' hooves. The landscape slowly alters before their eyes, and in the foothills, the first desert flowers bloom, perfuming the air with sweetness.

Hope barely notices. She is still reliving her night with Book. It feels as though there's a mark on every part of her skin where he touched her. Beautiful tattoos.

They set up camp, and Hope wonders what it is with words, why they're so difficult to say—the ones that really matter, anyway. Why couldn't she tell Book what she wanted to tell him? Why couldn't she express her real feelings?

Why didn't she convince him to come with her?

Stars explode in the sky as though someone flipped

a switch, and the only sounds in camp are murmured conversations, the nickering of horses, the quiet crackle of fires.

Hope knows that sleep isn't possible, and so she rises from her bed and edges away from camp. Solitude tugs at her.

She doesn't know what life was like in pre-Omega days, but as she takes in this enormous wilderness all around her—scent of sage and woodsmoke, final bird cries of the evening, a distant coyote nipping at the air—she vows to help protect it. To live in a world worth living, for *everyone*.

Without knowing why, she strains a hand upward and tries to touch the stars.

"Live today," she says aloud.

There's no one there to complete the thought.

EPILOGUE

THE DREAM WAS ALWAYS the same: racing across the prairie, fleeing from Brown Shirts, chased by an angry swarm of bullets. A hazy gunpowder hung in the air, wrinkling my nose with its acrid smell. My four-year-old hand was encompassed in my grandmother's, even as we ran for our lives.

And then, I discovered years later, it wasn't a dream. It happened. It was a *memory*. Soldiers were after us because I was a Less Than, and by letting me be captured instead of killed, my grandmother saved me.

Now when I race across the prairie, the smoke that hangs in the air is not from gunpowder but morning mist, rising lazily to the sky as the sun warms the damp earth. It's not the singing of bullets but birdsong.

Our hands are locked, Hope's and mine, our fingers intertwined.

We surprised each other in the night. As Argos and I left Libertyville and followed the soldiers' trail east, Hope was retracing her way west. We met somewhere in between.

"Book?" she asked, trying to confirm that it was really me.

"Hope?" I asked in return, not really believing it was her, there in the dark in the middle of the high desert.

She nodded. Argos barked.

"Come on," I said.

She stared at me a moment. "Where are we going?"

"I don't know, but we're about to find out. And wherever it is, it's going to be a hell of an adventure."

My hand took hers, and then we circled in place until we were dizzy. When we came to a stop, fighting to keep from falling down, there was a vast and untouched prairie in front of us, stretching as far as the eye could see.

"Which way are we facing?" she asked.

"Does it matter?"

She smiled, and without a word between us we began to run. My eyes landed on her wounded leg.

"Can you do this?" I asked.

"I can definitely do this," she said.

And so that's what we do. We run. Maybe not as fast

as in times past, and certainly not as desperately, but still we run, even as the stars disappear and the sun rises bright and golden against a blue dome of sky.

Although we have yet to open our hearts and say the things we want to say, we're together. And for once our running isn't because we're fleeing anybody, it's because we're headed toward something. To a future we can't yet guess. To a shared life.

Book and Hope together.

We run for the longest time, sometimes laughing, mainly just enjoying the sound of each other's breathing and our muted footsteps on the earth. Neither of us quite believes we're together.

"Wait," she finally says, coming to a halt.

My chest heaves, inhaling crisp morning air. Hope is red cheeked from running.

"I never told you," she says.

"Told me what?"

She hesitates, bites her bottom lip, musters courage. "How I feel about you." Those piercing brown eyes of hers look into me. *Through* me.

I give my head a slight shake. "You don't need to tell me. I know. Because I feel the same way about you."

A smile brighter than the sun lights her face.

"But there is something I need," I say.

"What, Book?" she asks, concerned. "What do you need?"

I slip my hands to her face, stroking those blush-
ing cheeks, those beautiful two Xs. I slide my fingers
behind her neck and pull her gently forward. Our lips
brush, hesitate, brush again.

"This," I say. "This is what I need."

My beloved.

ACKNOWLEDGMENTS

I BELIEVE IN COMMUNITY. Whether it's geography that brings people together, or a sports team, or putting on a play, there is value in the team.

As this final book of the Prey trilogy makes it into readers' hands, I want to acknowledge how honored I am to be a part of the HarperCollins community. They have championed this series from the beginning, and I can't thank them enough for their belief in this story and for all the hard work they do to publish and promote young adult literature.

I am indebted to senior editor Alyson Day, assistant editors Abbe Goldberg and Tessa Meischeid, copyeditors Renée Cafiero and Valerie Shea, designer Joel Tippie, marketing manager Jenna Lisanti, publicist Lindsey

Karl, and all the wonderful people at HarperCollins who tackle the countless assignments it takes to publish a book. Thank you, each and every one of you, for doing what you do . . . and doing it so well.

I want to give particular thanks to my editor, Alyson Day. For a number of years now we have worked on these three books, and with every single interaction Alyson has treated me with respect, with humor, with kindness, with gentle prodding (when needed), and always with utter graciousness. She does her job with efficiency and, just as important, with compassion. I am more grateful to her than I can possibly express.

The same goes for my wonderful agents—Victoria Sanders, Bernadette Baker-Baughman, Chris Kepner, Jessica Spivey. They bolster my spirits when they need bolstering and challenge my writing when it needs challenging. Again, there aren't the words to fully express my gratitude. I am honored to be on the VSA team.

As always, I want to thank my early readers who have accompanied me on this journey, in particular Ryan Gallagher and Katie Caskey. They asked the tough questions, even when I didn't always want to hear them asked. I'm grateful they persisted.

I've dedicated this book to my parents. Although they've both passed away, they continue to be with me: guiding, encouraging, supporting.

Finally, I want to thank Pat, my true companion.

She was with me when I had the idea for these books—when the notions of Book and Hope and Cat and the Less Thans first entered my mind—and she's been with me every step along the way. More important, she teaches me the three Ls: to laugh, to live, to love. I am the luckiest guy in the world to get to travel through life with her.